TEMPTATION OF A PROPER GOVERNESS

Mr. Severson slammed shut the door and walked directly to the dresser without seeing her standing in the far corner of the room. Isabel held her breath, uncertain of what to expect. He was taller than most men and, she sensed, stronger.

If the devil were to come to life to tempt women, this was the face he would choose. Slashing black brows, a lean jaw, and brown eyes so penetrating they appeared as if they could look into another's soul.

Her heart beat faster just looking at him . . . especially when she realized *he was looking at her, too.* He could see her reflection in the glass.

The pull between them was indefinable and powerful. His lips curved into a lazy smile, and she thought her legs would melt.

This man didn't see her as a servant or a governess. He saw her as a woman. And when he said, "Come here," she had no choice but to comply.

Romances by
Cathy Maxwell

CATHY MAXWELL

TEMPTATION OF A PROPER GOVERNESS

AVON BOOKS
An Imprint of HarperCollinsPublishers

AVON BOOKS
An Imprint of HarperCollins*Publishers*
10 East 53rd Street
New York, New York 10022-5299

Copyright © 2004 by Cathy Maxwell
ISBN: 0-06-009298-X
www.avonromance.com

First Avon Books paperback printing: September 2004

Avon Trademark Reg. U.S. Pat. Off. and in Other Countries, Marca Registrada, Hecho en U.S.A.
HarperCollins® is a registered trademark of HarperCollins Publishers Inc.

Printed in the U.S.A.

10 9 8 7 6 5 4 3 2 1

To Kevin Michael Maxwell

You were right, Max.
Life really is all about love.
It's the only thing that truly matters.

December 1803

As the *Sea Serpent* sailed through mist and fog toward the long ridge of land, Michael Severson leaned over the ship's rail, mesmerized by the first sight of his homeland in over a decade.

England.

He'd not anticipated this surge of emotion, this hunger for what he'd missed.

When they had left Canada, the leaves had fallen and the grass had gone brown. Now, although the season was more advanced and they had reached at a higher latitude, England was green. The sight of gardens and grassy knolls beyond the sharp rocks that compressed the waters into a narrow strait, coupled with the gloomy days at sea, gave this homecoming a sense of stepping back into a world he'd almost forgotten.

"So, this is civilization," his business partner Alex Haddon's unconvinced voice said from behind him.

Turning to him, Michael said, "Some claim it is the center of the universe." Neither man wore a hat. Salt spray dampened their hair, which hung down past their shoulders. Michael would get his cut when they reached London. He doubted if the half-Shawnee, half-white Alex would let anyone touch his. It had been a major concession for him to give up deerskin leggings and shirts for cotton and wool.

Michael had no such hesitation. One of his first acts in London would be to make an appointment with a Bond Street tailor. Society judged a man by the cut of his coat.

Ironically, Michael appeared more Indian than his blood brother. Alex's father had given him gray eyes and a hint of wave to his hair, while Michael's eyes were brown and his hair straight.

Alex leaned against the rail, frowning at the shore as if he wished to remove its existence. "You are making a mistake."

"In returning?" Michael shook his head. "I've

been preparing for this moment from the day they ran me out of the country."

"And what makes you believe they are waiting with open arms now?"

"One of them isn't. Aletta's killer will not be happy to see me at all. But the time has come. The man who did murder her and almost got me hanged for the crime will pay." It was the only way he was going to find a measure of peace in his life. Aletta's death haunted him. No, he might not have murdered her, but he'd been passed out drunk while someone else had done it.

He and Aletta had been occasional lovers, one of her many. As the reigning queen of the London stage, Aletta had been all the rage and she'd reveled in her popularity. Michael had been an earl's wastrel second son with empty pockets, good looks, and charm.

"I know this weighs heavily on your soul," Alex said. He paused as if wanting to say more.

"Go on."

"What if there are no answers?"

The thought was inconceivable to Michael. "There will be."

"How do you know? It's been ten years. Who will care about a dead dancer?"

The man who murdered her. That man waited for Michael to return. One could not murder an

3

innocent soul and not expect an accounting.

"I had the dream about Aletta's death again last night," Michael said. He'd first had the dream two months ago. It had been the impetus for his decision to return.

"Could you see the man's face this time?" Alex asked.

"No. He is still in shadows."

"But you know him?"

"Yes," Michael answered, and added with frustration, "If only I could see more of him."

"Your dream is speaking to you. In time, you will know. Just wait a bit longer."

"I've *waited* long enough," Michael answered. "I'm going after Elswick, Alex. He's the only one who wanted to destroy me."

"Because his son wanted to marry the dancer?" Alex retorted, his doubt clear.

"Because he feared his son killed her and he wanted me to take the blame," Michael responded.

"Do you think the son killed her?"

Michael nodded. "Yes." He'd thought hard about this. It was the only explanation that made sense. Otherwise, why would the powerful marquis of Elswick actively campaign to see Michael found guilty of the murder? He'd used all his influence, including printing flyers and passing them to the masses declaring Michael's guilt. The only thing that had saved Michael's neck was an honest judge who had demanded hard evidence. Not even his own family had supported him.

"Men kill out of jealousy," Alex said with a shrug. He knew the story. Michael had told it to him numerous times.

"It is usually the only reason men kill," Michael countered. "They want what someone else has. Henry wanted Aletta and killed her when he found me in her rooms." Henry was Elswick's son and heir.

Alex shook his head. "You're wrong. Men also kill for revenge. Remember that, Michael. Don't do anything foolish."

Michael glanced out the corner of his eye at his friend. "Is that why you insisted on coming with me?" he challenged.

"One of the reasons," Alex said, unintimidated.

"And the other reason?"

"Perhaps I thought it time to see the other side of the world. After all, we do own a ship," he said, referring to the very one beneath their feet.

"Or perhaps you have a thought to finding your father?" Michael surmised gently. Alex's father had been a British general who had betrayed his country to the French. To a man who valued honor the way Alex did, his father's traitorous actions and subsequent desertion had sent him back to his mother's people, where he'd saved Michael's life when he'd been captured by the Shawnees.

Since that day, almost nine years ago, the pair had been close friends as well as business partners. They'd hunted and trapped together, watching their fortunes grow alongside their friendship. Each had his own purpose for finding wealth: Alex to prove himself more honorable than his father, Michael to gain the resources needed to reclaim his good name.

Alex studied his friend a moment before admitting, "If my father crosses my path, we will talk."

"When Elswick crosses my path, we shall do more than talk," Michael promised.

He turned his attention back to England. Elswick would soon learn that Michael wasn't the same frightened, callow youth who had once run away. He was a fitting adversary now and one unafraid to take on the most powerful man in England.

One

❧❧❧

March 1804

*M*iss Lillian Wardley's bed was empty.

Isabel Halloran, her governess, greeted the sight with a combination of frustration and panic. Lillian had a reputation for being promiscuous. Curbing her wild ways was one of the duties Isabel had been hired to perform three months earlier.

Isabel did not need a clash of wills with Lillian tonight. She was fighting her own demons or rather, one demon, Lord Riggs, Richard, a man she once believed she'd loved until he had attempted to take her by force. He was a guest under this roof, and she was determined to avoid him. She didn't want him to know she was there. The pain of his betrayal was still too fresh.

Isabel had no desire to be out wandering the halls, looking for her errant charge.

She should have known Lillian was up to something. The seventeen-year-old had been too quiet, too accommodating, and had excused herself far *too* early for bed that evening. Her unquestioning obedience was out of character and had disturbed Isabel enough for her to rise from her own bed, throw her brown day dress over her nightgown, and check on Lillian.

It was half past midnight . . . and she had a sinking suspicion where Lillian might be.

Holding a protective hand around the candle flame, Isabel hurried across the hall to knock on Nanny's door. It took more than one knock to disturb the older woman's sleep.

The door opened. "Miss Halloran, is there something with the children?" Nanny rasped, squinting at the candle flame. She had the care of Mr. Wardley's three younger children by his second wife, a very buxom former tavern girl with ambition to match her husband's.

"Lillian is missing."

"Missing?" Nanny repeated without comprehension.

"She's not in her bed. I need your help finding her."

Nanny came awake. "Oh, dear." She opened

the door while she reached for her dressing gown hanging on a nearby nail. "The last time she did this we found her with the stable lad. 'Twas before your time. I know you've heard about it."

"I thought I was making progress with her."

"I thought so, too." Nanny slipped her arms into her gown, leaving her nightcap on her head. "The Master had the boy transported to Australia." Isabel had heard this story, but Nanny never tired of repeating it. "He begged for mercy, he did, but the Master would hear none of it. Them with the money makes the rules. That's what my mother used to say. Let's pray Miss Lillian's not got another young laddie in trouble."

"No, I think she has her sights set higher." Isabel started for the stairs at the end of the hall. Her nightly braid had come loose, but she wasn't going to waste time rebraiding it.

Nanny moved with surprising speed and caught Isabel's arm. "One of the guests? Why, the Master's friends are all rakes and scoundrels, even if they do have titles to their names. They'd gobble up a young girl, spit out her bones, and the Master wouldn't be able to do a thing about it."

"I know," Isabel answered. She couldn't answer for all of Mr. Wardley's guests, but Richard certainly fit that description.

"We could lose our positions."

"Yes." Isabel was relieved that Nanny grasped exactly what was at stake.

"We'd best hurry," the older woman said as she picked up a candle stub from the hall table and lit it off Isabel's. The two women hurried toward the stairs. "I wish the Master would marry Miss Lillian off as soon as possible. Yes, she's young, but she is going to come to grief with her wild ways."

Their master was Mr. Thomas Wardley, a merchant who had made his fortune brokering wool to the army and fancied his money could buy his way into Society. He was fond of expanding on how he was part of the "new social order," where a man didn't need a title to be accepted. But the servants knew he desperately wanted one; they often called him "Sir" Thomas behind his back.

And Isabel knew he was wrong about a new social order. The divide between the aristocracy and everyone else was deeper than the ocean. Richard had taught her that, just as he'd taught her that a title didn't make a man a gentleman. The five titled gentlemen visiting this week were supposedly there for hunting—although no one had gone hunting yet. Instead, the downstairs reeked of port and brandy, and Nanny and Isabel had their hands full keeping the children away from bad influences.

The two women reached the floor where the guest bedrooms were. Candles in wall sconces had the area ablaze with light. Mr. Wardley might be stingy with his servants, but no expense was spared for guests.

Isabel paused. The footman who usually sat in a chair at the top of the stairs leading down to the main floor was missing from his post. She felt a cold suspicion.

The quiet of the hall was broken by a burst of boisterous male laughter drifting up the stairs from the dining room where the gentlemen liked to play cards. "They are having a rowdy good time tonight," Nanny muttered.

"I don't know why Mrs. Wardley tolerates it," Isabel said.

"The Mistress is usually down there with them."

Isabel frowned but feared she'd already said too much. A governess walked a fine line. She was a servant and yet had a higher standing than the others. It didn't help the situation that

Isabel was not good at being subservient. Pride was her besetting sin, and she didn't like it when her employers pretended she was invisible.

"You don't think Miss Lillian is down there with them?" Nanny wondered in round tones.

"No." Isabel studied the closed doors lining the hall. "Which room do you believe is Mr. Severson's?"

The mention of the man's name brought forth a gasp of horror from Nanny. "You can't be serious."

"He's all she could talk about from the moment she saw him arrive this morning."

"He's all any of the maids can talk about, too. I went down to the kitchen after the children were in bed, and even Cook was sighing over his looks. Have you seen him?"

"No, and Miss Lillian shouldn't have either. Her mother took her downstairs for introductions. I don't know what Mrs. Wardley was thinking introducing her daughter to any of those men." *Especially Richard.*

"He's rumored to be very wealthy."

"Who?" Isabel asked, confused, her mind on Richard. In spite of his title, Richard was a fervent gambler who rarely had a penny to name.

"Mr. Severson," Nanny answered.

That was even worse. "I don't care how much

money he has. He's also been accused of murder," Isabel stated.

Nanny's jaw dropped. For the first time since Isabel had met her, the older woman was speechless.

"It happened years ago," Isabel explained. "He killed a woman in a jealous fit. The judge claimed there wasn't enough evidence to convict him."

"How do you know?"

"I just do," Isabel said with a shrug, realizing that she'd been so upset by Richard's appearance at Wardley Manor, she'd barely given a thought to a man who had once been of great interest to her.

Isabel knew of Mr. Severson's murder trial because she had her own secret—she was the bastard daughter of the marquis of Elswick, a piece of information she kept to herself. She was the by-blow of an affair between the marquis and her mother, who had loved him madly. That love had not been returned. Indeed, Isabel doubted if the marquis ever gave a thought to her existence.

On the other hand, Isabel had grown up aware of everything about the marquis. From the moment she could read, she had collected London papers to scan for mention of his name.

The windfall had been Severson's trial for the murder of an actress. From the stand, Severson had accused her half brother, Henry, Lord Tainter, of being the murderer. It had made for sensational reading. The murdered actress had been popular in London, and even in a parish as small as hers, people wanted details. Isabel had even been inspired to write the marquis a letter telling him she didn't believe anyone in their family could commit such a foul deed.

She had never received a response.

And now, the murderous Severson was a guest under the same roof where she was living, and she was more concerned with avoiding Richard.

Life took strange turns.

"That is the best bedroom, right?" Isabel nodded to the one at the end of the hall.

"It's the biggest," Nanny agreed.

There was another burst of crowing male laughter, then the crash of glass. Isabel drew a deep breath. "We start there. Keep guard while I talk to his valet."

"He doesn't have one," Nanny said, and added, "Servants' gossip. Only one of the lot not to bring a man with him."

Isabel nodded. Sometimes gossip was good. She walked to the door, placed her hand on the

14

door handle, and drew a fortifying breath. Who knew what sight would greet her on the other side of this door? Her mind flashed on the memory of Richard trapping her, attempting to force her to his will—

She pushed the shame aside and opened the door.

The room was in blackness. There was not even a fire in the grate. Isabel held her candle high. Its light shone on the huge, four-poster bed covered in blue silk that dominated the space in the room. In the middle of the bed, Lillian glared at her with open defiance.

To Isabel's eternal relief, Mr. Severson was nowhere in sight.

"Go away," Lillian ordered. "I'm not going upstairs with you."

"Yes, you are," Isabel said. She set her candle on the bedside table. "Now, we can do this rationally. You can get out of that bed and come with us, *or* you can be carried upstairs. The choice is yours."

"I'm *not* going," Lillian announced.

"Very well," Isabel answered. "Nanny, I'll need your help." The older woman left her post by the stairs to come to Isabel's aid. In a sweeping gesture, and before Lillian knew what to expect, Isabel threw back the covers, trying not to be shocked that the girl was stark naked beneath them.

"Merciful heavens," Nanny said under her breath. "The child knows no shame."

"I'm not a child anymore," Lillian declared, and would have snatched back the covers had Isabel not been quicker. She caught the girl by the ear, gave it a twist, and cupped a hand over her mouth before Lillian could scream. Nanny removed her own dressing gown and threw it over Lillian's nakedness. Together, the two of them herded the squirming, kicking girl out into the hall and up the stairs. It was a battle, but one Isabel was angry enough to win. She didn't breathe easy until they had Lillian locked in her room.

Isabel fell back against the door, exhausted. Lillian let the world know what she thought by pounding her fists against the wood and screaming at the top of her lungs.

"You are stronger than you look," Nanny said, gasping for breath. "I don't know that I was that much help."

"It took the both of us," Isabel assured her.

"She's going to wake the babies if she keeps that up," Nanny worried, and, as if on cue, one of the little ones gave a call for her. "You are on your own now," she whispered, and hurried across the hall to see to her charges, who shared the room next to her own.

"You think you are *so* clever," Lillian shouted, the thick door muffling her voice. "My father will be furious with you!"

"Your father will thank me for saving your reputation," Isabel corrected her, and was tempted to add, *such as it is*. But she didn't. She knew how important it was for a young girl to have someone believe the best of her. She was desperately attempting to do that for Lillian.

Lillian kicked the door and yelped upon hurting her toe.

"Go to bed," Isabel instructed her. "And *stay* there. We shall discuss this in the morning."

"We'll discuss *nothing*!" Lillian sounded as if she spat at the door. "Father wants me to be in Severson's bed. He wants me to have a rich husband."

"Husband?" Isabel turned and stared at the door. "How? By entrapping him?"

"Everyone knows you aren't the best governess. They know about you and Lord Riggs. They'll blame you for my getting into trouble," Lillian taunted.

The child had finally gone too far. "Of all the disgusting, deceitful, underhanded—"

She stopped. Why was she surprised? Mr.

Wardley had never impressed her as an honorable man. And Nanny was right, he wanted his daughter married off.

Murderer or not, not even Mr. Severson deserved Lillian. And no man would compromise her while Isabel was in charge. "Let me tell you something, Lillian, and you'd be wise to listen well. Whatever you heard about Lord Riggs and me is not the truth. He attempted to compromise me, but I fought him off. Do you understand? Just because I am a woman doesn't mean I don't believe in honor and integrity, two qualities I've been attempting to instill in you. As for this night, you and your father can give up your silly plan. Someday, you will thank me for it."

Lillian's voice sounded as if it were close to the edge of the door. "Silly, silly governess," she said softly. "I left my bracelet in his bed. I *am* compromised. He must marry me. Father says that Severson wants to be accepted in Society and will have no choice but to marry me. I am going to be a rich man's wife, and you will be dismissed."

Righteous anger welled up inside Isabel to the point she shook with it. There was a way of doing things in this life. An order. Principles meant something. And people, even women, were not to be used as pawns in a chess game. They were important. Her mother had been important, and so was she. The marquis should have done better for them.

"I'm going to fetch that bracelet."

"No!" Lillian slammed the locked door with her body as if to run through it and stop her, but Isabel was already on her way.

She'd left her candle in Mr. Severson's room. She didn't bother to pick up another off the hall table. She knew the way.

The guest passageway was still empty, and laughter echoed through the rooms downstairs. She could imagine fresh bottles of port being opened. That didn't mean she had time to spare. Someone could come upstairs at any moment.

The door to Mr. Severson's room was open. Neither she nor Nanny had taken the time to close it when they'd carried Lillian out of the room. Her candle still burned on the night table.

Entering the room, Isabel quietly closed the door and began a frantic searching of the sheets.

Nothing.

She felt under the feather pillow, then ran her hand between the mattress and the headboard, probing with her fingers for the delicate gold chain. She knew the bracelet. It had been a gift from Mr. Wardley to his daughter for her birthday a month ago. There was a small charm attached to it engraved with Lillian's initials.

Just as she pulled out the bedsheet, she caught a glimpse of her reflection in the looking glass over the chest of drawers across the room and was so startled she stopped. It was like staring at a stranger.

Her heavy dark hair had come loose from its braid and made her appear vulnerable. Her brown dress had ripped at the sleeves, probably during her battle with Lillian. She looked like a woman whose life had not played out the way she'd hoped.

And that was true. Regrets threatened to overwhelm her. She was tired. It had been a long day even without Lillian's escapade. She worked so hard to be everything proper and right, and this was where she found herself— searching a man's bedclothes in the middle of the night and working for such crass people as the Wardleys.

Her mother's death had changed her life. Isabel had never been a welcome addition to her stepfather's family. She was a reminder of her mother's past and that she had loved another. After her mother died, Isabel's stepfather had wanted her gone, just like Mr. Wardley wanted to rid himself of his troublesome daughter.

Well, life was full of disappointments, Isabel reminded herself as she turned from the mirror. Nothing was everlasting, especially love, words her mother had repeatedly said to her—

She caught a glimpse of gold on the floor near the table. *The bracelet*. She practically leaped for it, scooping it up from the floor. The delicate charm reflected the candlelight, and she released her breath with relief.

Isabel set to work remaking the bed. In minutes, it would be as if no one had been in the room.

She fluffed the pillows, threw them in place, and yanked the silk spread up on her side. The bed was too wide to finish making by leaning across it. She had to walk around to the other side. There was three feet of space between bed and wall, just enough room to allow it to be made with some ease. She pulled up the other half of the spread, soothed out any winkles, and was bending over to pick up a pillow that had been knocked to the floor when the bedroom door opened.

Isabel froze.

She hoped it was Nanny coming to help her.

It wasn't.

It was Mr. Severson.

She caught a swift glance at his dark head and started to duck, but then stopped. She had nothing to hide. If anything, he should be grateful she had rescued him.

Isabel closed her fist around the bracelet and forced herself to straighten.

Mr. Severson slammed shut the door and walked directly to the dresser without seeing her standing in the far corner of the room. Isabel held her breath, uncertain of what to expect. He was taller than most men and, she sensed, stronger. His boots gleamed with champagne blacking. His neckcloth was crisp and snowy white. He wore the best. Nor did his tailored jacket of dark blue superfine need padding to enhance the width of his shoulders. He was a Corinthian, a sportsman . . . a man in command of his world.

At the dresser, he placed a hand on each corner and braced his weight as he bowed his head. Isabel thought he was feeling the effects of drink. But then he faced the mirror, looking himself straight in the eye, and said with stone-cold sobriety, "Damn."

The concise, angry word was laced with a wealth of frustration. "Go back down there," he ordered himself. "Wait them out. One of them is the key."

The key to what?

Isabel pulled back in the corner, her courage disappearing. It wasn't just his size she found intimidating—it was his looks.

If the devil were to come to life to tempt women, this was the face he would choose. Slashing black brows, a lean jaw, and brown eyes so penetrating they appeared as if they could look into another's soul.

Her heart beat faster just looking at him . . . especially when she realized *he was looking at her, too.* He could see her reflection in the glass.

Panic paralyzed her until pride took hold. Her motives were honorable. She refused to flinch from meeting his gaze.

It was an electrifying moment. The chain in the palm of her hand became an afterthought.

Neither spoke.

Isabel moved to the end of the bed, staying close to the wall, his gaze holding hers. Her heart beat so hard against her chest, she was certain he must hear it.

She stopped.

The light of the bedside candle didn't reach that corner of the room and yet, she sensed, he missed no detail of her appearance. He was as aware of her bare toes peeking out from beneath her skirts as she. He knew she wore no undergarments, no smallclothes or petticoats. His sharp gaze brushed over her hair, her eyes, her nose, her breasts.

And he liked what he saw.

Just as she liked him. The pull between them was indefinable and powerful. His lips curved into a lazy smile, and she thought her legs would melt.

This man didn't see her as a servant or a governess. He saw her as a woman. And when he said, "Come here," she had no choice but to comply.

Two

❧❧❧

Michael watched the woman walk to him, her expressive eyes wide with apprehension—and longing.

Yes, this is what I need. Mindless sex would relieve the tension and frustration that had been building in him ever since he'd returned to England.

Elswick had shut him out. For close to five months, Michael's every effort to reclaim a place in Society had been thwarted to the point he'd had no other venue to pursue than the likes of Riggs, the profligate nephew of a duke whom few people accepted, and the drunken, fawning Wardley.

Not even his brother returned his calls. The

butler, whom he had known since boyhood, seemed to enjoy informing him they were "not at home."

Michael knew Carter was there, and his wife Wallis, too. He could feel them watch him as he left their doorstep. They wanted him to stay out of their lives.

Meanwhile, Alex had returned from a profitable trip to Spain. Their shipping venture was already returning their investment fourfold. He had suggested Michael go with him on their next trip. Michael refused.

There had been a time, before Aletta's death, when he would have taken the easy route, when he would have forgotten the past. Now, he was a man who got what he wanted.

And at this moment, he wanted this woman.

She offered a much-needed diversion—and an excuse not to return to feigning drunkenness with Wardley and his ilk. He'd had enough.

Nor was Michael unaccustomed to women presenting themselves to him. He wasn't vain about his looks, but he knew their power. Furthermore, money was a potent aphrodisiac. In spite of the rumors swirling around his name, women in London eagerly sought him out. But the incident with Aletta had taught him discretion. He'd not taken what was freely offered. Even in Canada, he'd rarely had lovers. He'd been too focused on building his fortune and preparing for the day when he'd return to clear his name.

However, this woman attracted him in a way he'd not felt for a very long time. Her shining hair hung in a loose braid almost to her waist, reminding him of the proud Indian women back home. She was tall, her straight back and high cheekbones giving her an aristocratic air. A most unusual woman for a servant . . . but then, in Canada, he'd met many who had been bold enough to carve a place for themselves in the world. He'd just not expected to find such pride under Wardley's roof.

The woman stopped as if unable to take the last step toward him. The flickering candlelight cast dancing shadows around the room. Her skin was smooth and without the artifice of the cosmetics that so many women used in London. Her full, black lashes framed apprehensive sherry gold eyes. Seductive eyes. The sort that lured a man with their innocence.

His mind warned she could be a trap. His instincts didn't believe it. She was as leery of him as he was of her . . . and yet as caught up in the moment as himself.

He lifted his hand toward her hair. She drew back. He held still.

"I want to touch your hair," he whispered. "I want to know if it is as silky and heavy as it looks."

This time, when he raised his hand, she didn't flinch. He took his time, slipping his fingers into the clean, shining mass. She smelled of soap, fresh air, and woman.

Just this light touch was enough to make him hard with a force that was astounding, and he knew he was going to have her. She shifted away, shying from him. He brought his other hand to cup her face. Her skin was softer than he had anticipated.

"Don't be afraid," he whispered. "I won't hurt you. I'd never hurt you."

Her gaze held his. "I shouldn't be here," she said, her voice so low he could have almost imagined her words.

"But you are," he responded just as quietly.

She nodded.

"What is your name?"

She wet her lips, the movement almost bringing him to his knees. He wanted to smell, touch, and bury himself in her.

"Isabel."

"Isabel," he repeated. Even the sound of her name was magical.

A pounding began in his ears. It was the beat of his blood propelled by the force of that blessed need that made him a man.

Go easy, he warned himself. *Take care.* But he could not heed his own advice. "I want to kiss you."

She didn't reply, her gaze solemn, and he took that as permission, placing his hand on her waist and gently bringing her closer. She didn't balk . . . or turn away when he lowered his mouth to cover hers.

His mind registered a moment's resistance, a hesitancy, but as he fit her to him, her lips softened. She sighed her acceptance, and he could finally kiss her properly.

Elswick, Riggs, Wardley, *the world* disappeared. For too long he'd kept his guard up, his drive for vindication taking precedence over other desires. Now, the urge for release pushed him as it never had before.

He could tell she'd not kissed many men, but she was an apt pupil. As their kiss deepened, her own uncertainty vanished. Her arms came up around his neck.

Michael deepened the kiss, and she responded, her breasts against his chest, her body fitting intimately to his.

His blood pounded in his veins. He was hard, ready. Dear God, why hadn't he thought of seeking out this release before?

Because no woman he'd met in London had tempted him as this one did.

Did she know how much he wanted her? What he would do to have her?

He began moving her back, toward the bed. When her legs hit the edge of the mattress, she startled. Their kiss broke.

Michael would not have her leave. Not now.

He gathered her closer and whispered coaxing words into her ear, enjoying the sound of each syllable of her name. *Is-a-bel.* He told her how lovely she was, how much he wanted her, how much he desired her. She melted into his arms, her mouth seeking his.

Michael knew this wasn't some wayward maid, the kind that gave a man a quick tumble while looking for a little coin, but he didn't want to ask any questions. Without breaking their kiss, he shrugged out of his coat and threw it aside. He wrapped his arms around her, pulling her skirts up her legs. She didn't wear shoes or stockings. He had already discovered she didn't wear anything else either under her dress.

She had his shirt bunched in her fist against his chest. "Unfasten my breeches," he whispered. "Touch me."

Isabel did not move her fist.

Michael was a patient man with an impatient need. He'd show her what he wanted. He covered her hand with his. Gently, he pried open her fingers. She held a thin chain.

So, she was a thief.

The stab of disappointment surprised him—but then she pressed herself closer against him, and Michael would have given her his whole purse to be inside her.

Warm, willing woman . . .

He rolled the chain out of her hand, not caring where it fell. Pressing her hand to his buttons, he begged again, "Release me."

This time, she attempted to undo the first button. Michael kissed her ear, her neck, her throat, his hand moving to her breast.

The moment he touched her, she gasped, stiffening slightly. Michael didn't move. Slowly, she relaxed, sighing as he circled her hard nipple with his thumb. The layers of material did nothing to hide her own aroused state.

She undid the second button. The tips of her fingers brushed his arousal.

Dear God, he was about to explode. His body moved toward her with a mind of its own. He wanted her naked and beneath him. *Now.*

Michael pushed her back onto the bed, his hands moving down to her thigh to pull her dress up her legs. He needed to feel her, to rest his weight on top of her, to—

His bedroom door flew open. The room flooded with the light from the hallway sconces and the branch of candles Wardley carried. His host practically stumbled into the room, followed by Riggs and the other two men, Foxner and Buddings, who were fellow guests for the hunt. All were the worse for drink and enjoying themselves mightily. Michael attempted to shield Isabel from their leering faces.

Once he had righted himself, Wardley demanded in a voice so dramatic it would have been comical, "What are you doing with my daughter?"

Michael blinked, his brain having trouble wrapping around the words. "Your daughter?" He'd met Wardley's daughter earlier. She'd impressed him as a precocious twit who was far too forward for her age. This woman was not his host's daughter.

"Yes, my daughter," Wardley stated. "She's the gal you're stretched out on top of."

Before Michael could respond, Mrs. Wardley pushed past the men to make her presence known. "Mr. Wardley, is something the matter?" She sounded as if she was reciting lines on a stage, and in her low-cut dressing gown and her rose-colored turban, she appeared far too presentable to have just been woken.

"I caught Severson with our daughter," her husband announced in ringing tones.

"Lillian?" Mrs. Wardley took a step toward the bed, clutching her breast. "Oh, my child, what has he done to you?"

At that moment, Isabel raised her head. "Good evening, Mrs. Wardley," she said with amazing composure. Her lips were swollen from his kisses, her hair tousled, and her skirts up to her thighs.

This time, Mrs. Wardley wasn't feigning shock. "Miss Halloran?"

"The *governess?*" her husband asked.

"Yes," Isabel replied in a small voice.

"Where's Lillian?" Mr. Wardley looked around the room as if expecting her to be standing right there.

"In her bed," Isabel responded.

"Her bed?" Mr. Wardley repeated. He gave

33

his wife a puzzled stare. "Wasn't she supposed to be in *this* bed?" he muttered to his wife.

Foxner and Buddings grinned like fools, thoroughly enjoying the scene. Riggs was white-faced. Michael knew this was one story that would be making the rounds.

They were also lewdly ogling Isabel. Even Wardley was taking an eyeful.

Michael rose, blocking their view and pulling down her skirts. He offered his hand. She came to her feet gracefully, her color high. He knew pride forced her to hold her head up.

"Do you mind leaving my bedroom, Wardley?" he said. "Miss—" He stopped, not remembering her name.

"Halloran," she supplied, her face reddening all the more.

"Miss Halloran and I have private business to discuss."

"I imagine you have been," the ruddy-faced Buddings chimed in before he and Foxner exchanged brandy-fumed smirks. Only Riggs had the decency to move back.

Mrs. Wardley discovered her voice. "I am *shocked*," she said, this time with true emotion. "Miss Halloran, you are not a fit influence for Lillian. You will remove yourself from this house first thing on the morrow."

"Yes, Mrs. Wardley."

"Do not expect references!"

"Wait a moment," Michael said, interjecting himself. "This is *my* fault." He had no idea why the governess was in his room. But then, what else could a gentleman do? "I take full responsibility."

"For what? Ducking the governess?" Wardley said. He yawned and let out a burp. "She's a servant. Come, gents, let's leave them to their sport. Unless you want a go at the lass?"

Foxner opened his mouth as if to take him up on the offer—until he took one look at Michael's face. He held his hands up to protest his innocence.

But Miss Halloran took that moment to slip past him and the others and run out the door.

Mrs. Wardley frowned at her husband. Some form of silent communication flowed between them, then his wife marched out of the room and down the hall, grumbling to herself.

"Sorry, Severson," Wardley mumbled. "Didn't mean to interrupt your fun. Better go see to my wife." He left.

Their hosts gone, Foxner and Budding, out in the hall, collapsed with laughter.

"I think you were almost trapped into marrying his daughter," Budding said.

"The look on Old *Wartley*'s face when he saw you were with the wrong woman was priceless!" Foxner agreed. "Could you believe it, Riggs—?" He looked around. Riggs had disappeared.

"Where the devil did Riggs go?" Foxner complained.

"Why don't you find him?" Michael suggested, shutting the door in his companions' faces. He turned toward the bed, frustrated . . . and then his gaze fell on the glint of a gold chain buried in his carpet.

In the upstairs hall, all was silent, except for the sound of Nanny's gentle snoring. Even Lillian had given up her battle and fallen quiet.

A burning candle stub had been left for Isabel on the hall table. Isabel picked it up and hurried to the haven of her room. She shut the door and crumpled to the floor. Never had she felt such shame.

All her life, she had struggled for respect. It hadn't been easy growing up as the village bastard. Her mother had bought respectability through marriage, but there were those who had believed the sins of the mother should be visited on the daughter.

Everyone knew her mother had been the

marquis' mistress. They *knew* who her father was. And they also knew how much her stepfather hated having under his roof a reminder of his wife's past.

Isabel forced herself to stand. Pity was a luxury she couldn't afford . . . and yet, for the moment, she wanted to wallow in it a bit. To let loose her frustrations. To rant and rail and throw a tantrum to rival any Lillian could imagine.

She set the guttering candle in the holder on the table by her bed. It was really little more than a cot. She pulled her valise out from under it and threw it down onto the thin mattress. Everything she had to her name could fit in the bag with room to spare.

Isabel raised her hand to her forehead. How could she have been so wanton?

Growing up, she'd had more than her share of unwelcome attention from men. They had sniffed around her like dogs. Village boys with dirt under their nails who felt she should give them a kiss. She'd stayed close to her mother, embarrassed to repeat some of the things they had said to her.

Richard was the first who had gotten past her guard.

Mr. Severson the second.

The difference between the two men was that Richard she had fought off; Mr. Severson she had encouraged.

And she didn't know why.

He was a stranger to her, and she'd met him kiss for kiss. She'd been as aggressive as he. After all these years of working so hard to protect her precious reputation, she had ruined herself in front of the worst possible audience.

What had come over her? She'd never reacted to a man that way. She had allowed him astounding liberties, and her body still simmered from the heat of his touch. She'd actually liked feeling the weight of his body on hers.

There was no excuse for her behavior. Mrs. Wardley had been correct to dismiss her. Isabel would have done the same.

She opened the valise and started to gather her meager belongings, uncertain what to do next. Two jobs, and she'd received references from neither of them—

Her thoughts were interrupted by the opening of her bedroom door. Richard strode in as if he belonged there.

He slammed the door shut.

Isabel groaned silently. "What do you want?"

His jaw tensed. "You. I want you. I've wanted you since I first set eyes on you."

There had been a time when she had thought him attractive. Now, after she had been in Mr. Severson's presence, Richard's handsome, boyish looks had lost their appeal. He seemed thin and ineffectual.

Nor was she intimidated by him. Not any longer. Something inside her had snapped.

"I'm sorry, Richard. I have just lost my position because of a man, and I really am not in the mood to deal with another."

A vengeful light leaped into his eyes. "He attacked you, didn't he? By God, he will answer to me."

Isabel's tenuous hold on her temper broke. "Answer to you?" She gave a sharp bark of laughter. "You have no rights over me."

"I would defend you." He took a step closer. She was thankful the bed was between them. "I'd protect you from anything, Isabel."

"Except yourself, or have you forgotten?" she answered, the memory of him holding her down very clear in her mind. But she'd known how to protect herself. She'd kneed him in the groin, the tactic she had learned to use against the village boys who had teased her.

"I'm sorry, my lord," she said dispassionately, "but I do not return your affections. Now go, Richard. Leave me be."

"You would take *him* over me?" Richard acted as if he couldn't fathom such a thing. Isabel reminded herself that he had been drinking. She wrapped her hand around the valise handle, preparing to use it to club him over the head if necessary.

"Yes," she answered, defying him to make a move toward her.

He didn't. Instead he whined, "Severson is a dangerous man. He's a murderer."

"I've heard. Makes me wonder why *you* associate with him."

Richard's mouth flattened. She knew the answer to her question. Mr. Severson was wealthy, and Richard needed money to pay for what he lost on the gaming tables. "I have my reasons," he replied.

"And I had my reasons for being with him, too."

"You are still angry with me, aren't you? Nothing happened that day between us, Isabel. I did release you."

"Released me? I *fought* you! Granted, you were the worse for drink, but then you followed through on your threat to see me dismissed.

You lied to your aunt, Richard. You told her I encouraged you."

He held his hands up as if irritated by the topic. "You make too much of it, Isabel. God made you for man's pleasure. With those looks, you weren't designed for a life in the school-room. You were meant to be cared for and cosseted. That's what I was offering. What I *am* offering if you'd only be reasonable. I could make you very happy."

"No, you couldn't," she said. A wiser woman might have spoken with more tact . . . but she knew tact was lost on Richard. "Look at you. You drink too much. You have no ambition, no responsibilities."

"I have a title."

"Yes, and like so many others, you believe it justifies your place in the world. It doesn't, Richard. Nor does it give you a right to me."

"You are wrong about me, Isabel. I made a mistake with my aunt over you. It seemed easier not to tell the truth."

"To *lie*," she corrected. "It was easier to lie and to let her believe *I* lied."

"If you wish to have it that way."

"I do."

His lordship's lower lip pouted out. He wasn't familiar with people telling him no, and

Isabel realized that a part of her wanted to believe there was something more to him than the spoiled, petted young lord he was. But then, what had she expected? There were no romantic heroes.

"You are so hard," he said. "If you aren't careful, I shall forget I offered to keep you. The world can be very cruel to a woman alone."

He was right. "You've already taught me that lesson, Richard."

For a moment, she feared she'd gone too far.

His jaw went hard, and his eyes turned murderous. It took all her courage to hold her ground.

"Very well," he said tightly. "I'll let you stumble a bit until you learn your place. But this time, I won't help you find a position. Oh, you thought you'd landed this job with Wardley on your own? No, my sweet Isabel, I had him hire you. Otherwise, *no one* else would have, not with everything my aunt had to say about you. So think long and hard before turning down my offer. Your looks won't last without a protector, and they certainly won't find you a decent position—especially after the stories circulate about you and, of all people, Severson."

With that prediction, he turned on his heel and left, slamming the door behind him.

Isabel stood stunned. Had Richard encouraged Mr. Wardley to hire her?

Dear God, what was she going to do?

For a moment, her resolve weakened. Caring for other people's children was not an easy task, or a gratifying one. She didn't mind hard work or scrimping and saving, but she hated being talked down to by people with less intelligence than she. Or by those who wouldn't pay wages on time. It was already a month into the new quarter, and Mrs. Wardley had not paid any of her servants. There was no greater insult than not to be paid for labor performed—although Isabel doubted if she'd see any money now that she had been sacked.

This was not the life she wanted to lead.

She wanted more. She didn't know what *more* was, but she vowed to find it. She must. She needed to believe there was more to her existence than waiting on the whims of others.

Hope gave her courage. Richard was wrong. She was not defeated, not yet.

As a sign of her renewed determination, she went out in the hall and gathered up all the bits of candles that were left on the table there. In her room, she started lighting one after another, setting candles in wax on her windowsill, the seat and back of a chair, all over the bedside table until their glow brightened even the darkest corner.

When she was done, she stood in the middle of the room by her bed. Each flickering flame seemed an embodiment of her spirit. She wasn't defeated yet. She didn't know what she would do on the morrow or even how she would eat, but she vowed to succeed. At all costs, she would not be beaten—

A knock sounded on her door.

Isabel whirled to face it. Why couldn't Richard leave her alone? Let him go find another bottle to drink or more friends to fleece.

He knocked again, the sound more insistent. She was tempted not to answer . . . except that would be cowardly, and Isabel was no coward.

She went to the door and threw it open, ready to send him on his way—but the words died in her throat.

Richard was nowhere to be seen.

Instead, Mr. Severson stood there in shirtsleeves, his neckcloth still disheveled, his eyes alive with anger. His presence filled the doorway.

He held up Lillian's bracelet, the charm swinging on its chain. "What the devil is going on?"

Three

Michael's patience was stretched thin. Wardley had attempted to trick him. He was certain of it. He wanted answers, and he expected Miss Halloran to give them to him.

Instead, that stubborn chin of hers shot up in open defiance a beat before she *slammed the door in his face*.

He stared at the painted wood, and his blood boiled.

He'd had enough.

He'd played "Society" games. He'd tolerated cold shoulders and outright rudeness. Gossip followed him wherever he went. They said one thing to his face, another behind his back.

Three weeks ago, a young idiot with too

much drink in his veins had publicly challenged Michael to a duel. He'd claimed Michael's presence in London was an "affront to dignity."

Michael chose swords and had shown the pup what a true "affront to dignity" was by disarming the braggart in a matter of seconds. He was later criticized because his method wasn't sporting, but he'd also achieved a new respect. No one was foolhardy to challenge him now—but for one governess.

And he wasn't going to take this sort of treatment from a servant.

Turning the handle, he opened the door and walked right in.

The ninny apparently hadn't anticipated such an action. She was bent over a valise, folding clothes—

Michael stopped dead in his tracks, taken aback by the array of burning candles. They were everywhere. Candle stubs of all sizes. Their flames generated warmth and filled the room with the sweet scent of hot wax and a golden glow.

"What's going on here?" he demanded, sounding more gruff than he'd intended.

"It should be obvious. I'm packing." In the

candlelight, she was even lovelier than he had first thought, and more spirited. Any other woman would have been intimidated by a man of his size intruding into her personal domain. Not Miss Halloran. She appeared more than ready for a fight.

But his temper had cooled, replaced by interest. "I was asking about the candles," he said. "My impression of Wardley didn't lead me to the conclusion that he is a generous or wasteful man."

"You are correct." She started to place the folded clothing in her bag, but then changed her mind, realizing her shoes should go in first. They were a well-worn pair of black slippers, the sort that was all the fashion in London. The leather looked to be kid. Shoes of that quality would be quite an expense for a governess, and she handled them as if they were pure silver.

She was also pointedly ignoring him.

Michael knew how to handle that. He plopped himself on the rickety bed, knowing she'd have to look at him. He just prayed the thing wouldn't collapse beneath him. "How could anyone sleep in such a flimsy thing?" he wondered aloud. "I'd prefer the floor."

Miss Halloran placed a protective hand on her bag, frowning at his audacity. "Usually," she said in a clipped tone, "when someone slams a door in *your* face, it means *you* are not welcome."

"I didn't expect to be," he answered, making himself comfortable by resting on one elbow. From that angle, he could see her feet. She was still barefoot, and he noticed that she seemed to have two hems. "What the devil are you wearing?"

She placed her precious kid slippers into the bag. "It is none of your business."

"You have on two dresses. Now, I understand why I'd had so much trouble figuring my way beneath your clothing. Every time I thought I'd found your laces, there were more."

Her face flooded with color. "Mr. Severson, please leave."

"I will," he promised, "after you explain this." He held up the graceful bracelet.

"Don't pretend to be naive," she answered, placing her clothes on top of the shoes in her valise, her actions deliberate and forceful. "Your friends grasped the situation immediately."

"They aren't my friends," he corrected carelessly. "And I want to hear the story from you."

"And then will you leave?" She shut the valise.

Absolutely not. Michael smiled. "If I must."

"You must." She moved to the other end of the bed. "Mr. and Mrs. Wardley had hoped to trap you into marriage by claiming you had compromised their daughter."

"But she is a child. Is she even sixteen yet?"

"She turned seventeen last month. Apparently, Mr. Wardley wants a rich husband for his daughter, and he chose you. Lillian liked you, too. It must be difficult to be so handsome women throw themselves at you."

He caught the sarcasm in her tone and heard the subtle rebuke of her own actions. "It doesn't always work that way," he said, keeping his voice light. "Sometimes I throw myself at them in return."

Her sharp glance told him she had not mistaken his meaning. "Not often," he added, watching her closely. "It's been a long time since a woman has caught my interest."

Her response was to cross her arms tightly, a clear signal that there would be no repeat of the earlier scene between them.

He understood. What had happened downstairs had been a lapse for both of them. She had slipped past his guard, just as he had hers.

"Lillian wasn't in the room when I came upon you," he said.

"No, I discovered what she was about, and Nanny and I bundled her back up here where she belonged."

"So why did you return?"

"The bracelet was a gift to Lillian from her parents. She has her father's cunning. She can barely write legibly, but she can scheme with the best of them. She left her bracelet in your bed as proof you had compromised her. When she bragged to me about what she'd done, I was angry enough to go fetch it. The rest you know," she finished, the corners of her mouth tightening.

Michael nodded, realizing he felt more than lust for the governess. He liked her. No airs, hysterics, or whining. She might have fears and doubts, but she would face them. He respected the kind of courage it took to be that brave. He'd been forced to rely on it himself. It's what had made him a man. "The candles?" He circled his hand to encompass the room.

Again, becoming color rose to her cheeks. "A protest," she admitted. She glanced around, and added, "A silly one."

He sat up, tossing the bracelet on the bedside

table. "I disagree. Any act of individuality in this country is to be celebrated."

His words brought out the governess in her and a bit of patriotism. "A *civilized* country needs rules," she responded as if by rote.

Amused, Michael challenged, "Rules that are bent or broken to fit the needs of the rich. The poor are left with gin instead of bread while the Prince and his ilk dine on dishes prepared by *French* chefs."

"We aren't at war with the French any longer. Nor is there a crime in enjoying their cooking."

"We will be again soon," Michael predicted. "And then the taste of all those sauces will sour in the bellies of *loyal* Englishmen."

"I don't know if you aren't the insurrectionist, Mr. Severson," she said stiffly.

"I'm not the one burning all the candles, *Isabel*," he replied, taking great pleasure in her name and the way the small intimacy infuriated her. "By the by, my given name is Michael. I believe we've moved a bit beyond formalities."

"I wish you would leave, *Mr. Severson*."

She combed her hair back with her fingers as she spoke, lifting it up and releasing it in a glorious mass of shining silk. The room filled with her scent. He knew it immediately and came to his feet, aching to touch her, to take her back in his arms and start where they'd left off.

A shadow of fear came to her eyes.

He stopped. "I won't come closer. You have no reason to fear me."

She didn't relax. "Your questions have been answered, Mr. Severson. I have nothing more to say. We are done with each other."

He didn't move. "Where will you go?"

Isabel moved back a step. "That is my concern."

Michael shook his head. "No, not yours alone. I played a hand in your losing your position. I wish to make some amends."

His words seemed to offend her. "I can take care of myself." She nodded to the door. "Now, please, leave."

Michael could not leave. He wasn't ready to let go of her, and he didn't like the thought of her unprotected and out in the world. "Let me take care of you."

It was the wrong thing to say. Her response was instantaneous. "I won't be any man's mistress," she said, her voice firm with conviction. Her eyes grew suspiciously shiny as if tears threatened, tears her pride wouldn't let her shed. "Do you believe you are the first to make such an offer? You aren't."

"I've never made such an offer to a woman before." It was true.

His response didn't mollify her. She wrapped her arms around her waist, holding herself close. "I suppose I can't fault you. After all, I've given you every reason to think I would be willing."

"We were *both* involved," he answered.

Her gaze slid away from his, and he knew he was losing her. He grasped at the only thing he had to barter with—his money.

"I can take care of you," he promised. "You'll never lack for anything—"

"I'm not for sale." Her hard words cut through the air between them.

"I didn't offer to *buy* you."

She met his eye. "No, just payment for service. Like the sort a draper or banker provides."

"I want to take care of you."

"As if I were a pet?" She shook her head, her doubt clear. "Or is it that you are bored and want to hire someone to keep you company."

Her accusations made him uncomfortable. "Isabel, be reasonable. We are both adults—"

"You came up here to make an offer for me, didn't you? Wanting to know more about Lillian's schemes was just pretense. You expected me to fall into your arms. And I almost believed

53

you were different from the others." She shook her head as if stunned by her own culpability. "I can't believe that after all this, I am still so naive."

"Isabel—"

"I'm sorry, sir. You can't afford my price."

Michael did not like being mocked, or that she had accurately read his intentions. It embarrassed him. He hid behind his own pride. "You might be surprised, Miss Halloran. I am embarrassingly wealthy. What do you want? A house, carriage and horses, jewels—?"

"Marriage."

The word seemed to suck the air from him, and she smiled, knowing she'd hit her mark.

"That's my price, Mr. Severson," she taunted. "Are you willing to meet it?"

"No." Michael had assumed that one day he'd get married, but that day was a long way off. He still had his name to clear, and, when he did marry, he had assumed it would be for all the right reasons—fortune, prestige, and power.

"I know," she agreed as if reading his thoughts. "It is too high a price; however, you aren't the only one with a vaunted opinion of himself."

Michael winced. "Your tongue is sharp, Miss Halloran."

"It needs to be, Mr. Severson."

He had to agree. "I like you, Miss Halloran."

"I take that as a compliment, sir."

"It is."

For a moment, they looked at each other in perfect accord. Michael moved first. He pulled out his card from his fob pocket and offered it to her. "I'm sorry for my role in this evening's work. Obviously, I was an unwitting stooge. Please, if you find yourself in need of a friend, contact me. My office is in a warehouse on the West Dock in London. Haddon and Severson. Or I have a house in Mayfair." He paused and added, "I'll expect nothing in return."

She studied him a moment as if searching for a sign of deception. He waited. Moments passed, then she took his card. "Thank you."

"You're welcome," he answered, and she actually smiled. It was a shy, slightly rueful expression that made him wonder if he was about to make a serious mistake walking out of this room.

Michael was no fool. If ever there was a danger sign to a man, that was it. He moved to the door and opened it. "Good night," he murmured, almost afraid to look at her again . . . but then he couldn't help himself. Perhaps his mind was playing tricks on him?

It wasn't. If anything, she was more lovely to him now than when he'd first walked into the room. She stood surrounded by candlelight, her dark hair curling past her shoulders, her bare toes peeping out at him from beneath her skirts as one finger traced the edge of the card she held in her hand. Her defensiveness was gone.

"Good night, Mr. Severson."

"Good night," he repeated more for himself than her. It took all his self-control to leave the room and shut the door.

For a moment, he stood outside, tempted to go back in. The draw between them was strong. His kisses had broken her resistance once. He could do it again—except he wouldn't feel right about himself. And eventually, she would hate him.

What was done was done.

He started down the hall. He was a third of the way to the stairs when he heard her door open. She called his name. "Mr. Severson?"

Michael turned.

The candles from her room flooded a square on the hall floor in which she stood. "Did you murder Aletta Calendri?"

Her question caught him off guard. People went out of their way *not to* mention the murder. No one ever asked.

"No."

She nodded as if he had confirmed something in her own mind. "I couldn't imagine you as a killer. Good night, sir," she murmured, and shut the door.

Michael stared at the point where she'd stood, letting his eyes adjust to the dark. Well, at least one person in England had the courage to speak of Aletta to his face.

However, it wasn't until he'd made his way down the stairs, that he realized she had called Aletta by name. Time had passed. Usually when he overheard the gossip and whispers that followed him, they spoke of a murdered "woman" or occasionally "actress." Few remembered the woman's name . . . but Miss Halloran had.

A niggling sense that there was something he should know about her, some connection he was not making, gave him pause . . . and yet, he could think of nothing. He was certain he'd never before laid eyes on her.

Downstairs, all was quiet. Apparently the others had gone to bed. It had to be close to three, and they were all planning to go hunting at dawn on the morrow. Sooner or later, even the most hardened gamester had to have sleep. Michael wondered if Wardley had settled matters with his wife.

A footman slept, leaning in his chair at his post in the hall. A few candles still burned, but a good number had been snuffed.

Michael walked to his room and wondered why he stayed in England. After three months, he had made no progress in clearing his name. If anything, matters were worse. His presence in London had revived interest in Aletta's death but no results. He'd attempted to look up court papers. There were no records. They had disappeared, and the people who had known Aletta had died or moved to parts unknown. Every door, every avenue concerning the murder was closed to him, and he was growing bloody tired of being the outsider. Perhaps his interpretation of the dream had been wrong. Perhaps he was a fool to have returned.

He opened his bedroom door, then stopped. Riggs sat in the chair with his feet propped up on the bed. A brace of candles on a table beside his chair provided the room's light. He swung a half-empty wine bottle between two fingers of the arm he dangled off the side of the chair.

"Where have you been?" he demanded.

Michael closed the door. "Out."

He didn't like Riggs, but the man, so far, had been his only entry into Society. They had attended school together. At one time, around the period of Aletta's death, they'd been gambling companions. However, the subsequent years had not been kind to Riggs. Lines of dissipation and disappointment were etched deep in his face and soul.

Michael also knew he was being milked for every copper Riggs could get off him; but having been a younger son himself, he understood what it was like to be expected to play Society's games and live on London prices without any expectation of income. "What are you doing here?"

"Staying *in*," Riggs said, mocking him. He raised the bottle and took a swig like a man who wanted to drink to forget.

"I'm tired," Michael said. "We're hunting tomorrow, right? I'll see you then."

Riggs didn't move. "You were with *her*, weren't you?"

Michael didn't need to ask to whom he was referring. Nor was there mistaking the jealousy in the man's eyes. "I was."

Riggs started laughing, the sound almost painful.

"I fail to see the jest," Michael said.

"Of course you don't," Riggs said, with an edge of superiority. "You haven't a clue."

"A clue to what?"

"Who she is." Riggs rolled up onto his feet, taking a moment to steady himself before facing Michael. "You have no idea."

"Are we talking about Miss Halloran?" Michael wanted to clarify.

"No other," Riggs answered. "I knew she was here with Wardley. Thought it would be amusing to bring you here, too. However, I didn't anticipate your reaction to each other. Aren't I the fool?" He took another drink.

Michael shook his head. "You are going to have to speak plainly. I'm too tired for riddles."

Riggs lowered his bottle. "I thought you were a quick one, Severson. A smart mind. And yet, what you seek is right beneath your nose, or beneath *you*, as the case may be."

"I won't let you insult Miss Halloran," he said quietly.

There was a long moment of silence. Riggs was drunk enough to take up the unspoken challenge. Michael wouldn't have minded a fight. He was in the mood to break someone's neck, and Riggs would do better than most. Few would miss him.

"Hall-o-raaaannnn," Riggs said, rolling the syllables out.

Michael frowned. What nonsense was this?"

"Halloran!" Riggs barked at him.

"I know the governess's name. What the devil does it matter?"

"Come now," Riggs jeered softly. "Do you not know Elswick's family name?"

Halloran. "God, I'm an idiot."

"I won't argue," Riggs said into the mouth of the bottle before he took another drink.

Michael shook his head. "This doesn't make sense. What is she to Elswick?"

"A daughter."

"He doesn't have a daughter."

"An *illegitimate* daughter," Riggs answered as if playing a trump card. "There is many a bastard who uses the sire's name." He turned the bottle upside down. It was empty. He dropped it to the floor and stumbled to the door. "I leave the rest up to you, Severson."

"Wait."

Riggs turned.

"Why?" Michael asked.

"To see if you can do better. I tried the lady. She wasn't to my liking."

61

Michael doubted that. He knew an empty boast when he heard one.

"An illegitimate daughter is the best I can do," Riggs was saying boozily. "You'll have to find your own way after that." He leaned against the door. "What you do with this tidbit of information is up to you. Of course," he sighed, "I do expect compensation for my services."

"It's the way of the world," Michael answered, silently adding, *with the exception of one headstrong governess.*

Isabel did not sleep that night. She blew out most of the candles shortly after Mr. Severson left, somewhat embarrassed at being caught in her pique of independence. It didn't take her long after that to finish packing what little she owned. She spent the last hours before dawn attempting to write a letter to her stepfather, asking him if she could return to his home until she could find a new position. The right words failed her.

Their relationship was strained. Perhaps it would be best to show up on his doorstep without warning and judge by his reaction if she should stay or go. She hated returning home a failure once again.

She was so miserable over returning to Lancashire a failure, she'd even toyed with the idea of writing the marquis—and rejected it. What could she say? *Dear Father, you don't want to know me, but I need a roof over my head.*

She'd never asked him for help, and she would not start now.

Instead, she counted her money. She could have used the wages Mr. Wardley owed her. As it was, she had just enough to make it to Higham and to pay her way for a month or two.

By the time dawn arrived, she'd convinced herself she would find a new position. She had to. Perhaps in Manchester, far from London, she could find a genteel family who wouldn't ask for references.

An hour later, she'd washed her face and styled her hair into the tight chignon she felt made her look older. She put on the one item her mother had passed down to her, a green velvet bonnet with yellow ribbons. In its day, it had been quite fashionable and very expensive. It had also been a gift from the marquis, and her mother had treasured it.

For a second, Isabel thought of Mr. Severson and his offer and felt a temptation to accept it.

Except what would she be left with? Would

she be like her mother and have nothing but a worn hat and a bastard daughter to remember him by?

Isabel picked up her valise and left the room.

Out in the hall, she took a moment to say her good-byes to a tearful Nanny. They hugged and wished each other well. Lillian was still fast asleep.

Downstairs, Isabel took her leave of the other servants, most of whom she didn't know well. She ignored the few smug looks sent in her direction. No, she wouldn't be able to find a position in this area. Servants gossiped, and the story of last night's scene would quickly spread through the parish.

The nearest village where she could catch the post was a good five-mile walk. She didn't mind stretching her legs a bit. Mist clung to the ground, and there was a chill to the spring air that added to the melancholy of her departure.

The gardeners were already at work with the lawns, and the grooms were bringing up horses from the stables to carry the hunters out into the fields. Mr. Wardley enjoyed hunting pheasant. He prided himself on being a crack shot and having the best bird dogs.

All too soon, he and his guests would be coming out of the house, and the thought was enough for her to hasten her step toward the brick pillars marking the entrance to the drive, especially when she saw one of the grooms leading a team of flaxen-maned chestnuts pulling a sporty phaeton. It was the vehicle in which Mr. Severson had arrived. She didn't want Richard or Mr. Severson to see her leaving.

She was almost to the road when she heard the sound of wheels on the gravel behind her. Mr. Severson pulled the vehicle up beside her. "Good morning, Miss Halloran."

She didn't think she'd ever seen a more handsome man. Contrary to her, he appeared well rested and ready for the day. His greatcoat was cut of the finest gray wool, and he wore it and his low-crowned hat with the dash of careless negligence. His boots shone in the morning light.

What pleasure it would be to wear shoes made of such fine leather. For a moment, she was tempted to take him up on his offer.

She started walking toward the road.

"I was hoping to catch you," he said pleasantly, as if she hadn't snubbed him. When she didn't answer, he said, "Here, will you stop for a moment?"

"I'm sorry, I must reach the Bull and Crown in time to catch the post."

He pulled the phaeton in front of her, blocking her path.

Isabel stopped. "All right then, what do you want?"

"To amend my offer," he answered smiling, his teeth strong and even. "You see, I've thought about it, and I've decided you are right."

"About what?" she asked, confused.

"Marriage," he replied.

Four

❧❧❧

*I*sabel wasn't certain she'd heard him correctly. "I beg your pardon?"

"You said your price was marriage." Mr. Severson spoke calmly, as if they discussed the morning weather and nothing more. "I've agreed. I will marry you."

It had been a long, disappointing night, and Isabel was in no mood for jests . . . especially since her heart did a little leap at the word "marry." No one had ever made her an honorable proposal. She was too honest not to admit to a measure of excitement over receiving one.

But she wasn't a fool.

He was almost blindingly handsome. Wealthy. Self-assured. *Everything* a woman could wish for in a man, including the fact that her toes curled when he kissed her. All he had to do was smile to set her pulse racing. She'd never met a man like him.

So it was with great pride that she mimicked his cavalier nonchalance, and answered, "You can't *agree* to marry me because I *didn't* ask you."

"Yes, you did," he shot back. "Last night you said your price was marriage."

"I was telling you that I would not be kept."

"Then I'm volunteering to marry you," he replied smoothly. His eyes danced with delight, as if he had anticipated her answer. He was enjoying himself immensely—*at her expense.*

She struggled with an urge to throw her valise at him. Seeing it hit him right in the head and knocking him off the high seat of the flashy, overpriced vehicle would give her no end of satisfaction.

"Why are you doing this?" She looked to the house. "Is this a dare you took with your cronies? Are they hiding in the windows snickering at the sight of you baiting the governess?" She gave him a look of pathetic sympathy. "Don't you think you've caused enough havoc in my life?"

She didn't wait for an answer but backed up and started to walk around the phaeton.

"Miss Halloran, you misunderstand my intentions."

She ignored him, hoping everyone, including the gardeners and the lads preparing for the day's hunt witnessed her giving him the cold shoulder. She'd arrived at Wardley Park a lady, and that was how she would leave it.

The ribbons of her bonnet had come undone. They never stayed in place, but she was not going to ruin the effect of her "walking away" by stopping and retying them.

"Miss Halloran, I'm speaking to you."

She smiled to herself. She was making him angry. Good. She liked getting in the last word.

Then she heard him jump down from the seat of his carriage, the stones crunching beneath his booted heels. He gave the horses a soft command, and she knew he was going to follow her.

Isabel lengthened her stride. She didn't want to appear as if she were running, but she might not have a choice.

Her rush was to no avail. His legs were longer and stronger. He was gaining on her. "Miss Halloran, don't be an idiot."

That made her stop. "What did you call me?" she demanded, whirling on him.

"An idiot," he dared to repeat.

Cathy Maxwell

She dropped her valise, her fists doubling. "If I were a man, I'd call you out."

"If you were a man, I wouldn't be asking you to marry me."

"That's not my point—"

"But it is a significant one," he interjected, "and I only referred to you as an idiot because it was also the only way I knew of making you stop."

"Well, it did, and it made me bloody—" She drew back from swearing. "It made me *angry*—"

"I see that."

"No, you *don't* see. This is a game to you. You and your friends—"

"Those men are not my friends," he corrected her.

"You drink with them."

"I don't drink. Thank you for giving me the opportunity to set the record straight."

"Well you have poor taste in companions," she replied.

"You might be right."

"I *am* right, and I'm also tired of you. Leave me alone."

She picked up her valise and walked around him. To her endless frustration, he fell into step beside her. "I'm sorry I called you an idiot."

Isabel didn't acknowledge him.

"I don't have *any* friends really," he said conversationally, as if they were having one. "Well, there is Haddon. He's my blood brother, and he is not anyplace close to Wardley Park. If he was, he'd assure you that I have never offered marriage to a woman before, and certainly I wouldn't do it as a joke. This is not some ruse or 'baiting the governess' game. I'm sincere."

From the direction of the house came the sound of the hounds being brought round. The dogs would be used to chase out the birds during the hunt. Their howling emphasized Mr. Severson's own doggedness. She kept her focus on the brick pillars and placing one foot in front of the other.

"You should consider my proposal, Miss Halloran."

"I have. I said no."

He hooked his hand in the crook of her arm and swung her around. "Isabel, listen to me. I am attempting to do the honorable thing. The devil knows I'm not a gentleman often, and it only seems right that when I try to be one, someone listen."

She looked into his eyes. He seemed sincere.

A tradesman's dray turned onto the drive from the road. Gently, Mr. Severson moved her over onto the grass to let the wagon pass. The driver in a felt hat with frizzy hair sticking out beneath it nodded to them with undisguised curiosity and continued on his way to the house.

A horse whinnied in the distance, and she realized Mr. Severson was not dressed for hunting. Indeed, he gave all appearances of taking his leave of Wardley Park.

Perhaps, he *was* acting alone.

Perhaps, he was *serious* about his offer.

The thought was riveting. Isabel forced herself to breathe. "You are offering me *marriage?*" She punctuated the last word with one gloved finger.

He gave a little shrug and nodded.

"Why?" The word practically burst out of her.

"You told me marriage was your price. I'm willing to pay it."

Isabel couldn't shake her doubts. "This is nonsense."

"The price is high," he agreed.

"Not about the price," she retorted, "but your willingness to marry *me*." She swallowed before admitting, "You don't need to fear someone is going to call you out on my behalf." She couldn't keep the bitterness from her voice. "I have no champion."

"You do now. *I'm* your champion."

A champion . . . someone who cared about her, who watched her comings and goings. She'd not had that since her mother died.

Something of what she was thinking must have shown on her face. "What is it, Isabel?" he asked.

She wasn't about to expose her deepest hurts to him. "A man doesn't just enter into a marriage on a whim."

"Actually most do," he argued. "Few have sound reasons."

"But *you* wouldn't," she responded more to herself than him. "In fact, you are not like the others. I wondered last night why you were involved with Richard—"

"Richard?"

Isabel dismissed the name with a wave of her hand. "Lord Riggs. What are you doing with him and Mr. Wardley and those others?" As if she'd conjured him, she could hear Richard shouting at his friends to leave their breakfasts and come out for the hunt. Soon, they would be charging across the countryside heading for the open fields in search of pheasant.

"We were in school together, and Riggs sought me out," Mr. Severson answered. "Wardley's invitation to this weekend came through him."

"He wanted to borrow money. He never has any."

"No, he doesn't," Mr. Severson affirmed. "But to his credit, he hasn't asked to borrow even a shilling."

"Then perhaps Mr. Wardley was paying him to find a husband for his daughter." She frowned. She had a larger mystery to consider. "Why would you even be willing to marry *me*?"

"Why would I not?"

Exasperated, Isabel said, "Don't patronize me."

"I'm not," he answered.

"Then why would you make such an offer?"

His answer was to let his gaze drop to her breasts.

With a will of their own, her nipples tightened immediately—and she wanted to go to him. All too clearly, she remembered the heat of his body pressed to hers and the discovery of needs she'd not known before.

He knew his impact on her. He raised his gaze and gave her a look so knowing and so intense everything inside her melted—including her resistance.

The hunting dogs, the house, her doubts . . . all vanished.

"I told you last night what I wanted," he said, his voice low, hypnotic. "I haven't changed my mind. I want you, Isabel, no matter the cost."

And she wanted him. He stirred her senses in a way she'd not known before.

Isabel grasped the handle of her valise with both hands. It was everything she could do to not fall into his arms.

"No," she said, her voice so faint she doubted if he heard her, but she couldn't speak louder. "I won't marry you. I won't marry anyone." She turned and would have run for those pillars except he still had a hold on her arm.

He pulled her back. "Why not?"

"Because I don't believe in love," she lashed out, wanting him to let her be. "And there is no reason to marry without it."

The words had just tumbled out of her mouth. She had no idea where they'd come from until she thought of her mother, who'd loved the marquis. Or her stepfather, who had worshiped a woman who could never love him even after he took in her bastard child. Better to be alone than expose herself to the possibility of making the same mistake.

"Then why do poets sing of it?" Mr. Severson challenged.

"Because unrequited love makes such delicious tragedy," she answered. "And don't be such a prig. I doubt if you believe in love either. You strike me as too pragmatic."

His quick smile made her knees weak. "Quite right, Miss Halloran. And yet every poet swears it must be worth the risk. I've taken more than my fair number of risks in my life. I'm not going to shy back from this one, especially when there is so much to gain."

They stood practically toe-to-toe. If she leaned forward, she would be able rest her head on his chest and hear the beat of his heart.

Isabel feared she wasn't as strong as her mother had been. She'd not recover losing in such a game.

Something of what she was thinking must have shown on her face because he asked, "What promise do you want from me? That I will never leave you? Very well. You have my word and my word is my bond. It's had to be. Trust me, Isabel. Believe in me . . ."

Those were heady words to a young woman who had nothing to her name and nowhere to go.

". . . Be my wife."

Isabel could not refuse.

He took the valise from her fingers, not waiting for her answer. He turned her around toward his horses. "We'll make arrangements in London."

She was conscious of walking beside him. He was strong and powerful, and she was safe.

In some part of her mind, she wanted to retie the loose ribbons of her bonnet before she climbed up on the perch of that high-flying phaeton. She'd never been on one before, but her younger half brothers, the sons by her mother's marriage, would think riding in such a sporting carriage all the thing. She used to race the boys around in the pony cart when they were little, before they went off to school and decided they were too old for games and too proud for their sister.

Her stepfather would be shocked if she showed up married to such a wealthy man.

In London, she might even cross paths with her real father.

Mr. Severson placed her bag in the phaeton's boot and came around to help her up onto the perch. She placed her hand in his. He gave her fingers a small, reassuring squeeze.

Isabel looked at him and, for a moment, *wanted* to believe in love. His eyes weren't as dark as she thought. This close to him, she could see the shades of brown and a hint of green as dark as the forest—

A shot cracked the air. The horses, so well trained they had been standing in place while she and Mr. Severson had been talking, tossed their heads and took a prancing step away.

Mr. Severson threw his arm around her, knocking her bonnet off her head as he pushed her to the ground.

"What is it?" she asked.

"Gunfire." He scanned the trees lining the drive up to the house. She looked, too. Mr. Wardley and two of his friends had already started the hunt, but they'd stopped when they'd heard the shot. She saw their figures silhouetted against the tree line. Even the dogs had picked up their ears and sniffed the air.

"I don't see anyone," Isabel said. "Are you certain it was a shot?" she asked.

"Yes. It hit me. In the back." He appeared startled by the knowledge and, for a second, she thought he jested until she looked behind him and saw the hole in his fine greatcoat.

"I think I shall need help . . . quickly," he

murmured, reaching for the side of the phaeton to draw himself up.

Isabel put her arm around him. Out the corner of her eye, she could see Richard running down the drive to them, followed by one of the stable lads. "Help," she called. "We need help." She started to remove his coat to see the wound and felt blood. Her mind scrambled for everything she'd ever learned about cuts and scrapes. She needed to stop the bleeding.

"Can't stay here," Mr. Severson said, his voice low.

"You can't travel," she countered. She got his coat off. The bullet hole went through the back of his coat and a rim of blood was spreading slowly seeping around it.

"Must go."

Richard reached them. Isabel could see that Mr. Wardley and his other guests were now hurrying toward them.

"It was a shot, wasn't it?" Richard said.

"Yes, it hit him," Isabel answered.

To her surprise, Mr. Severson straightened. "I'm fine," he said.

"The devil you are," Richard responded. "Look at the blood. You need to lie down."

Mr. Wardley and his friends arrived then.

"Severson's been shot," Richard told them. "We need to take him back to the house."

"Good heavens," Mr. Wardley said. "Who would shoot him?"

"Any number of people," Riggs answered.

"Bad luck it is," Mr. Wardley muttered. "I say, did you see who fired the shot?"

"We saw nothing," Isabel said. "What of you?"

Mr. Wardley snorted his answer. "Wasn't even looking in this direction."

At that moment, Mr. Severson sagged against her. Isabel almost dropped him to the ground. "Take me away from here," he said in a voice so low only she could hear him. It wasn't a request but a command.

Isabel looked to the circle of men watching them and felt uneasy. They didn't seem unduly surprised about the shooting, and whereas they might express concern, the cold way they appraised Mr. Severson belied their words of concern.

Or perhaps, her disquiet stemmed from the fact that all of them, except Richard, carried guns—and Richard's was held by the stable lad who had accompanied him down the drive.

Isabel wondered if there was a way to find out which one of those had been fired.

She didn't dare ask. Instead, she looked to Jack Pickett, the hound master. "Mr. Pickett, will you help me lift Mr. Severson up onto the perch."

"Now see here, Isabel," Richard said, upset enough to use her given name in company, "Severson will bleed to death if you go tearing off over the countryside with him."

Mr. Severson put his boot on the step, ready to hoist himself into the seat if he was able. Isabel pleaded, "Mr. Pickett, please."

"Oh go on, Pickett," Mr. Wardley said. "You can see the man wants to leave. Let him."

The master of hounds stepped forward, nodding to the stable lad to help. The boy handed Richard his gun and, together with Isabel, lifted Mr. Severson up onto the seat. To their credit, the horses seemed to sense the seriousness of the situation and remained still. Then, with Mr. Pickett's help, Isabel climbed up beside him. "Thank you," she said to the servants. Mr. Pickett picked up her bonnet from the ground and handed it to her. It was a miracle a horse hadn't stomped on it. She tied the ribbons to the bar around the seat and picked up the reins.

"I want you to know, I won't have his death on my conscience," Mr. Wardley said. "If you leave, you do so without my blessing."

Mr. Severson spoke for himself. "We're leaving." He sat quiet and erect, one hand grasping the front edge of the hard leather seat, the other the back.

Isabel raised the reins, and the horses started forward. She was conscious that everyone watched them.

"Can you drive?" Mr. Severson asked.

"I've driven a pony cart." A high-perched phaeton was no pony cart.

She heard the hint of a smile in his voice as he said, "Courage, Isabel. The horses know their job. Keep your hand steady."

They reached the brick pillars. Isabel held her breath as she turned the horses onto the road. A phaeton looked sleek and fashionable from the ground, but it felt absolutely unstable when one was driving it.

"Are they following?" Mr. Severson rasped, referring to Mr. Wardley and Richard.

"No," she answered.

He released his breath and slumped against her. "Doctor. Not much time."

Isabel fought panic. "Of course, a doctor," she said. "There isn't one in Glaston. Or, at least, not most days. We send to Uppingham if we need a physic. I don't know if you could make it to Uppingham." She was babbling.

Worse, Mr. Severson appeared beyond caring. "Whatever . . . you . . . think," he managed to say.

One of the horses stretched its neck, tugging at the reins in her hands, a sign of the animals' impatience to be on the way, and she knew she must make a decision.

"We'll go to Mr. Oxley," she said half to herself. "He's the rector at St. Andrew's, only a mile or two away. He was in the military. He'll know what to do."

Mr. Severson did not answer.

Isabel feared driving the well-sprung phaeton and Mr. Severson's very responsive horses. She feared overturning them.

She feared that Mr. Severson was going to die.

Her heart in her throat, she clucked the horses to start moving.

They'd traveled less than a mile when, his weight too heavy for her shoulder, his large body fell into her lap.

Isabel grabbed for him, afraid he would tumble to the ground. The horses did not like her sudden jerk on the reins. For one wild moment, she feared they would bolt.

They didn't. She shifted her weight, trying to balance Mr. Severson better.

"Please sit up. Can you sit up?" she begged.

He didn't respond. His forehead felt clammy to the touch. Fever would set in soon—if he didn't die of blood loss first.

She debated turning back, then thought of the hardness she'd glimpsed in Mr. Wardley's and Richard's eyes.

There was only one direction to go—*forward*. She went, praying every foot of the way.

Five

Michael did not dream. His was the sleep of the dead. He knew because he was in Death's presence.

He felt the presence of others, too. He recognized them without seeing their physical forms. They were companions he'd known, companions who had crossed over into the Darkness. They hovered on the edges of his mind, as real to him as they had been in life.

His first visitor was the young lieutenant he'd gambled with the night he'd arrived in Frenchtown. The lieutenant and his friends had entertained themselves by scaring the wits out of a very green Michael with tales of Indian torture, stories Michael dismissed as too incredible to

Cathy Maxwell

be true. A week later, Michael had been with the party of men who found what was left of the lieutenant's body in a clearing where he had been scalped and burned at the stake.

The Widow Coffey, who had cooked for so many on their journeys, was still her laughing self in this afterlife. She'd died of blood poisoning, but now she and her lover, a burly sergeant who had been the victim of a lightning strike, hovered close by his bed.

And his parents were there, too, silent and disapproving as always . . .

Most disturbing was Aletta.

His mind remembered her as she had been—vibrant and beautiful, with just the hint of dissipation around her eyes. She'd lived hard. Death had not freed her.

She knew who had murdered her, who had ruined his life. He wanted to know. Now, when earthly cares should no longer be his worry, he still needed the answer.

But Aletta would not share her secrets. Instead, she drifted away, teasing him to follow, just as she had done to every man who'd crossed her path.

He surged toward her, calling her name over and over. *She couldn't leave him, not when everyone thought he'd killed her. She must tell the truth!*

However, his body was not made of mist and air. Sharp pain ripped through him—

He fell back on the straw mattress, his shoulder throbbing in anger.

Gentle hands urged him to relax. "Please," a woman's voice begged. "You must lie still."

Another woman asked, "What happened?"

"He tried to rise from the bed," the woman holding him down answered.

"He's healing," a male voice said. "Makes them restless. Let's give him that draught Maribelle made. It will ease the pain."

But Michael didn't want a draught. He welcomed pain. It meant he was alive. It meant he had another chance at justice.

In the end, the choice wasn't his. Whether he wanted it or not, the draught was poured between his lips, and he swallowed it.

Then sleep came.

Now he dreamed, alone. There was no comforting presence, no companionable Death, no Aletta with the secret she'd taken to her grave . . .

Forrest Oxley did know what to do for Mr. Severson, although he warned they might be too late since he'd lost a great deal of blood and would lose even more when he dug for the bullet. Isabel had to leave the room because the rector searched with his finger, poking it into the wound. Mr. Severson was unconscious the whole time, but she felt pain for him.

When the rector had finished his doctoring, he told Isabel that Mr. Severson's fate was in the hands of the Lord. She was thankful that neither Mr. Oxley nor his wife questioned her decision to tend to Mr. Severson, although the rector's wife handled the more personal aspects of his care. They'd accepted her murmured claim about his being betrothed to her . . . although she sensed they had to know better. St. Andrew's was a small parish.

For three days, she had rarely left his side. They'd set up a cot for her in the other room, but after they went to sleep she would sneak in and lie on a blanket on the floor by his bed. There was a bond between her and Mr. Severson. She wasn't certain what would come of it, but she'd recognized that, like her, he was an outsider.

Her empathy manifested itself in a fierce protectiveness toward him. The coldness she had seen in Richard's eyes haunted her. *He'd* fired the shot. She knew it . . . and wondered why the others had lied for him.

Isabel tried not to worry. Mr. Severson appeared to be regaining strength and might soon return to consciousness, and when he did—then what?

She was uncertain of the answer.

However, she was taken aback when inflammation and fever had made him delirious, and he'd called out Aletta's name.

The rector's cottage was little bigger than a mousehole. Mr. Severson's room had space enough for the bed and a chair. Beyond the sitting room was a kitchen, then the Oxleys' bedroom. Hardly anything could be said in one corner of the house without every occupant overhearing.

So, Mr. and Mrs. Oxley heard Mr. Severson call out another woman's name, not once but over and over again.

Isabel had backed away from him when he'd shouted, going to a corner and crossing her arms. The despair in his voice had made the hairs on the back of her neck stand.

Nor had she been prepared for the sharp jealousy that had cut through her. She might pretend her motives were chaste and innocent. They were not.

Isabel didn't understand why God and Severson's enemies had placed him in her care. All she knew is that she had to give him time to rebuild his strength and keep him safe from Richard . . . and the ghost of Aletta Calendri.

Michael woke in stages to a dark world. It was night, and no candle burned anywhere.

The sheets smelled fresh, yet they lacked the cottony smoothness of his own. The air was close, but damp and cool, and he was glad of the heavy covers.

His legs felt like leaden weights, and his body seemed molded to the mattress. He lay on his stomach, and he, a man who never wore anything to bed, had on some sort of nightshirt that felt several sizes too small. It took him several moments of consciousness to remember being shot.

In the darkness, he slipped a hand along his arm to his shoulder and felt the bandages. The wound was tender to the touch, and he marveled at having been hit so close to his heart without bleeding to death.

"Mr. Severson? Are you awake?"

The hushed woman's voice gave him pause.

There was movement beside the bed. He sensed more than saw the figure stand. There was a scraping, the strike of flint on steel, then a flickering of light that grew as the candle on a table beside the bed was lit.

The brightness hurt his eyes. He turned his head away, giving himself a second to adjust before looking back. The first thing he noticed was the woman's silky black hair and, for the briefest moment, fear blocked his throat.

Aletta.

He silently mouthed her name even as she bent over him, and her face came into view.

This woman was not Aletta. She had the same glossy hair, but her features were more refined and lacked Aletta's Latin sultriness.

He recognized the governess just as she started to speak. "How do you feel? Is your fever gone?" She pressed a hand against his forehead, and it soothed away the inkling of a headache.

She smelled of the night air and roses . . . English roses. His memory came alive. He knew her touch, the taste of her kisses, and the way her body fit his. *Isabel. Miss Halloran.*

He remembered them arguing on Wardley's drive—he offering marriage; she refusing; he winning her over. His reasons for making such an offer exploded in his head. *She was Elswick's daughter.*

The upheaval of memories he was experiencing must have shown in his face. She started to pull away. He caught her arm at the wrist, amazed at how weak he was.

She hesitated. He held fast. At that moment, she was his only link to his surroundings, the only one he thought he could trust. She could have broken his hold. Instead, she lowered herself to sit on the edge of his bed, letting him hold her wrist as tight as he wished.

Yes, she was Elswick's daughter. Hers was a feminine version of his straight nose and high cheekbones. She even had his arching brows—only hers were tempered by compassion, an emotion he doubted Elswick had ever experienced, and they gave her face character.

"Miss Halloran," he said, in acknowledgment. His voice sounded rusty, and his throat was dry.

"Mr. Severson," she replied as quietly, and he couldn't help but smile. He had nothing to fear.

"How long have I been here?"

"Almost a week. We feared we'd lost you."

"I thought you'd lost me, too," he rasped, and was rewarded with her shy smile. He swallowed, finding his voice. "Where am I?"

"St. Andrew's rectory in Glaston. Mr. Oxley is the rector. He used to be in the military, and I'd heard he had some surgerying skills. He and his wife took us in."

Michael nodded, not having the strength for

more questions. He would sort it out later, when he was strong and could make decisions again.

She leaned over him, her expression anxious.

"I will live," he assured her.

"Someone wanted you dead," she whispered, as if revealing a great secret.

"Someone does," he agreed, sensing his hold on consciousness slipping away. He relaxed his grip on her wrist. "Thank you." He said the words on a sigh and wasn't certain if he had spoken them aloud or just imagined he had. Either way it didn't matter. He'd returned to the sweet oblivion of sleep.

Isabel sat beside him on the bed, waiting until she was absolutely certain his breathing was regular and normal. She rubbed her wrist where his hand had held her. Her skin was still warm from his body heat.

A sound came from the door, and Mr. Oxley poked his head in. "I thought I heard voices."

"He woke," she said. "He is going to live."

"I knew he would," he assured her. "He's a strong man. He should heal rapidly now." There was a beat of silence. He asked, "And what of you, Miss Halloran? You told us you were promised to each other?"

"Yes." She didn't elaborate. She wondered if Mr. Severson remembered their argument. He hadn't said anything.

The rector studied her a moment, and she wondered if he could see her doubts. He did, because with a frown he said, "Mr. Severson and I will talk when he is better. I will see he carries through with his responsibilities."

Isabel didn't know whether to be grateful or alarmed. She was infatuated with Mr. Severson but knew better than to trust him . . . especially when he called out another woman's name.

The next time Michael woke, it was daylight. His room was little larger than a corncrib. A window was cracked open to allow for fresh air. A bird called to another, a call that went unanswered.

Miss Halloran was not there.

He listened for signs of life beyond the half-open bedroom door and heard voices in quiet conversation. The smell of baking bread made his stomach rumble. He also caught the drift of pipe tobacco and a hint of roses. Miss Halloran was close by.

His mind was clearer, and he wanted to move. He tested his body by attempting to lift his left arm. Thank God, the shot hadn't hit his sword arm, and he was pleased that he had less pain than when he'd first come to his senses.

He wondered if he dared sit up. He leaned his weight over on his good arm. The bed was narrow. There was a braided rag rug on the floor. He focused on its bright, optimistic colors, his body complaining as he strained in an attempt to push himself up—

"Here now, don't do anything foolish," a man's voice said from the door.

Michael rolled back on his stomach, frustrated. The man walked into the room, his pipe in one hand. He was thin and short, with a bald pate and a tuft of gray hair sticking out over each ear. His eyes missed nothing.

"I'm Mr. Oxley, the rector of St. Anthony's." He closed the door behind him and took the step to the bed. "You've had a rough time of it, sir."

Michael nodded. He knew. "You took the bullet out?"

"Yes. It came easily enough. May I?" he asked, setting his unlit pipe on the table. He didn't wait for an answer but lifted the nightshirt, unwrapped the bandages, and began inspecting his handiwork. He grunted, a pleased sound. "The wound is clean. You should heal quickly now. I was worried about the inflammation, but you've come through the worst of it."

He straightened. "I put a stitch or two in, but you know how it goes. You'll have a scar to go with the others. You've lived an adventurous life, Mr. Severson."

"Out of necessity," Michael answered. "Sometimes I wasn't smart enough to dodge the bullet." The rector chuckled, as Michael knew he would. He liked this man. He was honest. "Do I have you to thank for saving my life?"

The rector rewrapped the bandage, and Michael pulled down the shirt. "I did the doctoring, but you'd not have made it through if not for Miss Halloran. She stayed by your side."

Michael remembered waking in the dark and her being right there. "I know."

"Do you, sir?" Mr. Oxley questioned, his expression grave. He picked up his pipe. "We are a small parish. Little escapes notice. Now, something like the Wardleys' governess snagging herself a husband, especially from one of the scoundrels her employer entertains, is fodder for the gossips for months."

"I imagine it would be," Michael said carefully.

Oxley studied him a moment before saying, "Yes, I believe you do. Miss Halloran is a member of our small church. She hasn't been among us long, but my wife and I are fond of her. We lost a daughter who would be about her age right now. She was our only child."

"I'm sorry to hear that," Michael murmured.

"Yes, well," the rector said, "it was years ago, but the pain is always fresh. Miss Halloran brings out the father in me. She is a fine young woman, a clever one. She'll make a good wife. I don't mean to take advantage of your weakened state, Mr. Severson, but you must marry her. She has no father or brother to speak for her. I helped her bring you back from the dead for that reason alone."

"I appreciate your plain speaking, sir," Michael said. "I have every intention of doing what is honorable."

"Good," Oxley replied. He hesitated a moment, and said, "I know your name. I've heard the rumors about you. I didn't know what to expect. I think I like you."

He could have no idea how much those words meant to Michael.

A quick knock on the door interrupted them. Without waiting for an answer, someone opened the door. "What is going on in here?" Miss Halloran said.

Mr. Oxley faced her, blocking her view from Michael. "We are having a men's discussion.

97

Go wait with Mrs. Oxley. I believe she is preparing a broth for our guest's lunch."

"I will do nothing of the sort," Miss Halloran returned roundly. She entered the room and moved to the foot of Michael's bed. The three of them filled the space. "If you are discussing me, then I will be present." She dropped her voice to add, "And I thought I made you agree not to discuss *any*thing until he was stronger?"

"Some things can't wait," Mr. Oxley said, putting his cold pipe into his mouth.

She turned to Michael, and he was struck anew at how lovely she was. However, her character transcended her beauty. He had not needed the rector to tell him all she had done. Such steadfastness was a trait he valued, one he'd not witnessed since returning to this shore and civilization—

He caught himself on the last thought. England was far from civilized, and he had a bullet in his back to prove it.

"I will not have you listening to a word he says," Miss Halloran instructed Michael. "You need time to heal."

"He needs to get his affairs in order," Mr. Oxley interjected.

Her answer was a scowl so dark it made the rebellious clergyman smile. And Michael, too.

He decided to speak for himself. "I *have* made an offer to you, Miss Halloran, and you said yes, didn't you?"

Something passed in her eyes, a shadow of disappointment that Michael didn't understand. "We shouldn't discuss this now," she said stiffly.

"There is no better time than now," Mr. Oxley informed her. He looked to Michael. "So, you wish to see the matter done right?"

"Yes," Michael said, and made an attempt to sit. He felt at a disadvantage having this discussion while lying on his belly.

Miss Halloran immediately came to his aid, pushing the rector out of the way. "You shouldn't try and get up," she chastised.

"I want to sit," Michael said.

With an impatient sound, she helped him turn over and sit up. Folding the feather pillow, she placed it under the small of his back. For one brief, disconcerting moment, their noses were less than an inch from each other—

The world came to a halt . . . and Michael was struck anew at how deeply he was attracted to this woman. She aroused him as no other ever had. If he leaned forward, he could press his lips to hers.

What's more, she felt the same magnetic draw. He could see it in the sherry gold of her eyes. Time stood still . . . until Mr. Oxley cleared his throat, reminding them they were not alone.

Miss Halloran flew back to the end of the bed, blushing in a most becoming way.

Michael wasn't surprised to see the hint of laughter in the rector's eyes. The old dog confirmed Michael's suspicions by saying, "You'll do, Mr. Severson. You'll do."

"As what?" Miss Halloran asked, regaining her prim composure. Michael liked that about her. She could be so cool and controlled on the surface, but it didn't take much for him to slip past her defenses to the hot-blooded woman beneath. And he knew she wasn't that way with every man. What lay between them was very rare.

"I'll do as a husband," he answered.

"But I refused your offer," she returned crisply, her pride getting the better of her. "You don't remember because you were shot, but we agreed to part company."

Michael frowned, uncertain. Would he have let her get away? He didn't think so.

"Everything has been changed now," he argued, wondering why she was so fiercely independent.

Or was it that she did not *want* to be associated with him in any way?

The thought was sobering, especially when she looked to Mr. Oxley, and said, "Will you please give us a moment alone?"

The rector sensed the change in attitude. He looked from Miss Halloran to Michael, wavering a second before saying, "I will be outside the door." He left, leaving the door open.

Boldly, she closed it, then, crossing her arms, walked to the window, her back stiff.

"You really have no choice," Michael said mildly.

When she didn't answer, he dared to ask the question uppermost in his mind. "I have a reputation, Miss Halloran. You know that." Memories were coming back to him, including her asking if he had murdered Aletta.

She nodded.

"The world is much smaller than we think," he said. "I've learned that the hard way. If you do not marry me and accept the protection of my name, such as it is, then you will be hounded by this incident for the rest of your days. Think on it. How would you support yourself, Isabel?" he asked, taking the liberty of

101

using her given name. It was like music. "The Reverend Oxley assures me everyone in the parish already feels you have overstepped the boundaries of propriety in taking care of me."

He had chosen his words deliberately, and they had the desired effect. She faced him, her eyes wide in alarm, a slow dark color creeping up her neck. "Mrs. Oxley saw to your more personal needs. I was just—" She stopped, at a loss for words. "I only did what was expedient," she replied in a small voice.

"And I am doing what is right. It doesn't make any difference what the truth is. What people think is what you have to live with."

Her voice so soft he had to strain to hear it, she agreed, "I know."

He pressed his case. "There is something between us. Something that draws us to each other. Do you not sense it as I do?"

He paused, silently daring her to be honest. A small frown had formed on her forehead. She did not wish to give him what he wanted, but in the end, her character would not let her lie. "I feel it," she admitted.

"Then that is all the more reason we should marry," he answered.

"If anything, it is a reason *not* to."

Michael frowned, unable to comprehend her reasoning. "Do you believe I can't take care of a wife? I assure you, Isabel, I am a wealthy man. And, rumors to the contrary, an honorable one. I can take care of a wife."

Her lips tightened, her face pale. Her resistance was an insult, and her capitulation, when it came, was hardly flattering. "You are right. I have no choice."

Immediately the door opened. "Exactly what I said!" Mr. Oxley declared, unrepentant over eavesdropping. He was followed into the tiny room by his wife, a woman with rosy cheeks and sparkling eyes. She carried a bowl of steaming broth in hands wrapped in a cloth. She was careful to set it down before crowding around Miss Halloran with open arms.

"This is wonderful news!" Mrs. Oxley said. "You are to be married, my dear. Your life will be so much better. You'll be raising your own children and not those of others."

Her husband rubbed his hands together in expectation. "We have work to do. The wheels must be set in motion. We'll have to post the banns and—"

"Excuse me, Rector," Michael interrupted, "but I insist on being married by special license."

Mr. Oxley frowned. He obviously preferred matters to be done the formal way. "The price the bishop charges for a license is exorbitant."

"The price is of no matter," Michael assured him, wanting to impress Isabel and win her approval. "A speedy marriage is. Besides, no one of my class marries by the banns. Send someone and make the necessary arrangements with all due haste. I'll pay well for the trouble." He added, "I must also insist on making a donation to your parish for all you have done for me. Will five hundred pounds be acceptable?"

Mr. Oxley's knees almost buckled. "That is too much," he protested.

"I assure you, it is little recompense when compared to how much I value my life," Michael answered.

Mr. Oxley took Michael's hand, shaking it vigorously with his excitement. "It is most generous, sir, most generous."

However, Miss Halloran's reaction was completely different and the opposite of anything Michael could have anticipated—she walked out of the room without a word.

Six

❧

*I*sabel walked straight out of the cottage but stopped in the front yard. The ground was damp from the previous day's rain. Shoots from hardy perennials were breaking the surface of the earth in Mrs. Oxley's garden. Beyond the yard, separated by a low stone wall, was the road. Isabel crossed her arms and stared at it, debating whether or not she should just keep walking.

Jingles, the Oxley's gray mouser, jumped down from the edge of the rain barrel where he'd been taking a sip. He glided up to her and rubbed his back against her leg, purring as he swirled her skirts.

Usually Isabel had time to give him a pat but

not then. Instead she struggled with pride and temptation.

"Isabel?" Mrs. Oxley's soft voice said from the doorway.

"Yes?" Isabel turned, forcing a smile.

The rector's wife came out onto the step, holding the door open. "Are you feeling yourself?"

"I am." Her throat tightened. "I need a moment."

She'd hoped that would be the end of it. It wasn't. Mrs. Oxley came out into the yard, closing the door behind her. "What is it, child? What troubles you?"

"I am hardly a child."

"Then what is it, *my friend*?" Mrs. Oxley corrected herself and Isabel was embarrassed by her churlishness. She had to explain. The Oxleys had been so generous, she couldn't shut them out.

"I barely know him," she said tightly. *And he'd called the name of another woman when he'd been unconscious.*

It was all so confusing. He claimed he hadn't killed Aletta, and her every instinct told her to believe him.

Then what *had* the actress been to him? A lover? Certainly. Something more? Deeper?

The jealousy Isabel experienced was unreasonable. She barely knew the man. This was a side of herself she'd not faced before. An object of her jealousy was a woman who had been dead a decade or more.

She'd thought she was different from her mother. More independent. Certainly more sensible.

But what if she wasn't?

She didn't say as much to Mrs. Oxley. The rector's wife enjoyed probing into other's reasons and motivations, and Isabel needed to keep all this close.

Mrs. Oxley smiled reassuringly. "I know the announcing of the banns gives a couple time to reflect, and this is all very quick, but sometimes it isn't always necessary to know the man you are marrying *too* well."

Isabel made her doubt plain. "It isn't?"

The older woman shook her head. "Sometimes our hearts know better than our heads."

The statement broke through Isabel's carefully nurtured reserve. She was tired, exhausted from days of worry. She laughed, the sound bitter. "That is not true. My mother's life was miserable. She should have thought with her head and not her heart."

"Why was that?" Mrs. Oxley asked, full of concern.

"Because she followed her heart and paid a hard price. The man she fell in love with, *my* father, didn't return those feelings. He was already married to another and happy with his life. Mother was his mistress and nothing more. By the time she realized he would never return her feelings, I was on the way. Nor did he want anything to do with me. It was as if her bearing his child made her distasteful to him. She went back to Lancashire and married a man who was a good provider. My stepfather loved my mother deeply, but her past was always between them."

"Could she not find happiness in her marriage?"

"There was always a deep sadness about her . . . and my stepfather. I think he wondered whom she loved best."

"Some men are like that," Mrs. Oxley agreed. "Always measuring themselves against another. However, I must speak out for passion. I was once promised to a man who would have been good for me to marry. He was well thought of and very respectable. Everyone admired him. He also came from money."

"What happened?"

"I jilted him."

"You?" Isabel asked, surprised.

"Yes, and I eloped with Mr. Oxley. It was the wisest move I ever made. We've been very happy." She placed a motherly hand on Isabel's arm. "I understand your fears and, considering your background, I can see why you would be afraid to act rashly. You might even believe it would be easier not to have to feel anything at all than to make the wrong decision."

"Yes," Isabel agreed, realizing Mrs. Oxley did understand.

"I've counseled several young women who were about to enter into the state of holy matrimony, women who had doubts like yours. I urge each of you to think with your heart *and* with your head. It's a difficult decision, Isabel, because there are no rules, no certainties. What seems right today may not last the morrow. We must all feel our way and pray the Lord helps guide us."

A chilly breeze circled around them, and Isabel glanced at the yard and the line of trees beyond, the first buds of spring giving their limbs a red hue. "I have prayed, Mrs. Oxley. Prayed, and prayed, and prayed. I don't know if anyone is listening."

"*Someone* is. And, perhaps, my dear, the reason you are feeling so conflicted is because a part of you wants to marry Mr. Severson. A part that right now, you don't trust."

Her words went straight to Isabel's deepest fears.

"And if you don't believe God cares enough to notice you," Mrs. Oxley continued, "then know *I* am listening." She tucked a strand of Isabel's hair that had blown free back behind her ear. It was a motherly gesture, and almost Isabel's undoing.

Tears threatened. She forced them back. "I just want something of substance in my life," she confessed. "Something I can trust and believe in." Dear Lord, she sounded like a fool.

"Like what?" Mrs. Oxley asked. "If it is money you wish, then Mr. Severson has all you could need and more."

"Money makes for a cold bed partner."

"You're right," the rector's wife agreed. "But what is it you want?"

To be loved. The thought leaped into Isabel's mind with a truth that was humbling.

She realized that was why she'd allowed herself to be charmed by Richard, even when later she recognized there was nothing charming about him.

Isabel looked at her friend, who seemed so wise and understanding, and knew she would never confess her thoughts aloud, not even to Mrs. Oxley. Such a confession would make her vulnerable. "I don't know what I want," she murmured.

Mrs. Oxley was not fooled. "Yes, you do. Isabel, you are too suspicious. I don't know what made you that way, and I won't pry. But I will ask that, at least this time, we trust that what is happening is God's plan."

"What if God is wrong?" Isabel shot back, expecting the rector's wife to fly into a tizzy.

She didn't. Instead, she shocked Isabel by asking, "Are you afraid Mr. Severson will hurt you?"

"No—" She thought of the painful jealousy she'd experienced when Mr. Severson had called out Aletta's name. "At least, not physically."

Mrs. Oxley pressed her lips together, her brow furrowing as if she heard what Isabel wasn't saying. "One would have to be blind not to see the attraction between you and Mr. Severson. I wish you could have more time to know each other better. I don't know your history, Miss Halloran, but I know you are not some village girl. There is quality about you. Oh, please," she said, when Isabel opened her mouth to protest, "we've all known. You move among us, but you don't belong here. Perhaps Mr. and Mrs. Wardley were too dense to see, but the rest of us haven't been. I don't know why you must earn your own way, but Mr. Severson is doing the right thing. If you refuse him, you may find yourself in very dire straits. There is a line a woman like you must not cross. If you do, there will be no going back."

Isabel didn't know what to say. Mrs. Oxley was a shrewd judge of character. She'd known. "What if I don't ever find my place?" she asked quietly.

"Miss Halloran, instead of preparing for things to go wrong, imagine them turning out wonderful. Life isn't a present where you have to be pleasantly happy all the time. You need the challenges to give it meaning. It would be nice if we could predict our lives or be able to see the future. We'd also be bored. At some point, a decision has to be made, and you must trust you've made the right one."

There was that word "trust" again.

Jingles gave a loud meow, a sign he wanted attention. Isabel picked him up, holding him to her chest, appreciating the diversion he provided. She looked at the petite older woman with new respect. "You are very wise."

"I've had more experience at life than you," Mrs. Oxley countered, giving a scratch to the point behind Jingles's ears he liked so much.

"You're right about me wanting to see the future. *You* seem to have no regrets over the decisions you've made, but what if you had? What advice would you give me then? You want to see an idyllic ending—"

"I do."

"But I *don't*. I see all the things that could go wrong."

"Like what, dear?"

Like falling in love with someone who could never love her.

And it hit Isabel that she *could* fall in love with Mr. Severson. She might even be halfway there. It should have been impossible . . . and she wasn't quite certain when it had happened.

"Oh, dear," she whispered, handing the cat to Mrs. Oxley.

"What is it?" her friend asked.

"I *can't* marry him," Isabel said.

"You have no choice."

"Yes, I do." Isabel started for the cottage, her mind made up.

"Miss Halloran—" Mrs. Oxley called, but Isabel didn't wait to hear her opinion. She was already through the door.

Mr. Oxley sat in his favorite chair before the fire, his eyes closed. Having caught him eavesdropping once, Isabel had no doubt he'd been about it again and was probably pretending to take a nap. She went directly to Mr. Severson's room and shut the door firmly behind her.

Mr. Severson rested on his stomach, his eyes closed, and he did not open them when she entered the room. The bed was too small for him. His broad shoulders and long legs filled it to the point where his feet hung over the bottom edge.

When they'd first undressed him, they had not been able to find a nightshirt in the portmanteau stashed in the phaeton's boot beside her own valise. Mr. Oxley's nightshirt didn't fit him well. Mr. Severson's arms were several inches too long. She'd not noticed those details when he'd been so sick. However, now she saw everything.

He opened his eyes. His mussed dark hair made his face seem paler. His features were drawn. He'd lost weight.

Concern welled up inside her. The bowl of cooling broth still sat on the table where Mrs. Oxley had placed it. Someone should have fed him but, what with the marriage nonsense, his nourishment had been forgotten.

With a frustrated sound, Isabel pulled the wooden chair up to his bed and picked up the bowl and spoon. The broth was warm to the touch, the perfect temperature really.

Mr. Severson frowned.

"I need to feed this to you," she said. "You haven't eaten anything for days other than Maribelle's sleeping draught." She leaned forward to spoon broth into his mouth, the angle a bit awkward.

"It would be easier if I sat up," he said. "Help me."

Isabel had no choice but to help him. However, this time she kept an arm's distance from him, her eyes carefully averted. She picked up the bowl.

"It would be easier if you sat on the edge of the bed," he suggested, "instead of that chair."

It would. "I don't think it would be wise," she responded primly.

Even weak, the light of a thousand devils could light up his eyes. "After what you and I have been through since we've first met, sitting on the edge of my bed is a relatively chaste act."

"We haven't been through anything," she announced breezily.

"My memory is hazy on some things that

115

happened when I was shot, but I clearly recall the night before the incident—"

Isabel shut him up by sticking the spoon in his mouth. "Keep your voice down," she whispered. She went to pull the spoon out, but he clamped his lips around it, refusing to give it up.

"What sort of game is this?" she asked.

He smiled and patted the bed.

"No," she answered.

He pulled the spoon out of his mouth, his good humor evaporating. "I can feed myself then." He reached for the bowl. She held it beyond his reach.

"It appears we are at an impasse," she said.

He patted the bed.

She didn't want to give in. She should leave. She didn't.

With a resigned sigh, Isabel moved to sit on the edge of the bed. He opened his mouth, and she ladled the broth into it. He had nice teeth, strong and white, and she realized that Mrs. Oxley had been right. She did want her own children.

Funny that teeth would make her feel that way . . . or perhaps it was because, as she was feeding him a second spoonful, Mr. Severson had placed his arm across her lap. It was a protective gesture, one of comfortable familiarity.

He watched her intently, as if waiting to see how long it would take her to bolt.

She didn't. Instead, she surprised him, and herself, by ladling another spoonful in his mouth. He looked tired.

"Very good," he murmured.

"Mrs. Oxley made it."

"It's been a long time since I've supped on broth."

"I trust you don't get shot often."

He smiled. "I try not to."

She couldn't help but like him. He was the most honest person she'd ever met. And there was that attraction between them that Mrs. Oxley claimed everyone could see.

For a moment, she fed him in companionable silence. He was hungry and made quick work of the soup. She put the spoon in the empty bowl. "Perhaps I should fetch more," she said, starting to rise.

He applied pressure to his arm, holding her in place. "We must marry," he said, quietly looking in her eyes. "I know there are those who would think you had lost your mind to marry me."

"I'm no catch either," she said.

"You are," he answered without hesitation.

His quick insistence touched her, but there was only one honorable thing for her to do.

Isabel set the bowl and spoon back on the table before looking down at him. She'd best tell him now. "I'm not what you believe," she confessed.

"You are not a governess?" He was teasing; she wasn't.

"I'm a bastard," she stated. She hated the word. She'd heard it all her life. Her half brothers, the village girls, the whispering women talking over their hedgerows had often used it about her.

"My mother was a man's mistress, and I am the result of their liaison."

"Do you know your father?" He didn't appear upset by this information.

"I know his name. We have nothing to do with each other."

He nodded. "And your mother?"

"She passed away a little over two years ago. She was ill for several years. I nursed her."

"So I'm not your first patient?"

"A bullet wound is different." She looked down at his hand resting on her thigh. "She had a wasting illness. She lingered a long time."

"It must have been hard."

"It was, for all of us."

"Who else is there?"

Isabel placed one hand on the edge of the

bed, relaxing slightly. "I have a stepfather and two half brothers."

"Where are they now?"

"In Lancashire. My stepfather is headmaster of a small school."

"Ah, so that is where you gained your education."

"Yes, he *did* teach me. I was actually a better pupil than his sons. My mother was well-read, too. Her father had been a village vicar."

"The vicar's daughter who became a man's mistress?"

Isabel shrugged. "He disowned her. I never met him though he didn't live far from us. He would have nothing to do with my mother or me."

"What about your stepfather?"

"He was genuinely in love with my mother. He could forgive her anything. He used to write the most atrocious poetry in her honor, but it all came from his heart. Even when she was sick, he'd write wondrous words to her as if she were whole and healthy."

"Perhaps he saw her that way."

"He *wanted* to see her that way," Isabel amended. "When she died, he behaved as if her illness had come as a surprise. And he seemed to blame me."

"Grief can do that."

"Either grief or the fact I wasn't his blood." She couldn't keep the bitterness out of her words. Her stepfather's rejection had hurt deeply. "What of you?" she asked, changing the subject. This was a personal conversation, but she didn't want to delve into deeper, more intimate feelings.

"What do you wish to know?"

Isabel shrugged. "Tell me about your family."

"My parents are dead." His bluntness surprised her. He frowned. "I didn't mean to shock you. They've been gone for years."

"You don't sound terribly unhappy about it."

Mr. Severson seemed to mull over her words a moment before agreeing with a small frown. "We rarely talked. I knew my nanny better than I did my mother. Furthermore, I was a disappointment to them. They died in a carriage accident shortly after I left England."

"I'm sorry."

He shrugged, and she sensed he felt their loss more deeply than he wanted to reveal. She moved the topic to a safer subject. "Where did you grow up?"

"My family seat is in Kent. My brother is the earl of Jemison."

"An earl?"

"Finally, I have your interest," he said with a grin. "Unfortunately, I'm not an heir. I understand he has two sons now."

"You understand?" Isabel repeated. She shook her head. "You don't *know*?"

"I believe we aren't talking."

"You aren't close?"

The humor left his eyes. "He wants nothing to do with me. I'm an unconvicted murderer, you know."

"I've heard," she observed dryly. He met her gaze with an appreciative one of his own.

"Thank you for that," he said. "I grow tired of living with Aletta's ghost. It grows heavy."

"Is she a ghost?" Isabel asked carefully.

"What do you mean?" he asked, equally as thoughtful.

Isabel lowered her voice, not wanting to give any hint of the jealousy she had felt, and yet, she needed to know. "Did she mean a great deal to you?"

Mr. Severson's hand curved around the outside of her thigh. "Did she change my life? Yes." His frustration was obvious. Nor did he shy from the topic. "Was I devoted to her at the time of her death? No. Aletta had many lovers. Any

121

number of men could have had reason and opportunity to kill her. I was just the last to be seen with her that night and too drunk to remember any of it. It was my word against the witnesses."

"There were witnesses?"

"To my being at her apartment, and a woman living next to her claimed to have heard us arguing. I don't recall."

It was riveting to hear him discuss this so matter-of-factly. "You don't seem to be whitewashing anything."

"How can I? I was a fool, Isabel. A selfish young man with nothing to do with his time except drink. I paid a high price for my laziness. I want you to know, I've changed my course. The man I am right now is what I made of myself in Canada. And I shouldn't be bitter about my family. My brother didn't stand beside me during the days of the trial. I'm the foolish one for insisting he see me now. He has the right to do as he wishes."

"Are you certain he knows you have returned?"

"Yes."

She leaned toward him, earlier misgivings gone. "It's hard, isn't it?" she said. "Family should be a refuge."

"It rarely is."

"I wanted it to be," she admitted quietly. "Everyone in Higham seemed to belong to someone but me. I was always the outsider . . . and I had to pretend I didn't care."

His hand curled around her leg, pulled her closer. She didn't mind.

"And it was still that way even after I left home," she continued. "I had difficulty finding a governess position. It was always that I was too young or too pretty—"

"I believe that," he said.

His compliment pleased her, but she pulled a face and made him laugh. However, when she was with him, she did feel pretty.

She could also see he was growing tired. He needed to sleep and still he hung on—for her.

Isabel was all too aware of the weight of the hand he'd placed possessively on her leg and the body heat that drew her closer. He pulled her to him as no other had before.

"I don't want you to think you *must* marry me," she said.

"I don't. I need a wife."

"You didn't need one before you came to Wardley Park."

"I need one now," he corrected.

Isabel searched his eyes, discovering that, in spite of everything she'd claimed, there was a part deep within her that wanted to believe he could love her.

His gaze lowered to her lips. His hand moved up toward her waist. "How do you know I would make you a good wife?" she asked, her breathing suddenly difficult.

"I imagine you do everything well."

The quiet, seductive baritone of his voice seemed to flow right through her. "I would try and make you a good wife, but perhaps you would prefer someone with a better background."

His lips twisted into a knowing smile. He knew exactly the power he had over her. "No one has ever made me do anything. I make my own decisions and my own choices." His hand stroked up her side, close to her breast.

Isabel's heart beat rapidly. It took all of her control to say, "What a blessing it must be to be so confident."

"What misery it must be never to make a decision at all," he returned, and slid his hand up behind her neck and pulled her down to kiss him.

They kissed very well together. It even seemed right and natural.

When he did break the kiss, she experienced a touch of disappointment.

His dark gaze met hers. "I *want* you to marry me, Isabel. I've never said those words before. I do not take them lightly."

And marriage to such a man would solve so many of her problems. "We don't know each other well," she pressed, arguing with her own doubts.

"Do any of us have the luxury of really knowing each other?" he asked, unconsciously echoing Mrs. Oxley's own thoughts. "I've lived a hard life these last ten years. I've witnessed things that would curdle your blood. A life can be ended in the space of time it takes to snuff a candle. We reach for what we can today, Isabel, and let the future take care of itself."

He was right. She'd tried planning her life, and it hadn't been very successful.

"Risk it," he urged. "Risk it all."

"On lust?"

"Is there anything better?"

Certainly not love.

"I suppose we should marry, Mr. Severson," she heard herself answer, as if in a dream.

He took her hand and kissed it. Something

stirred deep within, that old yearning for the "more" she couldn't quite define.

"I suppose we should marry, *Michael*," he amended. "That's my given name."

"Michael," she repeated. A strong name. She smiled. "The guardian angel of God."

"The *avenging* angel of God," he corrected, and without waiting for her response, he raised his voice and called for Mr. Oxley who was, as expected, standing close to the door.

Within the hour, a messenger was on his way to the bishop to purchase a special license. A friend of Mr. Oxley's was traveling to London, and Michael wrote a quick letter to be delivered to his London office and a man named Fitzhugh, who Michael said was his solicitor. "I'm sending for my coach," he explained to Isabel. "It will make our return more comfortable."

He then fell back into the healing sleep his body needed . . . and Isabel found herself sitting by his side, wondering what she'd done. She was marrying a man who owned ships and coaches. Who thought nothing of giving a draft of five hundred pounds to a parish and made decisions at the snap of his fingers and expected them to be carried out.

A man whose kisses had caused her to toss aside all modesty and propriety.

But marriage would make it acceptable, would make *her* respectable—wouldn't it?

The next day, when she met the magistrate, she started to have an inkling of the answer to that question.

Seven

❧

Isabel was outside helping Mrs. Oxley hang the laundry late the next morning when Mr. Oxley came out to inform them the magistrate had arrived and wanted to speak to her.

"Me? What of Mr. Severson?" Isabel asked, untying the strings of the work apron she had borrowed from Mrs. Oxley from around her waist.

"He's asleep," the rector answered. "I offered to wake him, but the squire prefers to discuss the shooting with you first."

Isabel nodded. Michael had slept the night peacefully and woken hungry. Broth was no longer enough to sustain him. He had wanted meat, and he was sitting up by himself. She and

Mrs. Oxley had cooked a big breakfast. He'd polished off everything, including three-quarters of a loaf of bread, then gone right back into a deep sleep.

Unlike Michael, Isabel had experienced a restless night. Her doubts were intensified when neither of them had mentioned their marriage to the other.

It was all so platonic—but that was what she wanted, wasn't it?

Not when she thought about Michael's kisses.

While Mrs. Oxley went ahead of them to greet their guest, Mr. Oxley took her arm and drew her aside before she walked into the cottage. "Squire Nolestone takes on many responsibilities, including that of local Magistrate, and he relishes each of them."

"What are you saying?" she asked.

"He's more than a bit officious, but generally harmless. Be patient with him."

Isabel nodded, uncertain what to expect. She was also anxious to hear what the squire had learned about who might have shot Michael.

Mrs. Oxley and Squire Nolestone were in the sitting room, teasing each other with the affection of a long friendship. Isabel knew the squire on sight but had never met him. He was obviously a man who enjoyed his puddings, roasts, hams, and anything else his wife put on his plate before him. He had a head full of curly, graying red hair and tiny brown eyes that reminded Isabel of buttons.

"I'll fetch tea," Mrs. Oxley offered. "I've already got it brewing. Miss Halloran and I were going to enjoy a cup after we finished our laundry."

"There, now," the squire said in a gruff, booming voice. "You don't, by any chance, have a spot of that mulberry liqueur you make so well? A little something to flavor the tea?" He gave his hostess a conspirator's wink.

Mrs. Oxley giggled, pleased he liked her homemade brew. "I imagine I can find some," she answered, and went into the kitchen.

Her husband made the introductions. "Squire, this is Miss Halloran."

"Pleased to make your acquaintance," the squire said. "My, you are pretty. No one quibbled on that point. If everyone agrees on everything else, then my job will be easy."

"You spoke to Mr. Wardley?" she asked.

"Aye, and a Lord Riggs. Please, sit down. Let us make ourselves comfortable, heh, now? We'll talk a bit, have tea and mulberry elixir"—

131

he raised his voice on the last two words to in-clude Mrs. Oxley in the kitchen—"and finish good friends."

He waved Isabel toward a straight-backed wood chair while he settled himself in Mr. Ox-ley's favorite upholstered chair before the fire. Mr. Oxley sat in his wife's rocker and picked up his cold pipe.

"I like this weather," the squire said. "It promises a fair spring."

"Yes," Isabel murmured, conscious that the squire's small talk was more than pleasant chitchat. His button eyes seemed to be con-stantly assessing—and she wondered why he was suspicious of her?

She decided to take the initiative. "What have you learned?" she asked.

The squire's eyebrows rose at her audacity in taking control of the interview, and she could feel him mentally putting a black check beside her name: *governess, pushy.* "Ah, here is Mrs. Oxley with that mulberry elixir."

"And the tea," Mrs. Oxley reminded him, setting the tray she carried on the table beside his chair.

The two of them would have happily chor-tled on about tea and liquors, but Isabel wanted information. "What have you learned about who shot Michael?"

"*Michael?*" the squire echoed, holding his teacup out for Mrs. Oxley to pour.

"Mr. Severson," Isabel corrected.

"I understand you and Mr. Severson were found in what we would call rather compromising circumstances," the squire said as easily as if he discussed the weather.

His directness in front of the rector and his wife stunned Isabel. She didn't know what to say and felt foolish because, of course, such a matter would be brought up. The Wardleys probably carried on to anyone who would listen about Isabel's disgraceful behavior. She had no defense and was painfully aware of her friends' presence in the room.

Mr. Oxley came to her rescue. "Miss Halloran and Mr. Severson are not guilty parties here," he gently reminded the squire. "They are the victims. Furthermore, the couple is pledged to each other."

The squire had not heard that piece of information, and his reaction was immediate. "You've promised yourself to a murderer?"

"Murderer?" Mrs. Oxley echoed, turning so abruptly to Isabel that she poured hot tea on the squire. With a yelp, he practically threw his cup and saucer in the air, splattering more hot liquid around. The pottery hit the floor at his feet, smashing into a dozen pieces.

Mr. Oxley was no less shocked. Isabel caught a glimpse of his concern and attempted to avoid it by scooting off her chair and kneeling to pick up the broken pieces of teacup.

Seeing that the Oxleys apparently didn't know the *true* character of their guest, Squire Nolestone took it upon himself to inform them. "Yes," he said in that officious manner Mr. Oxley had warned her about, "he stood accused of killing a young woman. An actress. They were—" He hummed for the right word. "They were *particular* friends."

"Oh," said Mrs. Oxley, not really understanding and then, as meaning took hold, drawing out the word, "Oooohhhhh."

The broken pottery pieces in her hand, Isabel stood. "The charges were dismissed against him."

Squire Nolestone sat back in his chair, secure in his opinion. "For lack of evidence. From what I hear, many believe the judge took too much upon himself. He claimed there wasn't enough information to convict Severson," he informed the Oxleys, putting a finger to the side of his nose, "even though there was a witness who saw Severson at that woman's apartment that very evening."

"And what does that mean?" Isabel demanded. "Just because he may have *seen* the woman doesn't mean he was the one who *killed* her. Many other men saw her that evening, too."

"It also doesn't mean he left her alive either," the squire responded, apparently not accustomed to being challenged.

Isabel wondered who had given him this information. Richard? If so, what did he gain by blackening Michael's name? Nor was she going to let Squire Nolestone smugly shirk his responsibilities. "Then, according to your logic, Mr. Wardley and *all* his guests—and the servants, too!—are guilty of shooting Mr. Severson. After all, they were all in the vicinity!"

"Nothing of the sort," the squire said, glaring at her for her impertinence. "I said *nothing* like that!"

In truth, Isabel didn't know what had come over her. She was usually more aware of her station in life, yet she was angry. She'd grown up suffering enough innuendoes from the smug and the self-righteous to last a lifetime. She wasn't going to tolerate it now, not when

Michael's life could be at stake. She demanded justice.

She dumped the pieces of pottery unceremoniously on the tray and told the squire evenly, "Then don't trivialize the attempt on Michael's life because you'd rather believe gossip than the verdict of a judge."

Mr. Oxley jumped in to soothe the bluntness of Isabel's words. "You must understand that Miss Halloran has been very concerned for Mr. Severson."

Squire Nolestone squirmed under her gaze. "I'm concerned, too. We don't like things like this happening in the parish."

"Of course, we don't," Mrs. Oxley said, and, using a fresh cup from the tray, poured another cup of tea for her guest, who accepted it with a wounded expression as if he deserved pampering after such an unwarranted attack. She further demonstrated her concern by picking up the broken pieces off the tray, and Isabel felt guilty.

She retired to her chair and sat. She placed her hands in her lap, forcing herself to be pleasant. No good came of losing one's temper. Wasn't that one of the lessons she had always taught her charges. "So what did you discover?" she asked the squire.

"That it was a hunting accident," he said, reaching for mulberry elixir to add to his tea.

Isabel's indignation shot to the surface. "It was *no* accident."

"Of course it was. Hunting accidents happen all the time," he insisted, stirring his tea with his finger.

"I was there. No one had started hunting, unless they were hunting for Mr. Severson."

"Then it is your word against Mr. Wardley's and Lord Riggs's," the squire said. "And quite frankly, they have the better character."

"*What* do you mean by that?" she countered. She sat up, her back straight. "Are you saying you believe that Mr. Wardley, of *all* people, has more integrity than I? Is that what you are saying?"

But the squire didn't answer. His beady gaze had shifted to a point beyond her shoulder, and his face paled considerably. He set his teacup back on the tray as if preparing to make a hasty exit, and Isabel knew Michael stood behind her.

He walked into the middle of their circle, his towering presence filling the small room. He wore shirt and breeches, and Isabel could only imagine how difficult it must have been for him to pull on his boots with one arm, but he had done it. To add to the drama, the shirt he was wearing was the one he'd been shot in. She had washed it and attempted to remove the blood-stain with limited success, but had not even tried to repair the hole where the shot had entered his back. That hole was damning evidence that someone had attempted to see him dead, and she was certain he'd chosen to wear it for that purpose.

"I'm certain this gentleman wouldn't say such a thing," Michael answered Isabel, his sharp gaze on the squire, "because that would be an insult, and he would not want to insult the woman honoring me with marriage."

"No," Squire Nolestone squeaked out.

Michael held out his hand. "Severson."

Obviously unnerved, the squire half rose from his chair. "Nolestone," he muttered, "*Squire* Nolestone," he added, as if needing the protection of a title.

"Please, sit," Michael said with the gracious air of host. "Is it possible that I could have a cup of tea, Mrs. Oxley?"

"Of course," his hostess said, and hurried into the kitchen to toss away the broken bits and fetch another cup and saucer.

Michael pulled another wooden chair around, one just like Isabel's, and placed it beside hers. He sat in it with the careless elegance of any town buck, the only person completely at ease in the room.

Mr. Oxley watched all of them, his cold pipe in his mouth.

Mrs. Oxley returned. "Would you care for some of my mulberry elixir in your tea?" she asked Michael.

"Thank you, but no," he responded.

"Should have it," the squire said gruffly, attempting to regain his composure. "Very good."

Taking the cup and saucer Mrs. Oxley offered, Michael said, "I don't take strong spirits."

"Don't drink spirits?" Squire Nolestone said incredulously. "What kind of man doesn't drink?"

"A man who values his scalp," Michael answered, reminding all in this room that he had lived another, very dangerous life.

"I hear tell that Indians can't handle drink either," Squire Nolestone was saying.

"Some can, some can't," Michael answered. "Just like white men."

The squire's brows came together in interest. "I'd heard you'd been out fighting savages. How dangerous were they?"

"Far less dangerous than the ones I've met in England," Michael answered. "And there isn't

139

a savage foolish enough to believe my shooting was a *hunting* accident."

Squire Nolestone's face flushed with the charge. "I've spoken with everyone at Wardley Park. They all agree. Even the servants."

"Which man admitted firing the shot?" Michael asked.

Isabel and Mr. and Mrs. Oxley looked at the squire for his answer.

He paused in the act of bringing his teacup to his lips. A dull red crept up his neck. "Never asked."

"Why didn't you?" The words popped out of Isabel's mouth before she considered their wisdom.

Squire Nolestone latched on to them as a means to get himself out of a tight spot. "I will not have you speak to me that way—"

"Be careful," Michael said, placing a hand on the back of Isabel's chair. The quietness of his voice did not lessen the effectiveness of his message.

"Besides, she is a witness, too," Mrs. Oxley said. She sat in one of the straight-backed chairs. "She told you she didn't believe it was a hunting accident." Frowning, the rector's wife said, "And I don't either. The whole incident doesn't make sense."

Isabel could have kissed her and, by his grin, Michael must have felt the same.

Squire Nolestone set his teacup on the tray and stood. "What do you want me to do? Tell titled gentlemen they are lying?"

"One of them is," Mr. Oxley said.

"I did what I could," the squire countered. "It's very political. One must be careful."

"But *thorough*," the rector insisted. "Can you not see the bullet hole?"

"He's alive, Forrest. Look at the man. He's not the worse for wear." Squire Nolestone shrugged. "Perhaps if he was dead, we could be more forceful. But there's no sense in upsetting everyone."

There was the naked truth. Nothing would be done about the attempt on Michael's life. The one person in the room who did not act surprised was Michael.

"It's not right. It's not justice," Isabel said.

Squire Nolestone pulled his waistcoat down over his belly. "It's what is best. It's all I could do."

Isabel found that unacceptable and would have said as much, save for Michael's standing. "Thank you, Squire," he said, offering his hand.

The squire came to his feet with obvious relief. "Wish I could have done better," he said, taking the offered hand.

"I know," Michael answered. He released the squire's hand. "By the way, whom did you interview at Wardley Park?"

"Wardley himself and Lord Riggs."

Michael nodded. "You know, Lord Riggs was infatuated with my betrothed. He was very angry she preferred me over him."

"Are you suggesting he would be jealous enough to shoot you?" the squire asked.

Isabel had not considered herself as a reason for Richard to shoot Michael, but knew he was capable of more than what most people imagined. She knew what he could do when crossed. Thinking back to the morning of the shooting, she didn't remember seeing Richard with the others immediately. He could have placed himself at the proper angle to fire the shot.

"No," Michael said, answering the squire. "I merely raise the possibility that Riggs might not be as honest in his answers to you as you wish him to be."

Squire Nolestone nodded, his frown deep. "I can do no more."

"I understand," Michael said.

The squire nodded to the Oxleys, ignored Isabel, and, taking his hat, left.

Mr. Oxley looked at Michael. "You should return to bed," he advised him.

"When should we see the messenger with the special license?" Michael asked.

The rector frowned. "I imagine today."

"How quickly can we marry?"

His question surprised Isabel. Mr. Oxley drew his brows together in concern. "Anytime you wish . . . once we have the license."

"We'll marry at the church?"

"You may," Mr. Oxley said.

Michael said to Isabel, "Come outside with me. I think we need a moment alone." He didn't wait but left, going through the kitchen to the back of the cottage, where the women had been hanging laundry.

As Isabel started to follow, Mr. Oxley stopped her. "You knew about his past?"

"Yes," she said. "He's been honest with me."

The rector studied her a moment. His opinion had changed. She knew he wondered if she was committing a grave error in judgment. So, he surprised her then when he said, "I believe he is innocent, too."

"Thank you," she replied, the words heartfelt, and left the room.

Isabel found Michael off to the side of the cottage. There, between the forest, the church building, and the laundry waving in the breeze, he'd found a modicum of privacy. He waited beside a stone wall and motioned with his hand for her to sit without looking at her, and she felt uneasy. She didn't move.

"What are you *not* telling me?" he asked.

His stern question brought her guard up. "About what?"

"Riggs," he said, at last looking at her.

"What makes you believe there is anything to tell?" she hedged.

"The moment I mentioned he could have shot me out of jealousy, a look crossed your face that led me to believe it could be true," he said quietly. "So, I'm asking what really lay between you? I knew he had wanted you."

"How did you learn that?"

"He told me. He was waiting in my room when I returned from speaking to you that night. He was drunk but very much interested in whether I'd been with you or not."

"Then you know everything you need to know," she replied.

"I haven't heard it from you . . . and I may be wrong, but I sense there is more here."

The words were on the tip of her tongue to deny it. After all, she was the one who had put herself in harm's way. Unfortunately, someone could tell Michael the story in London, and it would be the one Richard's aunt liked to spread.

Best he hear all from her first. "He attempted to rape me."

Anger flashed in Michael's eyes. "What happened?"

She didn't want to say. The story threatened to choke in her throat.

Michael crossed to her and pulled her down to sit beside him on the stone wall. Placing his arms around her, he repeated in a gentler tone, "What happened?"

Isabel looked over at the laundry she and Mrs. Oxley had been hanging on the line. "I should have been wiser," she confessed.

"I don't believe that," he answered.

"You don't? After what occurred between us?" Isabel lifted her head to look at him. A shadow of a beard darkened his jawline.

"Was that how it was with Richard?"

"No," Isabel said firmly. "I admit, I did fancy myself in love with him at one time. I worked in his aunt's household. He sought me out, and his attentions were a very heady thing. He would leave notes for me and occasionally flowers and trinkets." She could still remember her excitement the first time she'd found one of his gifts left in the schoolroom for her. She had been so foolish.

"One day, I found him in the pantry, of all places, with the kitchen maid. I was so stunned."

"What did you do then?"

"I refused to have anything to do with him—"

Her answer startled a sharp bark of laughter out of Michael. "What do you find amusing?" she asked.

"I doubt if Riggs ever had a woman treat him in such a high-handed manner. He was probably unprepared to receive a set-down from you."

Isabel realized he was right. "It upset him," she admitted. "He acted as if I should tolerate anything he wished to do. And that made me angry," she said, her spirit returning. "Instead, I dedicated myself to my charges. I was disappointed but surprisingly not as heartbroken as I thought I would be."

"I thought you didn't believe in love," Michael said.

Isabel gave him a sharp glance, surprised by the turn of his thoughts. "Richard is one of the reasons I don't," she said.

"Well, I can't imagine anyone with good sense being enamored of Riggs," he allowed before surmising, "since he forced himself on you because you ignored him."

It was a statement, not a question. Isabel nodded. "Yes. It was a miserable attack. He was waiting in my room at the end of a very long day and was a bit surprised when I fought back."

"What did you do?"

"I kneed him hard."

Michael almost fell off the wall, roaring with laughter.

Isabel couldn't help but smile, too. "I grew up illegitimate in a small village," she said, explaining herself. "My mother is the one who taught me how to defend myself."

"I wish I could have seen Riggs's face," Michael declared.

"It was funny," she agreed. "He was caught off guard. However, he was very angry." The memory wiped the smile from her face. "He shouted so loud, he woke one of the children, who woke the nurse. Then the duchess was summoned. They all blamed me. Richard claimed I had invited him to my room. I'd *tempted* him. The duchess dismissed me without references."

"Was the other night the first time you'd seen Riggs since then?" Michael asked.

"Yes." She made a motion correcting herself with her hands. "He'd sent a letter once, apologizing. I tore it up."

"What did he want the other night?"

"To ask me to be his mistress."

Her point wasn't lost on Michael. *"Touché,"* he said softly.

"Yes, it was a busy night for me."

She'd answered offhand and immediately wished she'd measured her words better—except, Michael didn't take offense. He laughed, as she would have wanted him to do. The doubt that made her restless and uncertain relaxed its hold a bit.

This was the sort of man she could admire. One with whom she could speak honestly.

He stopped laughing. They stared into each other's eyes. He held up his hand, palm toward her. She placed her hand against his. He had big hands, strong ones, hands that knew what it was to work.

In that moment, she wanted to believe in heroes.

"I must clear my name," he said.

"Yes," she agreed. "I will do what I can to help." She didn't believe he was a murderer. She would not have this faith in him if she thought he was guilty. "Do you have any idea who did kill her?"

He searched her face before answering. "I think I might know the man."

"Who is he?"

Michael's brows came together. She sensed he debated whether or not to confide in her. She was disappointed when he said, "This isn't the time for this discussion."

"I want to help."

"You will, in London," he assured her. "But for right now, this is what is important." And he showed her what he meant by drawing her up and into his arms.

Isabel lost herself in the kiss. Eagerly, she pressed against him, wanting to let him know she believed in him. She would make him a good wife, and he would never regret marrying her.

His tongue brushed hers. She wrapped her arms around his neck and held him tight, silently vowing never to let him go. Right or wrong, she was falling in love. It was a dangerous thing, this love was . . . and yet, how could she resist?

This bold, handsome man with a sense of humor wanted to be her husband. He valued her, and those childhood dreams of being loved, of being wanted, were about to come true.

She shoved all doubts aside.

Eight

❧❧❧

The sound of Mr. Oxley clearing his throat broke their kiss. He had tracked them down to their place in the garden.

"Perhaps you'd best prepare to spend the night at the Bull and Crown," he advised Michael. It was the best inn in the area, located two miles from Glaston. The Bull and Crown was also the post house.

Isabel worried for Michael's health. "I don't think he is well enough," she protested.

"If he can kiss like that, he'll manage until the morning and your wedding," Mr. Oxley said.

Michael laughed. "He's right. I'll be fine." He took her hands. "I'll see you tomorrow, at the church."

Isabel prayed it would be true. An hour later, as she watched Michael drive off in his yellow-and-green sporting vehicle, she struggled with the fear that he would not return.

All her life, whenever she'd really wanted something, she couldn't get it. Consequently, she'd taught herself not to expect too much in life.

Now, she felt as if she wanted everything.

Mrs. Oxley seemed aware of Isabel's unease. And Isabel was aware of how quiet her benefactress had become since Squire Nolestone's visit.

It wasn't until evening, when the fire burned low in the grate, and Mr. Oxley had gone to bed, that anything was said.

Isabel was trying to take her mind off her worries by reading a book. Mrs. Oxley was pretending to be knitting. Neither woman was very good at her task.

Finally, Mrs. Oxley lowered her knitting to her lap. "I admit I am rattled by the accusation of murder against Mr. Severson." She looked at Isabel, her brow furrowed in concern. "Both Mr. Oxley and I have concerns. My dear, do you really know this man?"

"I know him enough to trust him."

"No, you wish to take a chance on him. There is a difference."

Isabel closed the book. She hesitated, then spoke her deepest fear aloud. "Are you saying you don't think he will be at the church on the morrow?"

Mrs. Oxley appeared surprised. "Oh, no, he'll be there. He wants to marry you, and I don't mean this as a slight, but you haven't known each other very long. If it weren't for the fact he compromised you, I might wonder at such haste."

Her words went straight to Isabel's insecurities. "He is everything I imagined a good man should be," she reminded herself.

"He has an unsavory history," Mrs. Oxley said soberly. "I no longer know what to think. I'm not going to say whether the accusation is true or false. Certainly, before Squire Nolestone's call, I thought well of him. Well enough to encourage you to accept his offer." She leaned over in her chair, reaching out to cover Isabel's hand with hers. "My dear, be careful. Be very, very careful."

"He won't let any harm come to me," Isabel answered. "If I know nothing else about him, I know that."

"I pray you are right," her friend said.

Isabel looked into those older, wiser eyes. "I am."

Mrs. Oxley released her hold and sat back. "Good." She sounded as if she were attempting to convince herself. She put her knitting away. "I'd best go to my bed. Good night, Isabel. Sleep well." She left the room.

Sleep well. As Isabel took herself off to the bed Michael had been using while convalescing, she didn't think she would be able to sleep at all. The apprehension she had seen in Mrs. Oxley's eyes was a warning.

In the end, the moment her head hit the pillow, she went right to sleep and didn't wake until Mrs. Oxley roused her the next morning.

Her wedding day.

"I feared you were going to sleep right through the morning," Mrs. Oxley said, opening the shutter on the room's window. "Have you given any thought to how you will wear your hair?"

No, Isabel hadn't.

Fortunately, Mrs. Oxley had a talent for hair. After Isabel had dressed in her finest green wool gown, the only one with lace at the collar, Mrs. Oxley swept her heavy hair up high on her head and pinned it into large curls, leaving some to dangle free down to her shoulders.

"Such beautiful hair," Mrs. Oxley murmured. They sat in the sitting room, with Isabel holding a hand mirror so she could see what was being done. "It's a pity we don't have a bit of ornament for it. My tortoise combs are so small they would disappear, but you *should* have something. Hair like yours begs to be shown off."

"My mother had mother-of-pearl combs," Isabel said, remembering. "Our hair was much alike."

"What happened to them?"

"My stepfather must have them," Isabel answered, the memory going sour. He'd kept them.

"What's he going to do with them?" Mrs. Oxley wondered.

"Perhaps he is planning on another wife," Isabel suggested.

She'd said it lightly, but Mrs. Oxley was too shrewd to not pick up on the nuances behind the words. Her gaze met Isabel's in the mirror as she rested her hands on Isabel's shoulders. "I'm sorry. I should guard my tongue. Don't think on anything negative. It doesn't matter. We can't use them now."

"It's nothing you said. It was just, well, sometimes my mother's loss stirs me more than at other times."

"A wedding is one of those times," Mrs. Oxley said, understanding. She gave Isabel's shoulders a squeeze. "I know she is looking down from heaven right this minute and is very pleased."

"Do you think so?" Isabel had never sensed her mother watching her, even though she'd always told the children in her charge tales of guardian angels.

"Absolutely," Mrs. Oxley said, without hesitation. "Now, let us think of the future." She took the mirror away from Isabel and set it on a side table. "Mr. Oxley went this morning to meet with your groom—"

"Why did he do that?" Isabel asked, alarmed.

"It's what he does with all grooms, and he sent word back that Mr. Severson has arranged for a wedding breakfast. A very special one at the Bull and Crown. I've only eaten there once, and it was delicious. Mr. Oxley also sent word that he was quite impressed with your young man."

Isabel was a bit bemused by how Michael had gone from being a cause of concern to her "young man" overnight. He must be planning a very fine meal indeed . . . and he was doing it for her. His use of the word "we" the day before echoed in her ears.

Mrs. Oxley turned her around and, smiling, gave a last touch to her hair. "You look lovely. Exactly as a bride should. We have a custom here, one you've never seen since you didn't live in town, where the bride walks the length of the village to the church. But since we are already at the church, you will have to walk all the way to the end of the road and back. Everyone will come out and wish you well, and the children will give you flowers and branches of sweet myrtle."

"But few people know me," Isabel said quickly. "I doubt if anyone will wish us well. This is short notice." And it would be humbling to be snubbed, especially on her wedding day.

"You are a member of this parish," Mrs. Oxley countered. "You have worshiped with us, and everyone knows Mr. Severson's misfortune. Why, it has been all the talk for a week. The ladies find your story romantic, and the men in the pub have been hashing out the mystery of who shot Mr. Severson. The road will be lined with well-wishers."

And probably more than a few people who would want to see the infamous couple—and yet, Isabel was pleased. Something should make this day special.

Mrs. Oxley donned her own bonnet, pulled on her gloves, and opened the door. The sky was slightly overcast but held the promise of clearing. This would be a fine spring day. Isabel glanced toward the church. It didn't appear as if anyone was there. Furthermore, the street ahead of her seemed very "everyday." No one lined the road waiting to hand her flowers.

Isabel stepped out the door, following Mrs. Oxley. Her feet felt like lead weights. All her life, she'd had people leave her. First, her real father. Then her mother, to death, her stepfather, to his pride . . . and what of Michael? Wouldn't he be wise to run now before he found himself saddled with a wife? Especially one who had no dowry and offered nothing to a man of his station?

She stopped. She hadn't thought about the dowry, but now, it became a looming concern.

Mrs. Oxley turned to her. "Come along."

Isabel couldn't move.

With a sympathetic sound, Mrs. Oxley walked the few steps back and took Isabel's arm. "This is no time for cold feet."

"I thought the groom was the one to get cold feet."

"Anyone with half an ounce of sense should be nervous about marriage. But the moment has come, Miss Halloran. Trust us, my dear."

"Trust." Such a short, simple word with the gigantic possibilities. A decision sealed by a kiss.

Isabel started walking toward the gate.

She and Mrs. Oxley had just passed the church when a young girl ran out of a cottage, and said, "She's coming! She's coming!"

The bell in the church tower started ringing, and people came out of the cottages and shops that made up Gaston. Some of the faces Isabel recognized from those times she was allowed to attend Sunday service. Many she didn't know at all. However, they all came out to welcome her.

The first to hand her flowers was the girl who had alerted everyone. She held out a nosegay made of wild violets.

Tears came to Isabel's eyes. "Thank you."

The girl smiled, pleased that Isabel valued her gift.

"This is Meg," Mrs. Oxley said, introducing them. "She is always the first to give a flower to the bride."

The time of year was too early for many flowers, but the villagers were creative. Isabel was given many violets, trailing branches of sweet peas, wild daisies, someone's prized tulip, yellow dandelions—these were given to her mostly by small boys—and branches of broom and evergreen myrtle.

By the time they reached the church, her arms overflowed with flowers, and Isabel felt like the wealthiest of women. She felt like a bride.

Mr. Oxley came out to meet her, wearing the white collar of his station. He smiled at her. "Are you ready?"

"Is he here?" she asked, almost fearing the reply.

"See for yourself," Mr. Oxley replied.

Isabel walked past him through the door and stopped. In the cool, candlelit atmosphere of the Norman church, Michael waited for her at the altar. He looked so handsome. He wore a jacket of dark blue superfine and tall boots, as seemed to befit a country marriage. The white of his shirt and neckcloth seemed dazzling in the church's gloom. He smiled at her, and her knees went weak.

It was everything she could do to stop herself from running to him.

"Simon, you can stop ringing the bells," Mr. Oxley told his bell ringer. He had to repeat himself until the man heard.

Mr. Oxley took Isabel aside a step away from his wife. "I spoke to Mr. Severson this morning, and now I will tell you the same. Miss Halloran, you and your intended don't know each other well, but I'll tell you a secret—it's rare a couple truly knows each other before they are married, even if they have been friends for years. Marriage changes everything. However, I want you to remember something." He leaned closer. "I may be saying the words, but you and your husband are the celebrants of this sacrament. You aren't saying these vows to me but to each other and in the eyes of God. Don't hesitate to repeat them often over the years. You have only to look at each other with hearts full of love to make them sacred."

She nodded, her heart beating so rapidly in anticipation she wasn't certain she understood everything he said—but she would sort that out later.

Satisfied he'd made his point, Mr. Oxley offered Isabel his arm. "Shall we?"

She took his arm, and they walked up the aisle toward Michael. Mrs. Oxley and the bell ringer followed behind to serve as witnesses.

At the altar, Mr. Oxley stopped and placed her hand in Michael's strong and capable one. She told herself she didn't care if Michael loved her or not. It was enough that she was falling very much in love with him.

But then, that was the way love came, wasn't it?

Her mother had loved a man who hadn't loved her. In turn, she'd married Isabel's stepfather.

Life was never neat and tidy. Those had been her mother's words and had proven to be true.

However, standing beside Michael, listening to him repeat his vows, Isabel resolved to make the best of this marriage. She would be a good wife in every way.

Michael surprised her by having a ring. It was a simple gold band. Its heaviness felt good on her finger.

Mr. Oxley raised his hand over their heads. In a voice that rang off the stone walls, he said, "I now pronounce you man and wife. Those whom God hath joined together, let no man put asunder."

And that was it. She was married. *Isabel Severson*.

Isabel braced herself, waiting to feel different. Nothing happened.

The earth didn't shake. Lightning didn't strike. Not even a tingling certainty in her soul.

She felt as she always had.

And then, Michael's fingers laced with hers . . . and a small, quiet voice inside her said, *this is right*.

"You can kiss her now," Simon, the bell ringer, said slyly.

"I most certainly will," Michael informed him, and bent over to do exactly that. It was a short kiss, but a meaningful one when he said quietly, "Your first kiss as my wife."

Her doubts evaporated.

Mrs. Oxley offered her heartfelt congratulations and handed Isabel back the flowers she had been holding for her. Their small party went outside and waited for Simon to bring around a pony wagon for him to drive the Oxleys to the Bull and Crown. Michael's phaeton and horses had been tied to a post on the other side of the church. That was why Isabel had not seen it earlier.

He helped her up onto the perch before going around to the other side and taking the seat next to her. The pony cart and phaeton made a happy little parade as they rolled out of the village. The children chased them, and Isabel had never felt more lighthearted.

The Bull and Crown was located at the crossroads. The innkeeper, Mr. Graves, fell all over himself greeting them. Isabel found out why when they entered the establishment. Michael had ordered a table set in the inn's best private room. Its mullioned windows overlooked a running stream and the road. The food laid out was enough for a feast. There was roast beef and pheasant, numerous puddings, every imaginable delicacy, and the best of wines. The Oxleys were impressed, and Simon was beside himself.

Isabel overheard Mr. Graves confide to Mrs. Oxley that the last person to order up such a spread had been the duke of Rutland himself.

Michael sat Isabel beside him. He placed her bouquet from the villagers in the middle of the table as the centerpiece. The wine was poured, and he raised his glass. "To my wife. May she never regret marrying me."

Mr. Graves, who hovered by the door, couldn't help saying, "There's not a one of them that don't regret their choice sooner or later," and everyone laughed as he'd meant for them to.

"To your marriage," Mr. Oxley echoed and everyone—even the innkeeper—drank.

Isabel discovered she was hungry as they fell upon the food. Michael had just passed her the plate of pheasant when they heard the sound of an approaching coach. The vehicle of burled wood and ebony, pulled by a team of high-stepping grays and escorted by a party of well-armed riders, drew up in front of the inn.

Her reaction was curiosity; his was more succinct.

"Damn."

She looked at him in surprise. "Do you know them?"

"I'm afraid I do."

Mr. Graves had hurried out to meet these new guests, leaving the door open. Michael set aside the plate of pheasant and sat back as if waiting.

He wasn't disappointed. Within minutes, they heard Mr. Graves arguing that the men couldn't disturb Michael's party. A beat later, a lean, broad-shouldered man marched into the room, his pistol drawn. The hair beneath the rakish angle of his low-crowned hat was black as a crow's wing. He wore it pulled back in a neat queue that went past his shoulders. His gray eyes appeared ready for a fight, and he was flanked by the four others carrying muskets.

But what was really unusual to Isabel was that he didn't wear a stock. Instead, his shirt was open, and there was a flash of silver from the collar around his neck. He also had a silver bracelet on each wrist.

The man scowled at everyone before looking right at Michael. "Are you all right?" he demanded. He was much the same age as her husband.

"Perfectly fine," Michael said in greeting. He seemed the only relaxed person in the room. "Isabel, this renegade is my business partner, Alex Haddon."

"I received word you were shot," Mr. Haddon said, ignoring the introduction. "I expected you to be at death's door."

"He was," Mr. Oxley spoke up. He nodded to Isabel. "She saved his life."

Haddon swung his sharp gaze toward her, and Isabel sensed he missed nothing, including how close Michael sat to her.

Michael covered her hand resting on the table with his own. "I'm fine, Haddon," he said. "Now, would you care to join us? Or are you going to stand there frightening my guests?"

"Your guests?" Haddon gave another frowning look around the room as if to verify the truth of Michael's words before lowering his hand holding the pistol. The other men followed suit. "What exactly is going on here?" he asked without moving.

Instead of answering, Michael said, "Mr.

Graves, will you see to my men? Give them whatever food and drink they wish. They've obviously had a long ride."

The outriders relaxed, nodded, and murmured, "Thank you, sir. Very kind of you," as they willingly followed Mr. Graves out into the common room. At a signal from Michael, the serving girl shut the door behind them.

Haddon tucked his pistol into the waistband of his breeches and released a world-weary sigh as if this wasn't the first time Michael had tried his patience. "Would you please explain to me what is going on? We docked late yesterday evening, and I received the news from Old Fitzhugh that you demanded a draft of five hundred pounds and asked for your coach to be sent to this"—He waved a hand—"place. Where are we anyway?"

"Rutland," Michael answered. "By the way, this is my wife, Isabel."

If the earth had opened up beneath his feet, Haddon could obviously not have been more surprised. "You? Married?"

"Yes, me," Michael answered, enjoying himself.

Haddon tossed his hat to the serving girl and picked up a chair from the corner of the room.

He set it up at the table right between Michael and Isabel.

"What are you doing?" Michael demanded.

"Getting to know your wife," Haddon stated flatly, squeezing himself in. He refilled Isabel's wineglass, then poured a glass for himself. Her husband drank springwater. "Has Michael told you anything about me?"

"No."

"Well, let me fill you in on the details—" Haddon started, but Michael cut him off.

"Don't listen to a word he says," he ordered good-naturedly.

"You'd better," Haddon assured her. "I know all his bad habits."

"Are there many?" Isabel asked, charmed by their carefree camaraderie.

"We shall be here all night," Haddon assured her.

"The devil we will," Michael said. He rose and, before Isabel realized what he was about to do, grabbed the back of Haddon's chair, tilted it, and pulled his friend out from the table. He pushed him in between Simon and Mrs. Oxley. "Flirt with the serving girl," he whispered into Haddon's ear in a voice everyone could hear.

"I will," Haddon assured him. "It's not often

I find myself surrounded by such lovely women." He looked at Mrs. Oxley, who blushed at the compliment, while the serving girl giggled as she handed him a plate.

"Haddon is my blood brother," Michael told Isabel.

"Blood brother?" Mr. Oxley asked. "What does that mean?"

"It means I saved his life, and he was thankful for it," Haddon said, spearing pheasant.

"Hardly," Michael corrected. "I saved his scalp from a Mohawk war party."

"No one likes the Mohawks," Haddon confided.

"Bad sort?" Simon asked, wide-eyed.

"The worst," Haddon answered, and Isabel didn't know if he was teasing or not. It was obvious he liked a good joke, as did Michael.

"The name Haddon is familiar," Mr. Oxley said. "Wasn't there a general by that name?"

"Yes, the traitor," Haddon said.

"Are you related?" Mrs. Oxley asked.

There was a beat of silence, then Haddon said, "He was my father."

The awkward moment was dissipated by Mrs. Oxley saying, "No wonder you speak English so well."

Haddon smiled at her, charmed. Isabel didn't know what he had expected from them, but it certainly hadn't been Mrs. Oxley's optimism.

"Haddon speaks several languages," Michael said. "He's half-Shawnee."

"And that is why you wear silver," Mrs. Oxley said. Both she and her husband were completely taken by Haddon.

"The importance of a warrior is shown in the silver he wears," Michael explained.

"And I'm hoping to start a new fashion," Haddon added, and everyone laughed, especially since he kept their glasses full. The breakfast progressed smoothly from that moment, and Isabel sensed Michael was glad his friend was present.

She didn't know how Haddon felt. She noticed that his appraising gaze often fell on Michael's hand covering hers.

Ever so slowly, the wine and good food eased Isabel's overly suspicious nature. The innkeeper's wife, Mrs. Graves, came in and joined them, both she and her husband sitting at the table. The conversation was interesting and lively . . . but Isabel wasn't attending to most of it. Instead, she basked in her sudden good fortune.

Her husband. The words filled her with a combination of nervous anticipation and pride. She touched the ring on her finger, marveling at the smooth, solid feel of the gold.

She tried not to let herself think too far ahead. She lived in the moment, pressing into her memory every nuance, scent, word of this meal. She would always remember the way the candlelight flickered in Mrs. Oxley's eyes as she and her husband listened to Haddon and Michael's tales of Canada. She wanted to capture the sound of Mr. Graves's gruff laugh and memorize even the image of Simon pointing his knife to emphasize something he'd said. All these things she wanted to remember forever.

The light outside the window faded to twilight. Mrs. Oxley suggested that she and Isabel "freshen up" together. The women excused themselves.

Out in the hall, Mrs. Oxley took her arm. Her cheeks were rosy with good cheer. "You are such a fortunate young woman," she said. "Your husband is handsome, generous, and very exciting. The stories he and his friend tell." She shook her head.

Isabel was feeling the same things, too, along with the mellow effects of the wine. Of course, Mrs. Oxley was a bit *more* mellow.

The necessary room at the Bull and Crown was beyond anything Mrs. Oxley had ever seen, and they had to spend several minutes enjoying the luxury and tucking in the pins in Isabel's hair to preserve the style.

They finished their business and were following the hallway back to the private room when they passed a closed door, and Isabel thought she heard Michael's voice. She slowed her step to a halt.

Mrs. Oxley, her mind pleasantly numb, continued on her way, a hand on the wall for a little guidance.

Isabel leaned closer to the door where she'd thought she heard Michael. But it was Haddon who spoke, "I know you want to clear your name, but *this* is going too far."

"I've tried everything else."

Haddon made an impatient sound. "She's an innocent."

"She'll not suffer because of me."

Isabel realized they discussed her. Her mind was too wine-soaked to wrap itself around the meaning of their conversation.

"Be careful," Haddon warned. "If you aren't, the next bullet may kill you. According to the priest, he almost succeeded this time."

"He won't try again. Not now." Michael's firm voice sounded closer, as if he was coming toward the door.

Isabel didn't want to be caught eavesdropping. She practically ran for the private dining room.

Michael paused with his hand on the door handle. He looked to his friend. "I know what you are saying, but Alex, Isabel is the only way. I've exhausted other avenues."

"She's not a part of this, Michael."

"I know . . ." He shifted his weight, then confessed, "I didn't marry her because of her connection to Elswick. I *want* her. There is something between us."

Alex looked at him with new interest. "Has a woman finally gotten past your guard?" he wondered aloud.

"Is that so strange?" Michael asked, facing his friend.

"For any other man? No. For you? Yes." Alex walked up to him. "Be careful, Michael. You've been consumed with clearing your name, but your Isabel really does imagine you a hero, and I know women better than you do," he said, a reference to the near-celibate state Michael had previously practiced. "They all want brave warriors, but there is a price to pay."

He placed his hand on the door and would have turned the handle to leave but Michael stopped him. "What of you? Any word of your father?"

Alex's back stiffened ever so slightly. "He's in France."

"Will you seek him there?"

"I'd rather go to hell." Alex opened the door. "He's as one dead to me, Michael. I was foolish to have even had an interest in meeting him."

"Sometimes we have no choice but to meet the ghosts of our past."

"My father a ghost?" Alex shook his head. "Not hardly. A son always carries the sins of his father." He searched Michael's face a moment and then added softly, "Be careful that your son has no sins to carry. Be gentle with that son's mother." With those words, he opened the door and left the room.

Michael didn't follow. Alex's warning pricked his conscience. As had Mr. Oxley's private lecture to him that morning about the sacredness of wedding vows.

He wasn't going to let Isabel get hurt. He'd not allow anything to happen to her. He just needed to draw Elswick out.

And he was committed to Isabel. He would take care of her—and any of their children, if they had them. He would be her "brave warrior."

Thoughtfully, Michael went down the hall to the private room.

Mr. Graves and Mr. Oxley were deep in conversation with Alex. Mrs. Oxley yawned, as she and Mrs. Graves shared opinions.

Isabel watched the door for him.

Their gazes met, and he knew why Alex had been concerned. She was fragile and yet strong. Timid, yet bold. Aware of her weaknesses, but courageous enough to face life in spite of them.

His Isabel. So reserved and proper . . . except he had tasted her kisses. He knew her blood ran hot. He'd felt her heat.

Suddenly, Michael couldn't wait to have her alone.

He walked up to her. Leaning down, he whispered in her ear, "Come, it is time for us to take our leave."

Nine

❧❧❧

*I*sabel wanted to grab hold of the edges of her chair and hold on. It was too soon.

However, she could see in the faces of those around her, Michael was right. They expected her to leave. It just seemed so very public—especially since she knew what would happen next. They would go upstairs as man and wife. She knew what would follow, and it embarrassed her down to her immortal soul that everyone else did, too.

"If I must," she said, not intending for her words to imply what they did or to be overheard.

Of course, they were.

Everyone in the room seemed to have been holding their breaths for this moment. Michael's friend Mr. Haddon covered his mouth as if choking back laughter. Mr. Graves and Simon were not so kind. They elbowed each other and mimicked her "If I must" to each other in dying tones.

Isabel could have boxed their ears. But before she could lose her temper, Michael pulled back her chair. "We must," he assured her, and swept her up into his arms, the movement making her a little dizzy. She had to hold on by wrapping her arms around his neck.

"Ladies and gentlemen, we bid you good night," he announced, and carried her out the door.

As they moved down the hall to the back stairs, she studied his strong profile and tried to lay her apprehensions at rest. He was so sure about life and what he wanted. She wished she could be that certain.

Michael caught her looking at him and smiled.

His was a beautiful mouth. A good mouth for kissing—

"What are you thinking?" his lips asked.

She looked into his eyes. "That I may have had too much wine to drink."

He laughed. "You're fine," he promised. "Here, these stairs are too narrow for me to carry you up without banging your head on the wall. You'll have to walk the rest of the way." He set her down on the second tread.

She didn't release her arms from his neck. They were at eye level now. "Are you sorry you married me?"

Michael frowned. "Where did you come up with such a question?"

"Are you?"

"No, I'm not. I never will be."

Those were the words she wanted to hear—

"Are you sorry you married me?" he asked gently.

Isabel couldn't believe he'd even imagine such a thing. "This day has been beyond anything I've ever known in my life."

"It's not over, Isabel." He took her hand and looked down at the ring he'd placed on her finger. "I meant my vows. I will always keep you safe." He turned her around, coming up on the step behind her. Through the layers of their clothes, she could feel his arousal. His lips brushed her ear. "We'd best go to our room. I'm anxious to make love to my wife."

Make love. Her blood sang with those words. All doubts vanished. She began moving up the stairs, Michael right at her heels.

The door to one of the guest rooms located

midway down the hall was open. Isabel didn't need Michael's hand on her waist to know it was theirs. He guided her to the door—and she stopped.

Some unseen servant had made preparations. The bed was turned down. It was a four-poster with velvet drapes. There were flowers on a table, an arrangement apparently made from those the villagers had given her.

But what caught Isabel's breath were the candles that glowed everywhere. They were on the windowsill, the dresser, the mantel's edge, in the hearth, and on the bed's side tables. Their light was reflected in the room's mirrors and filled the space with their golden glow.

Isabel walked in, feeling as if she were entering a fairy world.

She turned and looked at her husband. "You remembered."

He released his breath as if he'd been holding it, anxious for her response. He closed the door. "Graves thought I was mad to want such a thing."

"But you told him any act of independence was to be celebrated in this country." Her words echoed those he had said to her the night she had lit candles.

"I did."

Her last remnants of doubt fell away. In that single moment, Isabel was suddenly overwhelmed with love, hardly able to believe her good fortune. She touched the ring on her finger. No one had ever given her such consideration and respect as this man had. He cared. The candles were proof.

She went to him.

She wrapped her arms around his neck, her breasts against his chest, and kissed him back with everything she had. He was her husband, the man she loved.

There was nothing she wouldn't do for him.

Isabel pulled on his coat, willing to rip it off, anxious to remove all barriers between them. His fingers tugged at her lacings. She struggled with the knot in his neckcloth. The urgency they had experienced under the Wardleys' roof came back full force.

She tugged at the buttons of his breeches, despairing of ever getting them undone if he kept teasing her ear with his tongue and soon finding her arms useless when he pushed her dress and chemise down over her shoulders. His mouth found her breast—

Isabel melted down onto the bed. Michael followed her. She pulled her arms free and buried her fingers in his hair, never wanting him to stop. No one had told her how good a man's touch could make her feel.

Her hand found a way to slip the last button of his breeches free. She stroked the hard length of his erection, and now it was Michael who was ensnared.

He covered her hand with his own. His gaze met hers. "Isabel," he whispered. Her name had never sounded so beautiful. He buried his head in her hair, which had lost all its pins, and whispered to her what he wanted. He covered her hand with his and taught her how to touch him.

Her cheek against his neck, she could feel the racing pulse of his heart, whose beat matched her own. Their bodies were bathed in golden light.

Michael's lips sought hers. He stroked her back, sliding her dress down over her hips. His hand touched her intimately, and she discovered pleasure. Her husband knew what she needed.

The time had come.

He sat on the edge of the bed to remove his boots. Uninhibited, Isabel kicked off her own shoes and slid her petticoats, garters, and stockings down. She lay back on the bed, watching her husband stand and pull his shirt over his head.

He was strong and powerful, his muscles lean and long. Life had honed him into the man he was. It had left marks; there were scars. But she also sensed he could take care of anything. He would protect her from the world, and, just as fiercely, she would protect him.

Isabel reached up to touch the bandage across his chest and back. It was white against his tanned skin. If his wound hampered his movements, she couldn't tell.

Michael stood to remove his breeches before facing her. His need for her was very evident, and Isabel was inordinately proud that this man was hers. As she came up on her knees to kiss him, his hands brushed her hair, stroked her back, and gently guided her back to the bed.

He covered her with his body. His weight felt good, and she sensed him positioning himself between her legs. Never had she wanted anything as much as she wanted this contact between them. Her body demanded this joining, but he hesitated.

"I don't want to hurt you," he said.

"You won't," she whispered.

He didn't.

He entered her with one smooth, fluid motion. There was a moment of discomfort. The feeling of him inside her was different than she had anticipated. Her body stretched to accommodate him . . . and it felt right.

"Isabel?"

She smiled, so full of love he must certainly be able to feel it flow from her. She touched his hair at the temples, and he began moving.

Deep within, a yearning built inside her for that which she did not yet understand. Her body met his thrusts, and she found herself whispering, "More." She wanted *more*.

The word that had haunted her now had definition and meaning. This closeness with *this* man was what she had been searching for.

Michael, the man who always seemed to be in control, now appeared as powerless against his needs as she was against hers. They moved together, finding a rhythm that was exactly right for them.

He whispered to her, telling her how beautiful she was, how unique and precious. She felt on fire—

Ecstasy caught her by surprise.

One moment she was of this world; in the next, her soul seemed to explode into a thousand stars.

She cried out Michael's name, holding him tighter.

He knew what she was feeling. His thrusts

became more powerful, deeper—and he buried himself to the hilt. His seed flowed into her. She could feel it. She held him close, never wanting to let him go.

Tears came to her eyes in the wonder of it all. This was a miracle. God's creation. Now, she understood—they had become One.

Slowly, his body relaxed against hers. He rolled over, bringing her with him. She felt him leave her, spent. Her body cooled, and he must have felt the same because he pulled the bedspread up over them.

She lay on him as languid and supple as a cat. Her ear against his chest, she listened to the beat of his heart. Never had she felt so drowsy or pleasantly sated. He kissed the top of her head, his arms around her waist possessively. She smiled, watching the flickering flame of the candle on the table beside the bed.

"Is it always like that?" she finally managed to ask.

"It's *never* been like that," he answered.

A fierce pride rushed through her. She lifted her head, her hair creating a curtain around them. "Ever?" she demanded.

"No," he promised. "Not ever."

He kissed the spot where her neck met her shoulder. It was a particularly sensitive place.

Deep, newly discovered muscles clenched. "And can we do it again?" she asked, already knowing the answer. The proud head of his arousal was already moving against her.

"As many times as you like, Mrs. Severson," he promised. He moved his hips.

"Are we going to do it now?" Her own voice now sounded breathless. Experimentally, she moved her own hips.

Her husband's reaction was immediate and swift. "Dear God, yes," he said—and so they did.

Michael didn't ever want to leave their room at the inn.

Isabel was like opium. The more he had of her, the more he wanted.

They made love with a need he'd never experienced for another woman. There were no days and nights. Beyond the four walls of their room, the world could have ended, and he could have cared less. He had Isabel. She was enough.

He was so besotted with her that he'd lie awake watching her sleep. Strands of her hair would curl around her neck and cheek. She looked so young in those moments, so innocent and pure. His wife gave without pretense or expectation of return, and it humbled him. Her generosity encouraged him to play to his best impulses, to be the man she wanted to believe he was. Isabel didn't trust easily. She trusted him.

Michael could have stayed in their room at the inn forever. Or so he thought.

Three days into their honeymoon, he woke in the middle of the night to find himself alone in the bed. He sat up, alarmed and didn't relax until he saw Isabel sitting in a chair by the window, wearing his shirt and staring out into the night.

"What are you doing over there?" he asked.

She turned, her face in shadows. "You were restless. You must have been having a bad dream. At first I tried to wake you, then I decided to leave you alone."

He didn't remember dreaming. "Did I say anything?"

Isabel drew her legs up, wrapping her arms around them and hugging them to her chest.

"What did I say?" he insisted.

"You called out Aletta's name." She paused, then said, "When you were fighting fever, you spoke to her as if she were in the room with you."

Michael put his feet over the side of the bed. "What did I say?"

"Nothing I could make out." She rocked back and forth in the chair seat a moment before asking, "Do you think you could ever set it aside?"

He wasn't certain he wanted this conversation now. "Set aside what?"

"Her death."

Michael lowered his head into his hands, not answering. From across the room, Isabel said, "If you don't ever learn who murdered this woman, will you ever be able to let it rest?"

"No." He looked up at her, wishing it could be different or that she didn't play a role in this.

He had set out to use her for his purposes and, in a bolt of insight, he realized this could be a wedge between them. She was too fine and good to be a piece in his game against Elswick.

And yet, what choice did he have? He'd already chosen his path. His only hope was that he could protect her.

Isabel studied him a moment before saying, "I didn't believe you could."

"If there was another way, I would take it," he answered. "It will be all right. Everything will be fine."

Isabel smiled at him then, the moonlight caught in her eyes. "Yes." She lowered her feet to the floor to stand. "Tomorrow is the Sabbath. Mr. Oxley will expect us to be in church."

Michael rarely set foot in a church. Michael wasn't a praying man—especially since God knew what game he played, but he could give her this. "Of course," he said.

Mr. and Mrs. Oxley were happy to see them at the Sunday service. Simon, the bell ringer and witness to their wedding, gave Michael a broad wink when he saw them. Michael winked back. Isabel looked back and forth between the two men, suspicious, but not offended.

Going to church, Michael decided, wasn't such a bad thing. Mr. Oxley gave a competent sermon. The passages read from the Bible were fine enough. Everyone enthusiastically sang a hymn, albeit out of tune.

But Michael didn't ever really connect to the worship and the prayers in the same way he sensed his wife did. No, instead, his mind chewed on other matters. His wound was healed, his mind clear, his resolve firm. It was time to return to London.

When he told Isabel, she didn't offer protest. Instead, she placed her hand in his, in a gesture of trust. Michael promised himself he would let no harm come to her. They spent their last day in the inn in the same manner they had been spending it—making love.

Only this time, for him, the pleasure was bittersweet. He was a man who believed in a reckoning . . . and he knew the time would come.

He vowed he would protect her at all costs.

The next morning, they left for London.

Michael told Isabel they would make it a two-day trip. And while Haddon probably had a stack of papers he wanted to foist off on Michael, there was no urgency to arrive.

"Does he read?" she asked. Haddon had taken the phaeton back, and the burled coach was spacious but cozy since her husband took up most of the room.

Isabel didn't mind.

"Of course," Michael answered, frowning at the card she had just discarded. They played to while away the time. "He just doesn't like details and he hates haggling. He claims Indians aren't good at negotiating against anyone but themselves, and he may have a point."

"Does he think of himself as an Indian?" she wondered. She didn't.

"He thinks of himself as a Shawnee, but he is also very conscious that he is half-white." Michael looked over his cards at her. "You must understand, the Shawnee believe there are Indians and then there are the Shawnee. They are quite elitist."

"But his father raised him, didn't he?"

Michael laid down his suit of cards, neatly winning the hand. "He lived with his father until the man turned traitor. Then Alex returned to his mother's people. Isabel, let me warn you, he doesn't talk about his father much. In his mind the man is dead."

"I wish I could be the same." Isabel gathered the cards, the game forgotten. "Every turn of the wheel reminds me we are on our way to London. My path could cross his. I should be more like Haddon."

Michael rested his hand on her leg. "I don't believe you could, any more than I believe Haddon has. I know what preachers say, but I don't believe man was meant to forget. I certainly haven't."

"No, Michael, we were meant to forgive," she corrected him.

"Have you forgiven your father?"

Isabel leaned back in the corner. "I just want him to acknowledge my existence. Is that too much to ask?"

"For some men." He put the cards into a wooden case and tucked it into the coach's pocket for storing such things. "On the other hand, I want it all . . . and I think you do, too."

"No, I've thought on this. I don't want very much from him."

"Good. You probably won't receive much."

He passed his verdict with absolute confidence, and a thought struck her. "Do you know the marquis of Elswick?"

For one fleeting second, she sensed him hedge, but then he said easily, "Everyone does. He is a man of great influence."

Of course. Isabel nodded, hearing something else in his words. "I shall have to make my peace with that, won't I?" she said thoughtfully. "I will have to forgive. The irony, of course, is that his son was also linked to that actress they accused you of murdering. He would be my half brother. You don't think he was involved, do you, Michael?"

"You think too hard on it, Isabel." He pulled her into his arms. "Forget Elswick. The man you consider your father is the one who raised you. That's my thought."

Her stepfather? She shook her head. "He never cared for me."

"He had the keeping of you. He did more than Elswick."

That was true, but still something in Isabel rebelled at the thought of giving her stepfather credit. It was her *real* father she wanted acknowledgment from. Her *real* father whom she must see—

Her husband pulled her up into his lap. "Don't think on it now, Isabel," he told. "Don't make yourself angry."

"It's important to me—"

He interrupted her with a long, leisurely kiss. But Isabel wasn't ready to let go. "Michael, you will introduce me to the marquis of Elswick, won't you?"

Michael looked at her as if he weighed something in his mind, then he shrugged. "Isabel, I have other things to think on."

"Like what?"

He moved her to straddle his hips, and she could feel his arousal. He wanted to make love. His fingers tucked at the lacing in the back of her dress.

Her initial thought was shock . . . then interest. "The coachmen will know," she whispered.

"That I'm making love to my beautiful wife? If they are men at all, they will hope I am." He pulled her lacings free.

Isabel felt herself blush furiously, and yet, she didn't offer protest as he pulled down the shades over the windows. It all seemed so wicked—and exciting. Michael had swept into her life and changed everything.

She found the buttons of his breeches and undid them with an expert's ease. Her husband kissed his way from her throat to her ear, knowing what she liked, covering her breast with his hand.

They didn't fully undress. There was no need to. Sitting astride, Isabel took her husband deep within her. The sway of the coach added to the pleasure of their coupling. He pushed her dress down, his mouth finding her breasts, and their movements took on more intensity.

Isabel no longer thought of the coachmen. Her husband had the power to make her think of nothing but him. Their passion overwhelmed all other concerns.

And when they were done, when they held each other in their arms, Isabel thought she was the luckiest of women.

Michael hugged his sleepy, well-loved wife close and didn't want to think of Elswick.

As he brushed his lips across the top of her head, drinking in the heady scent of her hair, he ignored the pang of conscience and promised himself it would all be fine. He would protect

Isabel, and heaven help Henry and Elswick if they had killed Aletta Calendri.

They stayed in an excellent inn that evening and left midmorning the next day. Their coach rolled into London late in the afternoon.

When Isabel had last left London, she had been in disgrace. Now she returned in far more style than even the duchess had known.

"You'll need to purchase a wardrobe," Michael said.

She frowned at her brown day dress, so aware of her inadequacies. Michael read her mind. "You are beautiful," he said in her ear. "Besides, I prefer you naked."

"That would make it awkward when I went out to do the marketing."

He laughed. "You don't have to do any of those tasks," he informed her. "Although my household hasn't been set up for a woman. Bolling, my butler, serves most of my needs. The two of you can talk, and you may do whatever you wish."

"*Carte blanche?*" she asked archly.

He caught the double meaning of her words. "Of course," he murmured indulgently.

The coach then turned onto one of Mayfair's

most fashionable streets. The homes were new, their limestone facades untouched by the elements.

The coach stopped in front of a hunter green door with brass trimmings. It was a magnificent doorway.

His arm around her waist, Michael gave her a little squeeze. "Welcome to your home, Madam Severson."

Never in Isabel's wildest dreams had she imagined this moment. It was as if she had become a queen.

The coachman opened the door. As they climbed out of the coach, the front door opened. Bolling was a tall, lean man with a hooked nose and that weary air of knowledge all good butlers should have. He was dressed in black as befitted his station.

"Hello, Bolling," Michael said.

"Hello, sir. Welcome home."

"It's good to be here," Michael said, escorting her into the house. The hallway was a round room with a huge bronze chandelier covered in prisms hanging from the ceiling. The white marble floor didn't have a rug to protect it, and the wall alcoves were empty. The only furniture was a chair by the door and a table for hats and candles.

"This is my wife," Michael said, introducing her.

Bolling made a bow. "Mr. Haddon informed us you would not be returning alone. It is a pleasure to welcome you, Mrs. Severson."

Isabel nodded, very conscious of her new responsibilities and anxious to explore her new home.

However, Bolling was not finished. "You have a visitor, sir. Someone you particularly wished to see."

Michael frowned. "Who knew I was coming?"

At that moment, the doors opened. A man stood there. He was of average height, and yet there was an air about him that made him seem larger than life. The man's sharp gaze flicked over Isabel with a rudeness that stole her breath.

Her husband's whole manner changed. He stepped between Isabel and the visitor, his manner definitely combative.

The two men took each other's measure, then the visitor demanded, "What in bloody hell do you think you are doing?"

"Gaining your attention."

"You've done it. Let's talk." Their visitor turned on his heel and went back into the sitting room.

Michael didn't hesitate. "Bolling, take Mrs. Severson upstairs to my bedroom. I'll be there momentarily." But she knew he'd already dismissed her from his mind.

He entered the sitting room and shut the doors behind him.

All of Isabel's earlier contentment vanished.

"This way, ma'am," Bolling said, starting up the stairs.

She didn't move. "Who is that gentleman?" she asked.

Bolling hesitated. He glanced at the door.

Isabel could put authority in her voice. "Who is he?" she repeated.

"The marquis of Elswick."

If the hand of God had come down from the sky, Isabel could not have been more stunned. That rude man was her father?

What astonished her even more was that she had not recognized him. She'd always thought she would know, that there would have been some bond between them that would have informed her.

He'd been a stranger.

"Mrs. Severson, this way please," Bolling said, reminding her of her husband's instruction.

But Isabel had no intention of going upstairs.

She had waited most of her life for that moment, and at last the hour had come.

She walked over to the sitting room and threw open the doors.

Ten

The two men were so involved in their conversation that they didn't even turn at Isabel's entrance. They stood in front of a carved marble fireplace that appeared never to have seen a fire in its grate.

The marquis was speaking in a low, angry voice, "Of course I'm here. I heard of your marriage and *whom* you married. You won't stop at anything in your attempt to get close enough to destroy me, will you? You are mad!"

"Sometimes I think I am," Michael answered. "You did your best to see me hang. If you weren't protecting Henry, why would you even care?"

She interrupted, wanting to make herself known. "So this is my father?"

Her quiet words were like a gunshot going off in the room. Both men looked up, startled. Her father's scowl grew deeper, and he muttered something to Michael that Isabel didn't catch.

Bolling came up behind her, apologizing, "I'm sorry, sir. Didn't realize she was going to do this and couldn't stop her in time."

Her husband waved him away, and said, "Isabel, I'll explain all in good time; but for now, go upstairs with Bolling."

"Explain all in good time?" She slammed the door, the butler having the intelligence to move back and save his nose. "The time is now, Michael. *Now.*"

Her father surveyed her with dispassionate interest, his irritation plain. She shared his thick black hair and determined chin. He, too, had flecks of gold in his eyes; but there was a harshness to his expression, an overall sense of disappointment with the world that she prayed would never imprint itself upon her.

"What did my mother see in you?" She'd not meant to speak the words aloud, but they came out all the same.

His brows rose. "I can't even remember what your mother looked like."

His words sucked the air out of the room.

Isabel struggled for breath—in her temper she found it. She wanted to rip his tongue out of his head. She charged forward, but Michael stepped into her path, catching her by the arms.

She whipped around to glare at him, seeing not her husband but a stranger. She jerked away from him. She didn't fully grasp the depth of his betrayal—it was too new—but she knew she had to put distance between them.

And then the marquis made a mistake. He smiled, the expression self-satisfied and grim.

Isabel raised her chin. "Go on with your questions, Michael. Ask him if he was the one who attempted to have you murdered?"

The marquis's astonishment to her charge appeared genuine. "Murdered?" He held out his hands. "I know nothing of that."

"Just as you know your son wasn't with Aletta Calendri the night she died?" Michael returned. This was obviously an old score between them.

"Aletta Calendri was a whore," the marquis answered. "She was with *many* men *every* night. You know that. You were there yourself."

"And so was Henry. We fought over her that evening," Michael said. "He was eaten up by jealousy—"

"Aye, because his friend was sleeping with the woman he loved," the marquis said. "His *friend*, Severson. That's what my son considered you, and you took his confidence and crushed it. Remember? You were all about conquest in those days. Too full of yourself to see the people you walked over. You had charm, looks, and Henry wanted to emulate you. He'd not listen to his father or anyone reasonable. Learning that *you* went to Aletta's each night after he left was a knife in his back." He looked to Isabel. "See what sort of man you have married? My condolences."

Michael held his hands up, palms out, as if asking for quarter. "I have no justification," he admitted. "I did think only of myself in those days."

"And you've changed?" the marquis drawled. His pointed look in Isabel's direction spoke volumes.

"Yes," Michael said bleakly. "I have."

"Only time will tell, won't it?" his lordship said. He shook his head. "Henry was angry that night. But he's not a killer. He didn't murder that girl."

"Then why did you try to pin the blame of her death on me?" Michael asked, and Isabel heard how much he needed to know the answer to this question. "Did you not consider that the judge could find out that you bribed witnesses against me? Or that you financed the printing of all those pamphlets accusing me? Why," he asked, "did you not grant me a moment of your time when I returned and was no longer a danger to you or Henry?"

"When was the time you weren't a threat?" the marquis countered. "Henry followed you like a dim-minded lamb. Once your influence was removed, he turned into a fine man. Castlereagh has him on his staff. He tells me Henry shows a true talent for diplomacy. There is no telling how high his star could ascend— then you return, asking questions, and protesting your innocence on a matter that has long been forgotten."

"Not by me."

"No, I suppose you couldn't," the marquis said. "But now you have returned, and people are linking Henry's name to yours and stirring up an old scandal that is best left forgotten."

"I can't forget it," Michael said. "I value my name as dearly as you do yours."

"Your name?" The marquis threw his hands

up in exasperation. "You are the only one in your family who has appeared to have made something of yourself. Certainly you are proving to be more useful to Society than the rest of your rackety family. That brother of yours pretends to be a high flyer without the blunt to pay even his grocer. Sold off everything that wasn't entailed. Fancies himself part of the Carleton set. Can you believe it?" He sniffed his disgust. "And the ironic thing is you wouldn't have accomplished half of what you have if you'd continued pursuing the path you were following before the murder. You'd probably be in debtors' prison or worse."

Michael fell silent, and Isabel knew he agreed.

The bluster left the marquis. He attempted a more conciliatory tone. "I mean no insult. I'm only protecting my son. There is no crime in that."

"No," Michael agreed, his voice heavy with disappointment. "But if I didn't kill Aletta, and Henry didn't, who else could have?"

"You really *didn't* do it?" the marquis asked as if still uncertain.

Michael shook his head.

The marquis considered the problem. "It could have been any of a number of men. She played every one of you for fools. Henry squandered every shilling on her, and I doubt if you were much better."

"I didn't have money. She took nothing from me."

"Well then," his lordship said, "if she was manipulative enough to exploit one man's affections after another for money, then offering her favors to you *freely*, I can see a temper unleashed. And what a perfect plan it turned out to be, because not only did the killer make her pay for her deceitfulness, but he also exacted revenge on you. Brilliant."

"Do you mind if I don't agree with you?" Michael asked dryly.

"Not at all," the marquis answered. "I'd feel the same in your shoes. Unfortunately, there may be no way of ever learning who did it. Too much time has passed."

"Except that someone is trying to kill him now," Isabel said. "Possibly the same person."

The two men looked up as if they had forgotten she was in the room.

"Of course, that is assuming," she continued, "someone doesn't have another motive for wanting to murder you." She could think of a few good reasons herself just then.

"Yes," the marquis agreed. "Of course, if these

attempts on your life are connected with Aletta, all you have to do is wait. The killer will come after you." He started toward the door. "Either way, I'm out of it. I wish you well, Severson. I shall be interested in learning the outcome."

"One last question, my lord," Michael said.

His lordship paused. "How did you know when to be waiting for me to return home?" Michael asked.

"My spies are everywhere," the marquis said arrogantly. "There was little you could do in this city and I not know. I always protect my interests." For the briefest moment, his gaze flicked over Isabel. He turned away. "Good-bye."

He opened the door and left. They could hear him asking after his hat. From her vantage point in the room, she could see him go out the door. It slammed behind him.

And she and Michael were left alone.

Only minutes ago, her life had centered around him. Now she wondered how she could have been so blind?

Self-consciously, she untied the ribbons of the bonnet. Taking it off, she recognized it for what it was—a faded, out-of-fashion, silly memento to a woman who had not been wise.

"You knew who my father was all along."

"Isabel—"

"Didn't you?" she demanded, her voice sharp.

"Yes. Riggs told me."

"So you decided to meet my price," she said, reminding him of their first conversation.

He didn't answer.

Better to stare at the yellowing lace ruching under the hat's brim than her husband. Everything inside her had gone hollow, even her mind. Her body had been one with his. She'd trusted him. She couldn't believe she had been gulled so easily. Not even her father's abandonment hurt as deeply as Michael's duplicity.

Bolling appeared in the doorway. "Is there anything you need, sir?" he asked Michael.

"No, Bolling. Shut the door."

"Yes, sir," the butler, said starting to withdraw, but Isabel suddenly needed to escape. She pushed her way out past Bolling—and realized out in the hall she had nowhere to go. She had nothing.

"I want to go to my room," she informed Bolling. She had to get away from Michael. Then she'd be able to think. She had a hard decision to make.

"Isabel, we must talk," Michael said from the doorway, but she was already going up the stairs, not even waiting for Bolling. There was no carpet to muffle sound, and she heard Michael's heavier footsteps behind her.

Glancing over her shoulder, she saw he was almost upon her. She threw the bonnet in his face, picked up her skirts, and, reaching the top of the stairs, ran for the first door, shutting herself behind it.

There was no lock. She had no choice but to try and bar it with her body. She was angry enough to believe she might make it work.

Her back against the door, she found herself in an ivory-colored room that had no furniture other than the bed and a chair. Everything appeared new. The spread and draperies were a sky-blue watered silk, the carpet the same ivory tones as the wall. It was a restful room that suited her tastes perfectly.

The door handle turned. Isabel dug in her heels. He stopped when he felt her body weight against the door.

"We must talk," he said through the crack.

Isabel stared up at the ceiling, noting the plaster medallions. She didn't have to say anything . . . then again, she did have one burning question.

"Tell me, Michael," her voice sounded incredibly calm in spite of the burn of tears in her throat, "now that you've discovered the marquis didn't have a hand in the murder, what are you going to do? You've taken the drastic measure of marrying me to no avail."

There was a beat of silence. She caught the scent of his shaving soap and leaned her cheek against the wood. Her heart hurt.

"It's not like that," he vowed quietly. "Isabel, let me in. Let us talk."

"Did you know he would be here when we arrived?"

"No." He lowered his voice so she had to listen closely. "I had no idea. He surprised me."

"But you expected to let him know about our marriage?" she guessed. "Sooner or later, I would have been your trump card . . . even though I'd told you he didn't give a care." Dear God, those words hurt. She had to grit her teeth, to be strong.

"I'm coming in. Let us speak face-to-face."

"I'm not ready for that."

"It doesn't matter. I must talk to you." He pressed the door. She wouldn't be able to hold him back, and she didn't want to see him, not when she hurt in a way she'd never thought possible.

Isabel pushed away from the door and crossed to the window. It overlooked the street. The roads were paved, and there was a charming fenced garden in the middle of the circle. She grabbed hold of the silk drape, clutching it as tightly as she could. Anything to keep herself together.

He entered and shut the door behind him. She could feel him staring at her. "I should have told you," he said.

That was the *least* of what he should have done.

"In the beginning it made sense to me," he said. "I marry you, and Elswick realizes he can't ignore me." He paused, and she could imagine him raking his hair with his fingers in that way he had when he was tossing something over in his mind.

"It all got mixed up," he confessed. "*I* lost sight of what was important. From the moment I saw you, I wanted you in a way I've never wanted a woman before."

She had to look at him then. She was pleased she was still dry-eyed. "Men have been wanting women that way forever."

"Yes, *forever*," he agreed pointedly.

"Are you reminding me of our wedding vows?" she asked incredulously. "I'm sorry. I don't want to think about them now. After all, I'm good and trapped, am I not?" She didn't attempt to conceal her bitterness.

His jaw tightened. "Our marriage seemed to be working—"

"Why? Because you thought your scheme would work? Or because you were getting everything while I received nothing?"

He jerked back as if she had slapped him.

Isabel turned away, holding the drape and pretending to look outside, although she would have been hard-pressed to say what was out there.

Still, he pressed on. "When I was shot, the game changed, Isabel. You were so brave. You saved my life."

No, she didn't want to think on any of this at all.

"I married you because you were honorable," he said, "and marrying you was the honorable thing to do. Accuse me of whatever you want, but I have the impression that you enjoyed our marriage. You were happy until you walked into this house and saw your father."

"He's no father to me," she said ruthlessly, angry at Michael for daring to say such a thing.

He immediately recognized he had made an error. "I know that now. I'm sorry I put you through an interview with him. But, Isabel, I had to know."

She didn't want to hear apologies. They

weren't what she needed. Slowly she faced Michael. "I trusted you," she whispered, "and it was all a sham."

"*None* of it was a sham," he said, his voice cutting through the quiet. He dared to take a step closer. "Be angry with me, Isabel. Rant and rave, throw things, be as bloody savage as you wish. But don't think for a second I don't respect and admire you. What we've had is rare . . ." He broke off as if just realizing the truth of those words. "You can't just toss it aside in a fit of anger."

"I'm not the one who tossed it aside," she said evenly. "You made me believe in those things when I didn't want to. And now I can't believe in anything. Certainly not you."

His hands fell to his sides. He looked completely miserable, as if he accepted all blame.

In another minute, she would break down completely, and her pride wouldn't let her do that. Pride was the only thing she had left. "I don't love you," she said, her throat tight. "I sold myself into marriage to you."

"You didn't sell yourself—"

"Yes, I did," she said cutting him off. "I was afraid to be on my own. Nothing I attempted to do on my own worked out. Then, when I was at the lowest point, and afraid, you made your offer and I took it. I will say this, Aletta Calendri was *wiser* than I was. She didn't let herself be *trapped*."

"You were not trapped," he came back, his temper rising. Obviously he didn't like the idea of being treated callously any more than she did. "You came to me of your own free will."

"And how I regret it," she answered.

His own temper caught fire. "Do you want *out*? Is that it?"

Was that it? Isabel didn't know. She felt as if she'd been ripped open, that her pain was there for him to see if he would only look. But of course, that would mean he must consider someone beyond himself.

In truth, it really wasn't his fault. He'd been honest from the beginning. His sole purpose was to clear his name. She was a detail.

She should have known. *Stupid, stupid, stupid—*

"Isabel, I don't want matters to be like this between us." His voice sounded tight . . . as if he truly had regrets.

"No," she agreed. "That's not the way men want it, is it? You believe all there is to marriage is what happens between us in bed." She walked over to that piece of furniture and lay down on the mattress, her fists clenched, her body stiff. "I'm ready, Michael. Whenever you want me, I'm here, waiting."

"Don't do this, Isabel," he warned.

"You don't want to make love here?" she asked, unable to look at him, fearing she would break. "Should I go down to the coach—?"

"Don't make fun of what we had," he answered through clenched teeth.

"We had *nothing*." She looked at him, wanting him to see how deeply he had hurt her. "This was all that was between us." She placed her hand on the mattress. "Don't you understand? There's nothing else."

Michael took a step back. His dark eyes snapped with anger. She braced herself, uncertain of what to expect.

He turned on his heel and walked out the door, shutting it firmly behind him.

Out of all the possible outcomes, she hadn't anticipated that reaction.

Isabel sat up. A moment later, the front door slammed.

As if in a trance, she rose from the bed and walked to the window in time to see his tall frame stride down the street and around the corner. He was gone.

And the house felt like nothing but an empty shell.

She had entered it with hopes and dreams, and now stood in the middle of unused grates and cold rooms.

Sinking to the floor, Isabel bowed her head and, at last, let the tears come.

Eleven

❦

Bolling had protested Michael's leaving alone. He'd wanted him to take along Langston, a footman. He'd said Mr. Haddon would have his head on a pike if anything had happened to Michael.

Michael wasn't in the mood to answer to anyone. And, as he walked out the door, slapping his hat on his head, he'd announced he would welcome a good fight.

Instead, he walked and walked and walked, not caring where he was going. It took a while before he could get his angry thoughts in order.

And when he did, he didn't like what he had done.

Isabel was right. He had used her. The extent

had only become clear to him after Elswick had left the house, and he'd seen the look on her face.

He'd been more concerned about getting his questions answered than the well-being of his wife. And what good had it done him? Elswick hadn't known a bloody thing!

But she was wrong in thinking he didn't care about her. He did. He had every intention of honoring his commitments. She'd not had anything to complain about yet, had she—?

Suddenly, he stopped. His temper leaving as quickly as it had come . . . to be replaced by an overwhelming emptiness.

Isabel was going to leave him.

He knew that, even if she hadn't quite realized it.

The woman he'd married had walls around her—just as he'd had. He was familiar with what it took to scale those walls—and he had done it. She'd put her trust in him . . .

The pain he had seen in Isabel's eyes was haunting—

Another piece of the puzzle fell into place.

He'd seen that expression before. In Aletta's eyes.

Michael reeled back. He looked around him, surprised to see he had walked himself halfway across London, moving toward the docks. Not far from there was a popular tavern, the Crow, that he'd patronized years ago. He took a deep steadying breath and let himself remember.

Aletta's angry words echoed in his ears. Words he hadn't been able to recall and, even now, had only vague recollections of.

A trio of burly sailors rolled down the street on their way back to the wharves. Michael stepped back, but one of them bumped into his shoulder.

"Sorry," the tar barked out, keeping pace with his companions—and Michael saw himself saying *sorry*. He'd repeated it several times. *Sorry*. Flippant, offhand . . . slurry.

He'd gone to Aletta for sex.

The details started to fly at him out of nowhere. He'd argued with Henry about Aletta earlier that evening, and after drinking a good portion of the night had decided he'd wanted her. Just that simple. So he'd gone to her apartment.

Disturbed by the memories, Michael began walking down familiar streets that grew more narrow and crowded as he moved along. Evening was coming. Those that had homes to go to were heading for them. Others milled about, making plans and moving toward taverns. Michael moved with them.

In his mind, he could feel himself sway, blind drunk the way he'd been the night of Aletta's death. She had wanted to talk. He hadn't. Looking back, he was amazed that he could have been that roasted and still hot and ready.

And, of course, Elswick had been right—Michael hadn't given a damn about Henry or Aletta.

But he and Aletta had not had sex. He knew that now. She'd told him she wanted something more. That she would give up everything for him, and he'd laughed.

He absently rubbed his chest where he'd been shot, feeling the plaster that covered the wound.

Aletta had been furious. She'd thrown things at him. He'd been on the bed, laughing, and it had infuriated her that he didn't take her seriously. But he couldn't. He was too far gone with drink to think of anything, and he recalled that he'd taken a pillow to protect himself, pulling it around his head, laughing to the point he'd started hiccupping.

God, what a cruel, bloody sot he had been.

Michael stopped at the corner, not far from the Crow. His old drinking pub was still as busy as it had been years ago. He tilted his head as if he could force the memories out of his mind. He recalled a muffled male voice. Aletta telling him to leave . . . *and then?*

It was no use. Try as he might, no more would come. But he did recall mumbling *sorry.*

He released his breath in a long sigh. He'd go mad before he figured this all out—

A tall, blond man removing his hat as he entered the Crow caught Michael's eye. Riggs— and he wasn't alone. He was with Henry.

His old acquaintance had changed over the years. He was heavier and looked older than his age. Elswick might be pleased, but Michael didn't think Henry looked at all happy with his life.

The pairing was suspicious.

Michael crossed the street to the Crow, neatly dodging a dray whose driver was too busy yelling at some boys to keep an eye on the road. He should probably send for Haddon and some of his men, but it would take a good forty-five minutes for anyone to come, and he might not have that kind of time to spare.

He wouldn't confront them. Just watch them and see what happens.

Inside, he didn't remove his hat. It wasn't necessary. This was a rough-and-ready crowd. More than a few punches would be thrown before the night was out. It also catered to a diverse clientele. Rakes and pickpockets mixed with Corinthians. Fops argued with post drivers. Merchants discussed trade with sailors, while thieves hobnobbed with bankers. The main room was smoky and noisy.

No one paid attention to Michael as he made his way along the edge of the taproom to a corner where he could spy on Henry and Riggs. They stood deep in conversation and didn't seem to notice anyone around them.

Michael would have handed over his share of the *Sea Serpent* to know what they discussed.

Suddenly, Henry turned abruptly from Riggs. He pushed his way toward the door. Riggs followed him, calling his name. Michael started to follow.

He'd reached the door when it opened and a new party of gentlemen pushed their way in. Anxious to follow his quarry, Michael tried to shove his way through. A man grabbed his arm, turning him around.

"Michael?"

"Yes," he answered, still moving out the door, and then stopped. He turned and found himself face-to-face with his brother. "Carter?"

Ten years ago, his brother had been a fine-looking man. The years had not been kind to him. Deep lines marked his brow, while the redness of broken blood vessels on his nose were a sign of his fondness for port. He'd also lost much of his youthful muscle strength and developed a slump in his shoulders.

His brother clapped him on the back. "Good God, yes, it's me. I've been looking everywhere for you. Come, have a drink." He didn't wait for Michael's reply, but swept him back inside.

Riggs and Henry were forgotten as Michael allowed himself to be presented to Carter's friends. "This is my brother," he said to the other gentlemen. They all wore the indolent, careless style of the Corinthian set, but their paunches belied their dress. Michael surmised they were more interested in wetting their throats than horse racing or fencing.

Certainly interested in him.

When the tankards were passed around, Carter snagged one for himself and Michael. "Cheers," he said, and drank his down. He held up his tankard to be refilled before steering Michael back to the corner where he had spied on Riggs.

Carter took a drink before saying, "So what have you been doing with yourself?"

It was an odd question considering the circumstances. His overt friendliness was a definite contrast to his past behavior. Michael said, "I called upon you. You refused to see me."

"Nonsense. I would have seen you if I had been in. I'm not home often."

Michael frowned. He was certain his brother or his wife had been in residence.

"Then again," Carter said, "I don't remember receiving a card from you."

"I didn't leave one."

Carter shrugged. "Well, there you have it. You can't expect me to return a call if there is no card."

"We're brothers," Michael reminded him.

"I know that." Carter took a swig and looked across the crowd as if ensuring his friends were still there. Not once had Carter met his eye. He was always looking somewhere else.

"I hear you are married." Carter's statement caught Michael off guard.

"Who told you?"

At last, Carter met his gaze. He smiled, his expression confident. "The bishop is a friend of mine. He couldn't help but notice the name on the petition for a special license. Am I too late to wish you happy?"

"We were married less than a week ago."

"Ah, the prime of a marriage. After that, it is all a bore." Carter smiled at Michael, the expression not reaching his eyes. "We shall have to meet your new bride. In fact, I'm surprised you are here tonight. The mattress has hardly been broken in on the wedding bed."

Michael didn't need love advice from his brother, especially on a currently sore subject. "How is your family?"

"Good, thank you." He contradicted himself with an exasperated sound. "The estates take up time. This bloody title is a nuisance. My oldest boy was just tossed out of Eton. We got them to take him back. Sounds like the two of us, eh? Of course, I hear you've done well for yourself."

"I've managed." Growing up, he'd idolized Carter. How could he not? Carter was the heir. He could do no wrong. Michael had striven to be like him in all things . . . including drinking, he realized, as his brother frowned into his now empty tankard. "Here," Michael said, pouring his into Carter's.

"Is it really as dangerous over there as I've heard?" Carter asked.

Michael shrugged. "The world is a dangerous place, anywhere you go."

"So true," his brother agreed disinterestedly. "Ah, Mullins is leaving." He clapped Michael

227

on the back again. "We'll have dinner together. Soon. Wallis will arrange everything." His sister-in-law had never really liked Michael. She'd thought him spoiled. She'd been right.

"Must go," Carter threw over his shoulder at him, already moving toward the door.

Michael didn't follow. He watched his brother elbow his way through the throng of drinkers toward his waiting companions. He didn't recognize any of them although he was certain he'd met Mullins before. The name sounded familiar. It came to him. Mullins and Carter had been drinking mates since before Michael left England, and it struck him that while his life had been changing, theirs had stayed the same—and not for the better.

He moved to the door. He doubted there was any sense in searching for Riggs or Henry. There was no telling where they could be.

Instead, his mind turned to Isabel, and, without really being conscious of making a decision, he started heading home. Fresh air felt good. The streets were not as crowded so there was room for a hack to roll up beside him.

The door opened. Michael braced himself, ready for anything.

Haddon stuck his head out. "Did you find

your good fight?" he asked, quoting what Michael had told Bolling.

"Are you offering one?"

His friend gave a resigned sigh. "Get in."

Michael obliged, taking off his hat to fold his tall frame into the coach. "Did you have me followed?"

"Yes. Bolling was smart enough to send a man after you. Michael, what are you thinking? Someone is trying to kill you. And don't give me that nonsense about not needing a nursemaid."

"I don't need to. I already have one—Bolling."

"He's a good man."

Michael shrugged, not willing to give an inch.

Haddon said in Shawnee, "I am worried for you, my brother. You are taking risks you should not."

"Only the bold discover the truth," Michael answered, also in Shawnee.

"Or the foolish." He switched to English. "Your wife knows why you married her?"

"Did Bolling share that with you, too?"

"He overheard a few things."

"It's a private matter, Alex."

"Your Isabel has a temper. That's good. You need someone who will stand up to you."

"Like you do?"

Haddon's teeth flashed white in his smile. "Perhaps."

And Michael had to admit it was true. He did admire Isabel's spirit. He also realized, he was not sorry he'd married her.

He didn't realize how quiet he'd become until Haddon suggested, "You may be falling in love with her."

The idea was so startling, Michael dropped his jaw.

Haddon laughed quietly. "I know, I know," he said, "I'm the romantic. You are the one too consumed with revenge—"

"I want *justice*," Michael shot back. Isabel had made the same accusation.

"Justice," Haddon patiently amended. "Be careful that in pursuing your quarry, you don't toss aside what you value most." He had changed back to Shawnee, the words musical when he spoke them. And prophetic.

Fortunately, Michael was saved from answering by their arrival at his front step. He opened the door.

Alex placed a hand on his arm. "I say these things in honor of our friendship," he said.

Michael answered in English. "I know." He hesitated. His feelings where Isabel was concerned were too new, too raw. He changed the subject. "I saw my brother this evening."

"Did he turn away or walk off?" Haddon knew of the calls Michael had made.

"He acted as if we were the closest of family. He'd heard of my marriage. I also saw Riggs tonight with Henry, Elswick's heir."

The light shining from the front door lamp reflected off the silver collar around Alex's neck. "Are you surprised at seeing them together? Is this not what you suspected?"

Michael shook his head. "I am not certain. This afternoon, Elswick convinced me Henry couldn't be involved."

"Fathers rarely know what their sons are doing," Haddon reminded him. "Mine certainly doesn't. Keep your guard up."

"I will." Michael got out of the coach. "You leave on the evening tide tomorrow."

"That's the plan."

"You like sailing that ship, don't you?"

Haddon nodded. "I have discovered freedom. No one can argue with me—unless I take you on board." He leaned forward. "Michael, we made more money than any two men should this last trip. I leave for Egypt on the morrow. I've been holding documents for you to sign. I understand if you are"—he nodded to the house—"involved. I can always do what I have been doing, forging your name."

"I'll be there in the morning," Michael promised, and why shouldn't he be? Perhaps a bit of distance from each other was what he and Isabel both needed.

"Make it early. We'll be loading."

"I will." Michael shut the door and nodded to the driver to be on his way.

Haddon stuck out the window to call out as he drove away, "Buy her something!"

"Who?"

"Your wife," Haddon said with some exasperation. "Gifts always make negotiating easier, and I'm not talking about cheap beads!" The hack rounded a corner.

Michael stood a moment. Alex was the one man he could trust. He valued his opinion, and perhaps he was right about taking a guard with him.

Unfortunately, he was wrong about Isabel. She couldn't be bought, unless he got her something he knew she wanted very much—?

Thoughtfully, he entered the house.

Bolling was sitting up waiting for him. "Glad to see you home, sir."

"I imagine you are," Michael said.

"You aren't unhappy with me for sending for Mr. Haddon, are you, sir?"

"Would it make a difference?"

"No, sir."

Michael sighed. "Go to bed." He didn't wait to see if Bolling obeyed but went upstairs, not even bothering with a candle.

The room he had been using was the largest one and located at the end of the hall. He knew Isabel wouldn't be there.

For a moment, he stood in front of the door of the room she had chosen out of anger and debated going in. His pride whispered to leave her be.

He tested the door.

It was not locked or barricaded against him.

He opened it. The room was dark, the shades drawn against even what little moonlight there was.

His eyes adjusted quickly and he could see her form on the bed. The even sound of her breathing drew him.

Without rationalizing what he was doing, he closed the door, undressed, and slipped into the bed beside her. It felt right to be there with Isabel. He'd grown accustomed to her presence, to the sound of her breathing and her soft warmth. Almost as if she felt the same, she rolled over to curl next to him. Her breath escaped in a soft sigh of contentment.

He'd never heard a more welcoming sound. Slowly, he lowered his arms to place them around her. She was still dressed, the worn material of the gown she had been wearing didn't inhibit her sleep. Her toes were bare, so she'd at least made herself that comfortable. Her sleepy warmth and the spicy, rose scent of her hair aroused him.

This would be the first night since their wedding they hadn't made love.

The first time he would sleep with *any* woman without sex.

He was tempted. He could slide into her and wake her with kisses. He knew Isabel. She would respond.

And then what?

As her body heat melded with his, a deep peace settled over Michael.

This, being close to his wife, was, for that moment, enough. He fell asleep.

Isabel woke the next morning to someone pounding on the door.

She pushed her hair back and looked around, not immediately recognizing her surroundings—then she remembered. She was surprised she had slept as well as she had. Her eyes had been swollen shut from crying when she went to bed, and she tossed and turned fitfully at first.

Sometime in the middle of the night, she must have finally relaxed.

And then she glanced over at the pillow on the other side of the bed. There was an indentation as if someone had slept there. Tentatively, she snuggled next to it and caught the clean scent of her husband.

Her senses went on the alert. She sat up, searching the bare room for more signs of him. There were none.

Isabel ran her hand over the sheets. They weren't warm as if someone had just vacated that side of the bed. Perhaps her imagination played tricks—

There was another knock at the door. "Mrs. Severson?"

She recognized the butler's voice. "Yes, Bolling?"

"I hate to disturb your rest, but you have visitors."

"*I* do?

Other than the marquis and the Oxleys, who knew she was there, or cared?

"What time is it?" she asked Bolling.

"Close to noon," a woman's melodic, cultured voice said, a beat before the door started to swing open.

Isabel pulled the covers up just as a magnificent creature with the blondest hair and the bluest eyes presented herself in the doorway. She had on the most wonderful confection of an emerald velvet cap. White and yellow ostrich feathers were pinned into place with a jeweled pin. Her dress was a lighter green with a lace jacket and matching gloves. Her shoes were the finest kidskin and dyed to match the hat. She had finished off the ensemble with a red walking stick as tall as she was and trimmed in white, yellow, and green ribbons.

The woman tapped the floor with the walking stick. "You are a sleepyhead," the woman said, her gaze boldly appraising Isabel. "I, too, could sleep the day away, but not when the finest dressmaker in all England waits upon my pleasure."

"Excuse me?" Isabel said.

"Madame Beaumain is waiting in your salon," the woman said. "She has an appointment to furnish you with a complete new wardrobe."

Bolling sought to interject himself, "The master ordered the dressmaker to come. He said you are to have *carte blanche*."

Michael had hired a dressmaker for her?

The woman had no difficulty understanding. Her eyes danced with anticipation. "Did you hear that? *Carte blanche*. Men are rarely so generous—to their wives. Come, come, Isabel! Up!" She walked across the room and threw open the drapes. The afternoon sun streamed into the room and made Isabel squint.

Holding her hand to shade her eyes and feeling like a veritable scullery maid in the presence of such elegance, Isabel felt it almost churlish to ask, "And who are you?"

The woman gifted her with a brilliant smile. "I am your sister-in-law, Wallis, countess of Jemison."

Twelve

❧

*I*sabel spent the most amazing day, and it wouldn't have been half as enjoyable if not for Wallis.

She was, indeed, Michael's sister-in-law. Isabel was more than a bit embarrassed that she didn't know very much about the family, a situation Wallis excused with a breezy, "Men never pay attention to the details."

"Now, hurry and dress. One doesn't keep Madame Beaumain waiting," her sister-in-law said. "And please call me Wallis. We are sisters now." She gifted Isabel with a brilliant smile before leaving the room.

A sister. Isabel wanted a sister or even a close female friend who was her age. Wallis was older, but she had a youthful spirit and, just then, when her marriage appeared to be a mess, Isabel appreciated the woman's diversion.

She also remembered, while she was washing her face, she'd heard of Madame Beaumain before. The duchess had used her and had once been in the foulest of moods because Madame had refused to make a costume for her to wear to a special ball. The duchess had made an offhand comment that had insulted Madame. It had taken weeks of gift buying and wheedling for the duchess to get back into Madame's good graces.

As Isabel pulled her forest green wool over her head, the dress she had married in, she knew she would not meet Madame's exacting standards.

Downstairs, Bolling hovered in the hallway with a worried expression on his face while a line of dressmaker assistants paraded in and out through the door carrying bolts of silks and muslins.

Madame stood in the door between the hall and the sitting room. She was a thin woman dressed in dark blue, with her hair in a tight bun and a mouth perpetually pinched as if she sucked lemons all the time. She watched Isabel come down the stairs, her disapproval plain.

"Hello," Isabel said. "Thank you for coming." She was so nervous, she almost offered her hand.

"I don't know if it is worth my time," Madame said bluntly. Her nasal voice gave her words a nasty tone.

Isabel was too shocked to comment.

Fortunately, Wallis was not intimidated. She sat on the settee in the sitting room surrounded by pattern books and stacks of material and looking completely at ease. Looking up from the French fashion gazette she'd been perusing, she asked, "Hasn't Mr. Severson paid you in advance?"

Madame stiffened. "You know this?"

"I know," Wallis said, meeting Madame's gaze with a guileless one of her own. "He has paid a fortune for your time, Madame. Knowing your reputation, you've probably charged him three times your costs to come to the house."

"I would do no such thing."

"Of course not," Wallis drawled with patent disbelief. She wore emerald earrings the size of Isabel's small finger.

Even Madame's assistants were dressed more finely than Isabel.

Wallis held the magazine up for Madame to

see. "What do you think of this style, Madame? Beneath those dowdy clothes, my sister-in-law is a true beauty. She will do justice to your creations, unlike the others. Women who can afford your prices are usually old and plump. Some of them look positively like cows in your creations. My sister-in-law will do you justice. I may even take her with me to Countess Varvarinski's rout next week. I promise, if I do and she is in one of your dresses, everyone will be in your shop the next day."

"Including the Countess Varvarinski?" Madame's beady gaze gleamed with avarice. She motioned for Isabel to enter the room. "Stop there, in the light." She walked around Isabel, looking her over from head to toe. "I could do wonders with her."

"Only you could make her what she could be," Wallis agreed.

There was a moment of suspense, then, with a sharp clap of her hands, Madame said, "*Tiens*, it will be done! Undress her. We must see her form."

Two of Madame's three assistants scurried to bring her will to fruition.

"Please, shut the door," Isabel begged, fearing they would strip her down in front of Bolling.

Wallis stopped them before they closed the door. "Wait, Mrs. Severson has not broken her fast and I admit I could eat a bit of something. What of you, Madame?"

"I could eat," the Frenchwoman said.

"Good," Wallis said. "Bolling, is it?"

Bolling nodded. He appeared as bedazzled by Wallis as Isabel was, especially when her ladyship bestowed upon him her radiant smile. "We will need some mulled wine, tepid, not hot. It's good for the digestion," she informed Isabel and Madame before continuing with her order. "Tea and perhaps some biscuits. I always prefer to eat light in the morning."

Isabel and Madame murmured that they did, too.

"However, for luncheon," Wallis said, "there is that stylish little shop no more than two blocks from here, Berry's."

"I know the place, my lady," Bolling said.

"They have the most incredible Portuguese ham, which they slice very thin. I'm quite partial to it, and their peaches they jar in syrup and cloves. Let us have that. Oh, yes, and next door is a marvelous bakery."

"I know that bakery," Madame said approvingly.

"I want some of their buns. Tell Emma, the

243

shop girl, you are shopping for me, and she will know exactly what I wish. But they must be hot. Whoever you send to fetch these things should know not to return without fresh, hot buns."

"Yes, my lady."

"Doesn't my husband have a cook?" Isabel dared to ask.

"Yes, ma'am—" Bolling said, but Wallis over-rode him.

"Cooks are *passé*. Is that not true, Madame?"

"*C'est vrai.*"

"And today is a special day," Wallis said, leaning back on the settee. "We should all treat ourselves. I am certain my brother-in-law would not mind."

"I don't think he would," Isabel agreed, and even if he did, she was still very angry with him. A decent lunch was the least he could do.

"Then it is decided," Wallis said happily. Bolling started from the room, but her voice called, "Wait a moment. Isabel, do you have a maid?" As an aside to Madame, Wallis explained, "She's just arrived from the country. You know how difficult it is for country servants to make the change to city ways."

"*Impossible,*" Madame answered with a world-weary shrug.

"Isabel must have a maid," Wallis declared.

244

"Bolling, send someone to my address and tell Becky to come. I told her there might be a possibility we will need her here. You will like her, Isabel. She's young but eager to learn. My Annie has been training for this past year. Becky has such a way with hair."

"Thank you," Isabel said.

"What are sisters for?" Wallis said.

What indeed? Wallis must have sensed her feelings because she held out her hand for Isabel to take. "Now," she said turning her attention back to the pattern books, "I believe Isabel must have something made in that soft ivory muslin over there. And she definitely needs a dress for this evening."

"What is this evening?" Isabel asked.

"You are dining with us. A small family occasion. Didn't Michael tell you?"

Isabel didn't want to share that she and Michael had had a fight, and she felt slightly foolish not knowing his plans at all. "He left early this morning," she said.

"And you are newly wed," Wallis said. "Thoughts of family dinners are second place in a new marriage. Is that not so true, Madame?"

"*Vrai, vrai,*" the Frenchwoman agreed.

"So, do you like this ivory muslin?" Wallis asked Isabel.

"I do."

"And don't you think this green-and-lavender tissue shot through with gold threads would make a lovely foil. You know, as a shawl, something light?" Wallis asked.

"Of course," Isabel said, finding the colors dazzling. The material must cost a fortune.

"This is the first dress, Madame," Wallis said. "You must have it ready this afternoon in this pattern so that my sister-in-law can wear it tonight. Her husband will be stunned when he sees her in it and will probably order many more dresses from you."

"There are expenses to doing a dress in a day," Madame said.

"Of course there are," Wallis agreed. "Discuss that with my brother-in-law. In the meantime, you need to collect Isabel's measurements. And, Bolling, why are you still here?"

Realizing he'd been dismissed, Bolling left to see to Wallis's wishes. Isabel placed herself in Madame's and Wallis's capable hands. It was not the easiest of endeavors. She was undressed and poked and prodded while everything was ordered from smallclothes to evening dresses.

Wallis had no hesitation about spending Michael's money. She seemed to know what he was worth down to the penny—and if what she thought was true, Michael was far more wealthy than Isabel could ever have imagined.

They drank tea and mulled wine in the morning, feasted on a delightful lunch, and nibbled on cheese and fruit all afternoon. The maid Becky arrived. She seemed a willing young woman, anxious to prove her mettle.

From time to time, Wallis would order something from Madame for herself. Not dresses but scarves, shoes . . . a petticoat.

The first time she did it, Madame raised a skeptical eyebrow. "I can place this on your outstanding account?" she suggested.

"Oh no, I'm certain my brother-in-law would wish to cover this himself. You know how difficult my husband can be."

"*Mais oui,*" Madame answered, her expression one of disbelief. Obviously, she didn't fear offending Wallis over money. "What do you think, Madame Severson?" she asked Isabel.

Wallis had done so much for her; Isabel couldn't imagine Michael would mind. She could not have handled Madame by herself.

And let Michael discover a wife wasn't just some tool for his own uses. Let him realize he was getting more than he bargained for!

"Of course, my husband wants Lady Jemison to have the scarf," Isabel said. "In fact, I believe she should have five of them, including one made out of that tissue she liked so much earlier."

"The one for your shawl?" Madame queried.

"Let me have the same fabric," Wallis said smoothly, "but in different colors. Then we shall complement each other," she told Isabel, and so it was done. After that, though, neither Wallis nor Madame asked permission. It was assumed.

Isabel had too many other decisions to make to worry. There were stockings and shoes to order, cloaks and wraps, undergarments of all sorts, and dresses—carriage dresses, opera dresses, dresses to promenade in, dresses to dance in, dresses for sitting at home. The whole affair was both exhausting and exhilarating—but worth every moment when, late in the afternoon, one of Madame's assistants returned with the ivory muslin made into a dress.

The lines were simple but the color brought out the creaminess in Isabel's skin. It had been trimmed in lavender and green ribbons, and when she put it on she felt as if she'd changed into a princess.

"Do you have the right shoes for it?" Wallis asked.

"I have a pair of kid slippers," she said, thinking of the ones that had belonged to her mother.

"Good, then you are ready for this evening." Wallis rose from the settee where she had spent much of the day directing things. Madame and her assistants were packing.

Isabel took Wallis's hand. "Thank you. I could not have handled her by myself."

Wallis smiled and gave her a wink. "Madame will do anything for money." She leaned closer. "Speaking of which, do you have the money for the vails?"

"The what?"

"The gratuities for her assistants?" Wallis whispered.

"I must pay them."

"A little something, especially since they are in your home."

Isabel thought of the meager hoard of coins in her purse. "Yes, I can get some." She started for the door, but Wallis, still holding her hand, pulled her back.

"Send Becky."

"Yes, Becky," Isabel agreed overwhelmed. The maid was already on her way out of the room. Apparently, while Isabel had been trying on clothes, the clever maid had been familiariz-

ing herself with the house and Isabel's posses-
sions. She was back in a blink with Isabel's cloth
purse.

The vails were appreciated. Isabel wasn't certain whom to tip. She didn't believe Madame
was eligible and yet, the dressmaker held out
her hand.

There wasn't much money left by the time
she was done.

"You appear exhausted," Wallis observed after the dressmakers had left. "Perhaps you
should have Becky rub your feet."

"What I'd really like is a bath," Isabel confessed.

"Becky?" Wallis prompted, and the maid
hurried to see it was done.

Wallis gave Isabel an indulgent smile. "You
aren't accustomed to servants, but you soon will
be. Michael must hire more. Your staff is absolutely down to the bare bones. And furniture!
You must buy furniture. I know a wonderful
decorator. He's brilliant. By the way, Becky's
wages are twenty-five pounds a year and an al-
lowance for board."

"That high?" Isabel had been fortunate to be
paid that as a governess.

"A good lady's maid is worth her weight in
sterling," Wallis assured her. "Now, let me be

on my way. I have much to do before this evening." To Bolling, who hovered outside in the foyer, she said, "Call a hack for me."

The butler hurried to comply. Isabel wished she had Wallis's sophistication, especially around servants.

Her sister-in-law placed her green velvet hat on her head at a rakish angle and picked up her gloves and shawl, moving with elegant ease.

Bolling came in. "I have a vehicle for you, my lady."

Wallis acknowledged him with a shrug. "Until this evening, dear sister. Half past eight," she said, taking Isabel's hand for another sisterly squeeze.

"Are Michael's sisters as kind as you?" Isabel asked.

A look of doubt crossed Wallis's face, but she answered, "I will let you form your own opinions on Margaret and Sarah. However, I believe you and I shall be the best of friends."

"I'd like that."

"So would I. Other than my children, I have no one close."

"Not even your husband?"

Wallis's smile froze on her face. "Of course, we are close."

There was something there, something that

perhaps, in time, Isabel would learn about her. But at present, she wouldn't pry. "What are your children's names?"

"I have two sons," she said proudly. "Jeremy and Wallace. That last is a bit of vanity," she said, referring to her second child's name. "I was named after my father Wallace, and it seemed right to carry his name forward."

"I'm certain your son is proud to bear it," Isabel said, walking with Wallis to the door. "It's an honor to be able to claim your lineage."

"I like you, Isabel," Wallis said. She gave her a kiss on the cheek. "Until this evening."

"Yes," Isabel said.

Wallis took a step toward the door and stopped. "By the by, do you have a bit of coin for the hack. I left my funds at home."

"Well, yes . . . I do." Isabel handed over to Wallis the last of her savings.

Wallis didn't touch the money. She gave Bolling a pointed look, and the butler stepped forward. He went outside to pay the driver.

"It was a wonderful day, Isabel. *À bientôt!*" Wallis went out the door.

Isabel stood in the hallway, feeling as if a whirlwind had struck and gone. She had no idea where Michael was or when he would return. She assumed he'd be home before half past eight—

She remembered her bath, and her spirits lifted. She went up to her room to find Becky busy making preparations. The maid had located a very deep tub, had set it up in the bedroom, and had organized the heating of water in the kitchen.

"I can't locate your scented soaps, ma'am," she said.

Because I don't have any Isabel could have said, but didn't. She was aware of how unsophisticated she must appear to the Londoners—including the maid.

Tactfully, Becky suggested, "There is a shop around the corner that sells Lady Jemison's favorite scents. Do you wish me to run out and purchase some for your bath?"

"It's that close?"

"Ma'am," Becky said, "in this section of the city everything is close. The shopkeepers want to cater to the people who own houses in Mayfair."

That made sense. Still, Isabel had another problem. "I don't have any money," she admitted.

"You don't need any. I'm certain the per-

253

fumer will extend credit. Lady Jemison never uses money. She says it is *de trop*."

Isabel doubted if Becky knew what *de trop* meant. And her country common sense warned her that money was a commodity that would never go out of style. Still, the idea of scented soaps was very appealing.

"See what you can do," she told Becky with a fair imitation of Wallis's breezy air. The maid didn't have to be told twice.

An hour later, Isabel found herself luxuriating in a warm bath scented with the attar of rose petals and Mediterranean peach kernels. She'd never thought of such a combination, but it made for a heady fragrance that soothed away all the pressures building in her mind.

Her intention had been to bathe quickly. She'd posted Becky at the top of the stairs with instructions to inform her as soon as Michael stepped into the house.

They had to talk.

She wasn't certain what she would say. The marriage could not be annulled, not with the activity they had been practicing over the past week . . .

Perhaps if she discovered she wasn't with child, they could manage something.

The thought made her sad. Her poor marriage. Over before it had even begun.

She sank into the fragrant water, wishing she could disappear—

Becky gave a knock on the door before entering. "Ma'am, your husband is home."

Michael was most anxious to see his wife. It had been a frustrating day. The paperwork and accounting had been endless. Their man of business Fitzhugh had cornered him with numerous questions that begged only Michael's attention.

But he was home at last—and he had a problem that would take the wisdom of Solomon to resolve.

Bolling met him at the door. "Did you have a good day, sir?"

"Fine. What of Mrs. Severson?"

The butler's raised eyebrows was a clue things had not gone well. "What is it?" Michael asked. "Was she not pleased with the dressmaker?"

"Yes, sir."

"Did she not order a dress or two to wear?"

"Oh, yes, sir." His tone spoke volumes.

"She spend a pretty penny?" Michael asked, pleased.

"Yes, sir . . . and more than a few hundred guineas."

Michael frowned, then decided the money was worth it. Isabel needed a wardrobe but Bolling didn't act as if he were finished. "What is it, man?" he asked with a touch of irritation.

"Lady Jemison was here today with her."

"My sister-in-law?" The last time he'd seen Wallis she had publicly given him the cut direct, snubbed him in front of everyone. "Why?"

"She helped Mrs. Severson with the dressmaker, and if I can make an observation, I believe, Mrs. Serverson appreciated her help. Lady Jemison left this for you."

Michael took the note from Bolling and cracked the seal. Wallis had terrible penmanship. In her childish scrawl, she reminded him they were having dinner together that evening.

"I knew nothing about an invitation for dinner," Michael murmured to himself. It had to have something to do with his seeing Carter the night before—and it really wasn't important to him. His true desire was to see his wife. "I've already had Gus put up the coach, and this is too short a notice. I don't believe we will be going anywhere this evening. Where is she?" he asked Bolling.

Bolling didn't need to be told who "she" was. "Upstairs, sir."

"Thank you." Michael took the stairs two at a time. He and Isabel needed to talk.

However, he didn't expect to have his way barred by a fierce pink-cheeked maid in a mobcap. "I'm sorry, sir, Madame is not at home," she informed him boldly.

Michael frowned. "Who the devil are you?"

"Becky."

"Well, Becky, this is my house, and I want to see my wife."

"She's not at home," Becky repeated stubbornly, placing her hand on the doorjamb to block his way.

Michael was stunned at the effrontery of the girl. "Did she tell you to do this?"

The maid's chin lifted. "She said she is not at home," she repeated, but he could see that she was starting to wonder if she was wise in defying him.

He pointed his finger away from the door. She pressed her hands against the jamb as if determined to hold her ground, but then, wisely, capitulated. She scurried out of the way, and he reached for the door handle—

The door swung open before he could touch

it and when Michael saw his wife standing there, all he could do was gape.

Isabel stood there, but this was not the same woman he'd left in bed this morning.

This woman was the very height of fashion. She wore a dress of soft ivory muslin that made her skin glow. Her hair was swept up in colored ribbons, the style emphasizing her long neck. A shawl of lavender, green, and gold threads reflected the light with her movement.

She was a goddess.

At that moment, every penny he'd spent on the dress was well worth the money.

"You're beautiful." The words fell out of his mouth before he'd thought them. They sounded trite. He'd said them to her before. "Stunningly beautiful," he managed.

For the barest of moments, he thought he saw her lower lip tremble.

"Isabel, we must talk—"

"We are already close to being late to dinner at your brother's house," she said. She came out of the room, sidestepping. "I think it best we have separate rooms."

"I don't."

"It's done," Isabel said, sounding for all the world like a governess chiding an unruly pupil, and he didn't like her high-and-mighty tone at all.

"I'm not going to dinner with my brother," Michael stated.

"We must," she answered. "They are expecting us."

"I've put up the coach and let Gus have his evening."

"Then we'll take a hack," she informed him, and started down the stairs.

For a second, he debated not going after her. And then he caught a whiff of her fragrance.

He started down the stairs.

And perhaps they should go to his brother's house. Why not? A hired hack was suddenly a good idea. It would be close quarters, and she couldn't escape him then. They would have privacy without an insolent lady's maid listening in.

At the foot of the stairs, she glanced over her shoulder. "Aren't you going to dress for dinner?"

He stopped in midstride. Who did she think she was? She'd never given a toss for how he dressed for dinner before?

A part of him wanted to stomp down the stairs and shake her back into being *his* Isabel, back into the woman he'd fallen in love with—!

His whole world suddenly tilted upside down.

He had fallen in love. Haddon had seen it. He'd known. He'd warned him.

Slowly, Michael sat down on the stairs, completely stunned. He was the blind man who could finally see. He was in love. Deep, mad, inescapable love.

At last, life made sense.

It all started and ended with Isabel.

She stood in the foyer, pulling on long gloves, studiously ignoring him, and he noticed she still wore her wedding band. All was not lost.

He knew she was hurt. Suddenly, he understood the pain he'd heard in her voice last night. He had the power to hurt her.

Michael rose from the steps, a different man than the one who had sat on them a moment earlier. Clearing his name no longer took precedence.

"Let me change," he said.

She looked up, mistaking his meaning. "We are late as it is. There is no time for you to dress for dinner."

He was tempted to correct her but realized it was not the time to declare himself. Later, when they were alone and she'd worn thin her temper, then he would tell her what he'd discovered in his heart.

"They'll wait," he answered, and went to dress. The battle between them was far from over, and it was one he planned on winning.

Thirteen

❧❦❧

*M*ichael was taking his time getting dressed. They would be late, another sin Isabel could lay at his door.

She crossed her arms, tapped her toe, then stopped. Bolling stood company with her, and she didn't want to appear peevish—even if she was.

If she could have her preference, she would have left without him, except she had no money to pay the fare. She didn't even know where they were going.

Isabel felt she'd managed to hold her own so far, but opening that bedroom door and seeing him standing there had challenged her resolve. Especially when he had spoken to her in that hushed tone of appreciation. When Michael told her she was beautiful, she felt beautiful.

And having him so close played havoc with her emotions. She was so angry, so terribly betrayed, and yet, she wished everything could be different.

But she did have her pride.

She just didn't know what to do with it.

A sound on the step told her Michael was coming. She turned to the door, wanting to make her displeasure with his tardiness known.

Bolling stepped forward, but he wasn't the one to open the door for her. It was Michael. He reached around, placing his hand on the small of her back.

She tried not to look at him or to notice that he'd taken an extra minute to shave. Something about the scent of the soap he used always made her heart skip a beat faster. She would have to change that. She would have to force herself not to notice him at all.

But Michael wasn't a man a woman could ignore.

Isabel couldn't help stealing a glance and was stunned by how tall and handsome he appeared in black evening wear. The formal, elegant cut of his coat suited him, and the snowy folds of his neckcloth were a good foil for his dark hair and eyes. How easy it would be to lean back into his arms, to pretend he hadn't hurt her.

Instead, she ran down the step to the waiting hack.

The driver helped her into the narrow confines of the hired vehicle. Isabel attempted to fit herself into a corner so that she wouldn't have to touch her husband. It was impossible. His large frame filled the space. He placed his hat in his lap and knocked on the roof for the driver to go.

The cab swayed on bad springs, throwing them closer together, if such a thing were possible. Isabel leaned back, too aware of her husband's thigh against hers.

"Do you remember the last time we were in a coach together?" he asked.

She gave him her back, preferring to stare out at the passing scenery. He wasn't about to be ignored.

"Say what is on your mind," he urged her quietly.

"I said it all last night," she responded briskly. She crossed her arms, finding it difficult to be this close to him.

"When you get your temper up, you remind me that you were a governess."

A flash of anger shot through her. She stared out the window, refusing to look at him.

"I'm sorry," he said.

Isabel didn't answer.

"I shouldn't have used you," he continued, his voice measured as if he was feeling his way carefully.

"Apologies have never been easy for me. If I could do it over, Isabel—" He hesitated. "—If I could do it over, I would do exactly the same thing, because otherwise you would not be with me now. You would have marched off that morning to wherever, and I would be alone. We'd *both* be alone."

He was right.

And did she truly regret meeting him?

Before her life had been boring. Now . . . ?

"Years ago, Isabel, in a court of law, I was given a second chance. I tried to make the most of it. I pray you give me a second chance now. I will never hurt you again."

She closed her eyes, fearing she would cry. Kid gloves made it awkward to dry tears, but that wasn't the real reason she wanted to shut him off.

Isabel didn't know if she *could* take another risk with him. It hurt too much.

And yet, she loved him.

"I'm so pathetic," she said, not meaning to have spoken aloud.

"No, you aren't," he corrected. "You are right to be angry."

"You used me." Her words revealed her pain. She could not help herself.

"I did."

"Are you using me now?" She dared not look at him. He appeared to feel as miserable about the state of affairs between them as she did. She had to maintain control.

"No," he answered.

"But there are no guarantees, are there? You could change your mind."

"I won't. I want you to believe in me," he said. "That's all I ask."

"You ask too much," she said, yearning to forgive him. It was a weakness. She should be stronger.

"Don't say that, Isabel. Please, don't say that."

Before she could respond, the hack rolled to a stop. The cab rocked as the driver jumped down.

"We're here," Michael said, stating the obvious. She could tell he was frustrated. "We're not finished with this, Isabel," he warned. "Not at all."

The door opened, and he had to get out. He held his hand for her.

Even this casual contact was almost too much for her. She ignored his hand and climbed out on her own. A footman opened the front door, and Isabel hurried up the step. She left Michael behind to pay the driver.

A butler held open the front door. Isabel stepped inside. Michael came up behind her and handed his hat to a servant. "I'm having the hack driver wait for us," he said.

She nodded.

Wallis came out of the front sitting room to greet them. She was dressed as fashionably as she'd been earlier, but still wore the same emeralds. "Welcome, Isabel."

"Hello, Wallis," Michael said.

Wallis blushed. "Was I ignoring you, Michael? How thoughtless of me." She placed a dutiful, sisterly kiss on his cheek. "Welcome home. I'm certain you will find everything unchanged."

"It wouldn't be home if it was," he murmured.

There was a current of distrust between them, but Isabel couldn't quite fathom why. Wallis linked her arms in both of theirs and steered them into the sitting room where a man who must be Michael's brother waited. He stood by the fire, as if posing for a picture titled, *The Earl at Home*.

Carter Severson, Lord Jemison, must have

once been almost as handsome as Michael, but drink had destroyed those looks. The gray at his temples gave him a distinguished look, but there was a heaviness about his face, and the slump in his shoulders aged him beyond his forty-plus years.

And yet, she sensed, Carter's mind was working like the gears of a clock. He missed nothing. He caught every detail, including that she and Michael stood a distance apart.

"Here he is," Wallis said grandly, announcing Michael. "Our family black sheep, returned to the fold."

Isabel knew her husband hated being labeled in this manner, but she wasn't going to defend him. If she did so, he would believe she was ready to relent, and she was nowhere close to doing so.

Instead, she concentrated on her surroundings and was surprised to note that, for a woman who boasted her association with a decorator, Wallis's sitting room was in great need of restoration. The carpet was threadbare and the upholstery well-worn.

Michael had said his family were gamblers. Isabel didn't think they won often if that was the case. Nor was his brother what she had anticipated, especially after spending the afternoon with Wallis. He appeared lifeless in comparison to his vibrant wife.

The couple did not like each other.

Everyone was relieved when a moment later dinner was announced.

Carter offered Isabel his arm. Wallis and Michael followed them. It all seemed so formal for a family dinner.

The chestnut-paneled dining room was far too large for such a small party. The table leaves had been removed, and the setting for four seemed adrift in the space. Footmen stood at the four corners, ready to see to their every need.

Lamb was served along with bottle after bottle of wine. Remembering her wedding dinner, Isabel didn't overimbibe. Michael didn't drink at all.

Wallis and Carter made up for the two of them.

"I say, Michael, how did you earn all your lovely money?" Wallis asked.

"I worked."

His sister-in-law laughed as if he'd made a great jest.

"He did, Wallis," Carter said flatly.

Her laughter died. "What sort of work?"

"Trading. I sold furs, land, and anything else I could get my hands on," Michael answered.

"You are a merchant?" Wallis asked faintly. Isabel could almost hear her wonder what she would say to her friends.

"Our new venture is in shipping," Michael said. "Is that better?"

"Our?" Carter asked.

"I have a partner," Michael said.

His brother frowned. "You do?"

"Yes, Alex Haddon."

"I've never heard of him.

Isabel sensed Carter didn't accept anyone if he hadn't heard of him or knew his family. "Haddon is half-Shawnee," Michael said.

"What is that?" Wallis wondered.

"He's Indian," Michael answered, and seemed to take enjoyment at his brother and sister-in-law's raised eyebrows.

"Interesting," Carter murmured. "Where is this Haddon now?"

"On his way to Egypt. We are trading British copper for cotton."

"My, you really are a tradesman," Wallis wondered aloud, slightly dismayed.

"A very successful one," Isabel couldn't stop herself from interjecting.

"And you approve?" Carter asked. As he drank, he grew more sardonic, a quality Isabel did not admire.

"Yes, I do. In fact, I've never understood the genteel class's acceptance of position in government, law, or the church—and yet they sniff at the actually doing of business."

"Because money trading hands is so common," Wallis said.

"Unless it is at a gaming table?" Isabel countered pointedly. "I'm sorry, but I've watched many a lord turn up his nose at work and yet throw away the wages of a small village on the turn of the cards." It was only after she'd spoken her mind that she realized she could be considered critical of her hosts, who looked at her as if they had let a leper loose in their midst.

They were right. She had been too outspoken.

Her cheeks turned hot. She should apologize, but then Michael came to her rescue.

"I married a freethinker," he said.

"I don't believe it is wise for women to have such strong ideas," Wallis said stiffly.

"I do," Michael answered. "Isabel possesses intelligence and conviction, qualities I admire."

"She's also beautiful," his brother added.

"Quite right," Michael said. "As are you, Wallis." He'd said the last as if an afterthought. Carter didn't say a word, but continued to stare at Isabel, making her feel uncomfortable.

A tightness appeared around Wallis's mouth.

Here was a woman with regrets. Isabel had seen the same expression on her mother's face.

Except that, instead of sympathizing with her mother, she felt a flash of annoyance. Her mother had had so much in her husband and her children, and yet she'd longed for a man like the marquis.

"Tell me about the children," Michael said to Wallis.

The transformation in her sister-in-law was immediate. Her two sons Jeremy and Wallace were her pride. Had Michael known this? That he would flesh out her personality was something Isabel could admire. It was kind, a trait she didn't associate with most men . . . and some of the distrust she had felt for him eased a bit.

He was trying.

Perhaps he did mean the words he spoke in the coach?

Wallis talked enthusiastically about the children, while her husband kept making small, disparaging asides.

Isabel decided she didn't like Carter very much, especially when he finally said, "Enough, Wallis. If you aren't boring Michael and Isabel, you are boring me."

"You don't like to hear anyone talk but yourself," she countered.

"Quite right, my dear, quite right." Carter turned to Isabel. "Let me give you a tour of the house. Michael, you don't mind if I monopolize your wife?"

"I wouldn't mind going with you," Michael said.

"But then who would stay with Wallis," Carter replied smoothly.

Michael's gaze met Isabel's. She couldn't read what he was thinking. She wasn't particularly anxious to accept Carter's offer, but when Michael said, "Of course not," she felt she had no choice.

"Shall we?" Carter said helping her up from her chair. Out in the hall, he took her arm at the elbow. "Let us go to the library. There is something I think you will find interesting."

Isabel slowed her step, uncertain if she wanted to be alone with him. "Such as?"

"A portrait of Michael and me as boys." He mentioned the one thing that could make her go with him.

She started walking, and Carter fell into step beside her. "The house was a gift to the second earl of Jemison for service to the Crown during the great fire," he said.

"What did he do?" she asked.

"I don't know. Never gave a thought to it before," Carter admitted. He lit a candle for himself and one for her from a hall table and opened a door. "This is the library."

Their candles cast an eerie light on the bookshelf-lined walls. Isabel noticed the books didn't appear to have been taken from their places on the shelves very often. She'd learned ago not to trust a library where all the books were shelved by height and the spines were lined up evenly. Those were the libraries whose books were rarely read.

What did catch her eye was a portrait over the room's desk. Immediately she recognized Michael. Carter was a young man and Michael a boy of about ten. He held the reins to a bay pony and looked up at his brother with so much admiration in his eyes it gave the portrait life.

The artist had also caught their similarities despite their age differences. Even as young as he was, Michael had the shape of his brother's head and shoulders. They even held themselves in the exact same way, a mannerism Isabel recognized as true even today.

Isabel moved closer. She was fascinated to see the innocence in Michael's face. This is what *their* son would look like if she stayed in the marriage.

"My brother is fortunate to have a woman like you love him," Carter said.

Isabel started. She'd almost forgotten his presence. "What makes you say such a thing?" she asked, wanting to know.

"The way you defend him. You have a good head on your shoulders, Isabel. You married wisely."

"Some would not agree with you." She tried not to show emotion. It was hard, because contrary to every resolution she had made in the past twenty-four hours, Isabel knew she still loved Michael.

She was as trapped as her mother had been.

"Look at him," Carter said. "Who would have thought he would become wealthy. He was never good at his studies."

"Were you?"

"No," he said decisively. "However, Michael was always lucky."

"He worked for his money."

"I'm not talking about the money." His gaze met hers. "I'm talking about women. He always had charm."

"You must have charm, too," Isabel suggested, taking a step toward the door, which she was surprised to see had been closed. He must have shut it while she was so taken with the portrait. "After all, you have Wallis," she reminded him.

"And her lovers."

Isabel parted her lips in surprise. Carter smiled grimly. "You didn't know about those. There have been a number over the years. This last one—" He rolled his eyes. "He was young enough to be her son. Lord Riggs. Chases anything in skirts. I told Wallis that. She is growing less and less discreet with age."

"Lord Riggs?" Isabel repeated, uncertain if she'd heard him correctly.

"You know him?" He looked at her expectantly.

Isabel wondered if he was teasing. The coincidence was too great. "We've met."

"If *I* meet him, it will be with my sword. Well, shall we return to the others. They'll start to wonder where we are. Of course, I wouldn't mind seeing if Wallis can get jealous, although I would not want to insult my brother."

That statement got Isabel moving toward the door. Matters were complicated enough without this sort of nonsense. Michael's family was strange. She now believed he had good reason to keep a distance from them.

However, a thought struck her as she reached the door. She faced her brother-in-law.

"Do you believe Michael when he says he didn't murder Aletta Calendri?"

277

"No."

"You are so certain?"

"Absolutely," Carter responded.

"And why is that?"

"I was there."

Fourteen

❧

Isabel closed the door. "You were there?"

Carter nodded.

"You saw him—" She couldn't use the word "murder." It had suddenly taken on a very real connotation.

"No . . . but I was there afterward. Michael sent for me. I helped him home."

"How did Michael send for you?"

Carter gave his head a little shake as if he were surprised she would question him. She thought of the wine he'd imbibed with dinner. He was probably clearing the fumes.

"He sent a servant," Carter said.

"Who didn't testify against him in court?"

Carter sliced the air abruptly as if warding

her off. "They didn't find him. The lad bolted, not wanting to be part of it all."

"But what reason would Michael have to hurt her?" she wondered. She touched her wedding band. Funny, but through everything, she'd not removed it.

"Jealousy. Isn't that the motivation for all murders?"

"Starting with Cain and Abel?"

Carter nodded. "Exactly so."

Isabel searched her mind to remember the stories she'd read years ago during the murder trial and was frustrated she didn't know more details. "What of Lord Elswick's son? Michael believes he may have done it. Henry and Aletta were lovers. Henry wanted to keep her."

She watched Carter's expression in the candlelight closely, searching for any sign that his memory could be wrong. Almost as if in response to her scrutiny, he drew back slightly into the shadows.

"I don't know," he said stonily. "Aletta was a victim of her own indiscretions. She played many men against each other."

"So there could have been many men who could have killed her?"

Carter's expression turned shuddered. "Possibly."

"Probably," Isabel corrected him. "Isn't that what the judge decided? There was almost no evidence against Michael that couldn't have been leveled against others?"

"A gentlemen in the building saw him."

Isabel shook her head. "If that was true, the judge would have convicted him."

Her brother-in-law was obviously not accustomed to being challenged. "My brother is fortunate to have such a passionate advocate for his defense." He sounded angry.

"I'm only stating what is true," Isabel answered. "And if you know differently, why did you not testify at his trial?"

"He's my brother." Carter nodded at the portrait on the wall. "I am the head of the family. I must think of our name."

"But, according to Sarah, your name was dragged through the trial as it was."

"You have a very sharp memory, Isabel." He wasn't paying her a compliment.

"I was a governess, my lord," she informed him. "I've had my wits honed by ten-year-old boys and the most wayward girl imagined. I listen to everything."

Carter's eyebrows rose with understanding. "I did not know you'd been in service."

"You don't approve?"

"I didn't say that," he answered, coming toward her and reaching for the door handle, a signal their interview was at an end . . . but Isabel had one more question.

She blocked his way. "Has it ever bothered you over the years that there was no justice for that woman's death? That her ghost must cry for vengeance?"

"Do you want me to turn over your husband?"

They stood close to each other, their faces in the circle of the candle's glow. "I just wanted to know if you had a conscience, my lord." God knew Michael did.

Carter frowned. "I do what I must for the good of my family."

Was that not why the marquis protected his son? And also his reason for ignoring her? She was inconsequential. A by-blow of nature taking its course. Nothing more, nothing less.

The ruthlessness behind such an attitude went against everything Isabel believed. The marquis and Carter seemed to believe they had the divine right to order the world as suited their whims.

"You must not be pleased that Michael returned," she said.

Carter dropped his voice very, very low.

"Poor, poor Isabel, in love with a man who has taken one woman's life. Do you fear for yours?"

His quiet taunt caught her off guard. What kind of a person said such things about his own blood?

"Not at all," she replied, her spirit returning. She pulled open the door and ran into her husband in the dark hallway. Wallis stood beside him.

Michael's arms came around her. He felt good and solid. "I wondered where you had gone off to," he said.

Carter came out with the candle. "I showed Isabel the family portrait. Seeing you with your pony almost brought her to tears . . . or was that laughter?" he suggested lightly, as if they had been having a good time.

"Laughter, I'm sure," Michael answered. He looked down at Isabel. "Are you ready to leave? It's been a long day."

"Yes, it has," she quickly agreed, wanting to get away from Carter's unsettling presence.

Michael led her to the front hall. The butler waited with Isabel's gloves and shawl. They didn't linger over saying good night. Unsettled by her conversation with Carter, Isabel was anxious to be away. She was convinced that

Wallis deserved a lover, even one such as Richard.

They murmured their good-byes, then her husband took her arm and steered her outside. The moon hid behind clouds that threatened rain for the next day. The hack waited for them across the street, its lamps lit.

The driver held the door open for them. His fuzzy hair sticking out from under his hat caught Isabel's attention. She didn't remember noticing it earlier, but then, she'd been very upset.

However, Michael stopped. "Where is the driver who was here before?"

"He's my brother. Sent a message for me to come and take over. He probably wanted to check on his wife. She hasn't been well lately. Stomach problem."

"Do you know where we are going?"

The driver gave Michael's address. Satisfied, Michael removed his hat and took his seat next to Isabel. The driver closed the door. He didn't wait for Michael's signal but started the horses.

Isabel sat back against the hard leather seat, realizing that in spite of everything, she felt safe with Michael. It was Carter who disturbed her.

"What happened in the library?" Michael

asked. He rested his ungloved hands on his thighs. His was a big hand, with long, tapered fingers—a swordsman's hands. She remembered that Aletta had been strangled.

"Charles talked to me about the murder," she said.

There was a beat of silence.

"Are you surprised?" she asked.

Michael leaned back into his corner of the cab. "No. In fact, that is more in line with the distance he kept when I returned to London. I didn't understand his sudden friendship. Apparently, he wanted to blacken my name further with you."

"So much for close family."

"Yes," he echoed. "What did he say?"

It didn't even cross Isabel's mind not to be honest with him. It wasn't in her nature. "He said he was with you that night."

"I don't remember." His fist clenched in frustration. "That sounds ridiculous. I should remember, but I don't. Nor am I taking you for a fool. I don't, Isabel. I've already made one mistake in not trusting you. I won't make another." He hesitated a moment, then said, "I want another chance at us."

And she did, too. Against all logic, she loved

her husband. The initial pain of his betrayal had been dulled by other concerns.

She would not commit at once. Her pride wouldn't let her. She was glad she'd never confessed her love. And, she'd be wiser this time around. But, oh, how she wanted the closeness they'd had before they came to London. She just feared being played the fool again.

So, she didn't comment on his declaration. She focused instead on the murder. "So you don't remember Carter being present at all?"

"He told me he saw me home. All I know is I woke up the next morning with the worst case of cup-shot I'd ever had and magistrate's men pounding on my door."

"He said someone saw you at Aletta's apartment."

"A neighbor. The judge wouldn't accept his testimony because he never actually saw me. It was dark in the hall, and all he really noticed was the silhouette of a man. Of course, he was willing to testify it was I, but since he was half-blind, the judge didn't allow it." He made a sound of disgust. "Exasperating, isn't it? I have tried to relive those missing hours of my life, and I can't. I've searched my mind, and it isn't there."

"Do you ever think you could have done it?" she asked softly.

His response was immediate. "Dear God, at one time I feared I had." The pain in his voice ripped through her. She reached over and took his hand.

"Then what made you return to clear your name?" she asked.

He searched her face, and she sensed now he was wondering whether to trust *her*.

"Do you believe in dreams?" he asked.

"As in foretelling events?"

"Yes . . . or in allowing you to see what you hadn't before?"

Isabel shrugged. "Sometimes I think I've done something I've dreamed only to realize it was probably a real or similar event I am recalling. I'm not particularly superstitious."

"The Shawnee are," he told her. "I was never either, and yet, when you are around people who believe dreams have great power, you start to wonder."

"Did you have a dream?"

"Yes . . . but it was one I'd had before, or thought I'd had. Right after the murder, I dreamed it often. But once I'd left England, it stopped. Then, about six months ago, it occurred again. Only this time it seemed more real, and now I'm beginning to wonder if it truly is a dream at all. Lately, memories have been coming back to me. I had such a strong sense that I needed to get to you when you were in the library with Carter. I felt you were in some danger."

"Your brother has an odd sense of humor," she said, *and absolutely no family loyalty*, "but I didn't feel I could come to harm." Although, she had felt uneasy. "Tell me your dream."

Michael leaned close as if not wanting to be overheard. "I see myself in Aletta's apartment. I'm lying down, but it's not in a bed. She is in another room arguing with a man. I hear his voice, but I can't make out who he is."

"What are they arguing over?"

"I don't know. There is a moment of blackness, and when I next see Aletta she is dead, and I know who killed her. I can't see the man's face, but I know him."

"Does the dream end there?"

"No," he said. "I leave. I walk home, but I move unsteadily as if I'm drunk. And, it is night and I am afraid."

"What happens next?"

"I wake then. My fear wakes me. I know she is dead, and it all seems so real to me. I can recall every emotion I felt that night."

"How did you feel that night?"

"Senselessly drunk."

"And what emotions do you feel in the dream?"

He made an exasperated sound. "Irritated at having my sleep disturbed when I hear the argument. Sick to my stomach when I realize Aletta is dead. And, finally, panic."

She sat back, amazed by how vivid his dream was. "What makes you believe you didn't kill her?"

"I didn't kill her," he said firmly. "I know myself better now than I did then. I've fought in battles. I've taken lives. I've done things I'm not proud of, but I've never hurt an innocent." He faced her. "I remember other things, too. Isabel, Aletta loved me. That's why Henry and I argued. She'd turned down his offer because she wanted me."

"Did *you* love her?" The words she had promised herself she'd never ask were out of her mouth before she could blink.

"No," Michael said. "I was too selfish and usually too foxed to think of anyone but myself." He paused, then said, "Did I detect a note of jealousy in your voice? Could it be that you still care for me?"

Could he hear how loud her heart beat? "I don't know what I want yet," she confessed.

"I do," he answered.

The hack had pulled to a stop but neither of them had registered they weren't moving until the door on Isabel's side was thrown open and she was rudely hauled out of the coach. She started to scream. A gloved hand was slapped over her mouth. They weren't anyplace close to Mayfair. All was black night save for the moon and the feeble light from their coach. Her assailant smelled like fish.

The hack driver jumped down from his perch, a horse pistol in his hand, and growled, "Pull her in the bushes and finish her off." He raised his voice. "Do you have him, Tom, or do you need my help?"

The answer was the ominous sound of a body dropping to the ground.

At the realization that Michael might be dead, Isabel went mad with rage. She kicked and twisted, reaching back with her nails ready to claw the man who held her. "Help me," he said to the hack driver, but his accomplice had his own problems.

As if coming out of nowhere, Michael dropped from the roof of the coach onto the driver. The pistol went off. The horse bolted with a scream.

Isabel's captor released her and took off into the night. She fell to the dirt road, then tripped on the hem of her skirt as she came to her feet to help Michael.

"Stay back," her husband warned. "He has a knife."

Almost too late, she saw the gleam of the blade in the man's hand. She stepped back.

The hack driver waved the knife menacingly, but Michael laughed in his face. "You'll have to do better than that."

The driver jumped at him. Michael stepped out of his way and caught his wrist. There was a snapping sound, and the knife fell to the ground. The driver cried out in pain and doubled over.

Michael had the knife in his hand in a blink.

Rolling on his back, the driver started begging for his life.

"I'm not going to hurt you," Michael said, "or call the watch. But I'll break your bloody neck if you don't shut up."

The driver closed his mouth.

"And your friend Tom is still alive," Michael assured him. "He will wake with a headache, only little the worse for wear."

"You didn't kill him?"

"Not yet," Michael warned softly. "Isabel, are you all right?"

"I think so." She was shaking and a bit

roughed up but otherwise fine. He didn't recognize their surroundings. The buildings were low, and she could smell fetid water. They must be close to the Thames. The horse had not run far but stood wild-eyed by a wall some hundred yards away.

The driver decided to try his luck running. He scrambled to his feet, but Michael had anticipated the move and tripped him. The man sprawled out in the road close to his friend Tom. Michael put his boot on the broken wrist.

"No, sir!" the driver cried.

"Then tell me who hired you," Michael ordered quietly.

Isabel's eyes had adjusted to the night. She could see that the driver was a weasel of a man, wry and mean, but there was something familiar about his frizzy hair.

"I can't," the man said.

She made the connection. "You were the dray driver in Rutland. You drove past us while we were arguing. You shot him."

"No, I didn't!" the driver said, his voice rising an octave and betraying him.

Michael tossed the knife up in the air and caught it, the point aimed at the driver's heart. "Who hired you to kill me?" he asked as pleasantly as could be, and Isabel realized he was in his element.

The driver grasped that, too. He babbled information as quickly as he could. "I don't know his name. No names, just money. Met him at the Crow. And it was a different man who tracked me down to let me know you still lived."

"Do you know how to get in touch with him?" Michael asked.

"Honestly, sir, I don't. They found me. They were both working for someone. I know that. They spoke of a gentleman. They said they were servants. You could tell by the way they talked about him. Said I had to finish up, or it would be my neck."

"Did they pay you well?" Michael asked.

"They didn't want to pay me, but I insisted, and they had no choice, did they?"

"No, none at all. And as much as I admire a man who sees a job done," Michael said dryly, "this is one you won't be finishing up."

A groan from Tom as he started to regain consciousness punctuated his words. Tom tried to lift his head, but fell back down again.

The driver saw this, and answered, "No, sir. You're a bit quicker than I am."

Michael moved his foot. "Go and take your friend with you. If anyone contacts you again because I am still alive, come to me. I pay better. If you don't, I'll make a trophy of your scalp."

"Yes, sir, thank you, sir." The driver said this as he was rolled to his feet, favoring his wrist. He reached for his pistol on the ground.

"No," Michael said, and the driver swerved away from it and went to help his friend Tom up.

"By the by, where is the hack driver?" Michael asked.

"Paid him off, sir, paid him off."

"You made a great deal of money for a bungled job," Michael said.

"Aye, sir.

The two men hobbled toward the hack. Michael's voice stopped them. "Sorry, gents, the hack and horse are mine now."

They didn't argue. In a minute, they vanished between the warehouses and were gone.

Growing more aware of exactly how grim their surroundings were, Isabel sidled closer to her husband. "This isn't anyplace close to home, is it?" she asked.

"No." Her husband's jaw tensed. "I should have been more aware." His arm came down around her protectively and, without conscious thought, she put her arms around him and hugged him close. Their arguments no longer mattered. She was so thankful neither had been hurt.

"Are you all right?" he asked.

"It all happened so fast." The colorful ribbons that had held her hair in place were gone, along with her pins. She pushed her hair back. "I'm fine. It was all so horrid. It was just like it was the day they did shoot you. I . . ." She swallowed, unable to go on.

Michael kissed the top of her head. "Isabel, don't think about what could have been."

His calm response helped her regain her composure and with it, her courage. "What do we do now?"

"That's my girl," he said approvingly. He took her hand and started toward the hack. "I'm going to take you home."

She stopped. "Are you going to stay with me?" She doubted it.

He confirmed her suspicions when he said, "No, I'm going to confront Elswick and his son."

"Are you certain it is they?"

"Who else has the money to see me dead? Or could gain anything from it?"

A coldness stole around Isabel's heart. She had no doubt that if Michael hadn't acted as quickly as he did, they would have killed her, too. "He would want me dead also."

Michael didn't contradict her. "I believed Elswick two nights ago. He'll need to convince me again."

"And me," Isabel responded. "I'm going with you."

Michael frowned. "No, Isabel. I don't know what to expect, and I want you safe."

"I *must* go," she said, standing up to him. "I want to see the look in his eye when he sees you. He has much to answer for, first for being a coward who hired someone to do his dirty work."

Her husband studied her a moment, then agreed, "Let us go." He picked the pistol up off the ground. "Tonight, we finish this."

Fifteen

❧❀❧

Michael drove the hack. Isabel sat by his side. He'd suggested she ride in the cab, but after their recent experience she wanted to be out in the open with him.

He'd found a blanket beneath the driver's seat and placed it around her legs. She didn't mind the chill in the night breeze. The fresh air reminded her of how good it was to be alive.

She tucked her hand in the crook of his arm, not only for his body heat against the night air, but also because she wanted to lend her strength to his. They didn't speak. They didn't need to. They were in complete accord. Together, they would defeat all enemies—starting with the man who had fathered her.

The buildings grew closer together, and more traffic appeared on the streets. Isabel quite liked sitting up on the driver's seat and, if they caused comment from those who noticed them drive by, all the better. Michael navigated the hack as if he were born to the trade. The streets grew wider and less populated as they traveled into the residential areas.

The marquis lived in the older section of the city. The houses were larger than the ones in Mayfair. Isabel knew because once, when she'd been working for the duchess, she had made the effort to see the marquis's house. She'd debated going up to the door, but her courage had left her. It would not leave her that night.

As they turned into his street, they could see his house was well lit, with a line of vehicles and horses outside waiting for guests. Coachmen and footmen gathered in small groups, gossiping.

"It appears he's entertaining," Isabel said. "Perhaps we should wait."

"Absolutely not," Michael said, and drove the hack right up to the front door.

A footman in blue livery broke from his conversation to greet them. He opened the hack door, then frowned as he realized no one was in it.

"We're up here," Michael said, jumping down from his seat. He came around to Isabel's side and held out a hand to help her down. "Keep the hack right here," he told the wide-eyed footman, setting her down on her feet. He tossed the man a coin. "We'll be out in a moment."

As they approached the front door, Isabel raised a self-conscious hand to her hair, wishing she had a moment and pins to style it.

"Don't worry," Michael said. "You look beautiful."

His saying so was all she needed to relax.

The door opened before they could knock. The butler was an imposing man whose black livery offset his white-blond hair and colorless eyes.

"I'm here to see Elswick," Michael said.

"I'm sorry, he is not home," the butler said, even as male laughter came from the vicinity of where the dining room must be located.

He started to close the door in their faces, but Michael was quicker. Taking Isabel's hand, he shoved the door with his shoulder, hitting it so hard, it knocked the butler back. "We'll announce ourselves," Michael said coolly as he passed the stunned servant, moving toward the sound of voices. Isabel was right at his side, her hand in his.

The dining room was the second door down the hall and open. They marched right into the room and found themselves in the middle of a dinner party of twenty or so men and women. The marquis sat at the head of the table.

All conversation stopped at their appearance.

"My lord," Michael said, "we need to have a private word with you."

At that moment, the butler ran up behind them, flanked by footmen. He rudely grabbed Isabel. She gave a sharp cry and shoved him away. The butler had not been expecting her to fight and, losing his balance, stumbled backward into his companions. He righted himself to meet the fist of a very angry Michael, who dropped him to the ground with one sharp punch.

One footman attempted to attack Michael from behind. Michael tossed the fellow over his shoulder onto the dinner table. Plates, silver, glasses, and food went flying. Chairs were knocked over as guests scrambled out of the way, even as Michael sent the second across the table after the first. It all happened so fast, the women forgot to scream.

Holding his bloody nose, the butler came to his feet. He doubled his fist, preparing to take an angry swing at Michael when the marquis's voice stopped him—

"That will be all, Roberts." Of everyone in the room, he appeared the most at ease. He still sat at his place at the table and didn't seem to have moved a muscle.

Roberts frowned as if debating disobeying his lord. Visibly taking himself in hand, he pushed his hair back and bowed. "Yes, my lord."

"Take the footmen with you," the marquis said.

The servants were only too happy to escape the dining room. Both wore the evening's meal on their uniforms and faces. They were not happy.

Isabel and Michael faced the marquis. His lordship took in their disheveled appearances with a bored eye. Isabel met his gaze with a disdainful one of her own.

To her surprise, he smiled. Turning to his guests he even went so far as to introduce them. "Let me present to you all Mr. Severson, you know, Jemison's brother. The lady standing next to him is his wife."

Several eyebrows were raised as if they recognized the name. "Is this the one accused of

301

murder?" the woman closest to the marquis's right asked.

"Yes," the marquis said as if he enjoyed the word.

It was then Isabel saw Richard. He'd bent down to pick up a broken glass, rising slowly when her gaze met his. He didn't appear happy to see her.

Michael didn't flinch from any of them. "I wish a word with you now, my lord, or I won't be the only one who stands trial."

His words had the desired effect. A murmuring ran through the elegant company.

The marquis rose. "I suppose if you must," he drawled.

"I must," Michael assured him without sympathy.

"Excuse me," the marquis said to the room in general. He started toward them, then stopped by the chair of a very attractive, gray-haired, blue-eyed woman. Of the assembly, she had been the only one who hadn't moved to scramble out of the way during Michael's battle with the footman. Isabel saw that she couldn't have. She sat in a wheeled chair.

She also, in spite of her brown hair, bore a remarkable resemblance to Isabel's mother. They would have both been of the same age if her mother was still alive. The woman wore diamonds around her throat and at her ears and, by the deference the marquis showed her, Isabel realized this was his marchioness.

"You shall see to everyone won't you, my dear?" the marquis asked.

"We shall await your return," his wife replied calmly.

A part of Isabel, the childish one, wanted to announce who she was. To let everyone in the room know what her father would deny.

And then the marchioness smiled at her, an expression touched by sadness and compassion.

She knew.

Isabel drew back toward Michael, her gaze inadvertently meeting the marquis's. He'd been waiting for her to denounce him. She realized that now. He had anticipated her creating a scene, and part of his cool demeanor had been in preparation for such a thing. He cared what his wife thought. Seeing this chink in her sire's armor humanized him in a way she'd not thought could be possible. It didn't excuse the hurt she'd felt by his disregard . . . but it gave her the chance to be the noble one.

Michael placed a possessive hand on her elbow as they followed the marquis down the hall to a library. It was a man's room, lined with books and paneling and smelling of leather. Its books had been read.

The marquis shut the door after them. His calm veneer vanished. "What the devil do you think you are doing charging into my house that way, Severson, and threatening me?"

"Threatening you? No, I wanted to surprise you," Michael answered. "After all, your attempt on my life failed, and I thought it best to inform you in person."

"My attempt on what?" the marquis said, shocked.

"You hired men to attack my wife and me while you sat in the middle of a dinner party," Michael stated. "You were probably entertaining while I was being shot in Rutland, too."

"I told you I had nothing to do with that. Or this."

"I won't accept your word any longer," Michael said.

The marquis straightened. "I should call you out—"

"I wish you would!" Michael said, not backing down. "Pistols or swords, I don't care. You have much to account for, my lord, and the time has come for a reckoning."

The door was thrown open. They all turned. A man close to Michael in age stood in the doorway. He had a vague resemblance to the marquis, and Isabel knew immediately this was her half brother Henry. He had thick, wavy brown hair and gray-green eyes. His features were softer than their father's. His mother's influence, no doubt.

"Stop it, both of you," Henry said, entering the room and closing the door behind him.

"Leave us," the marquis ordered. "This isn't your fight."

"I'm sorry, Father, it is. It sounds as if you have been working on my behalf, and yet I know nothing of your activities."

"I haven't done anything," the marquis said.

"Did you arrange for Severson to be murdered?" Henry asked quietly.

The marquis recoiled as if such a question from his son was an abomination. "I did not."

Henry released his breath, and Isabel realized he'd feared the answer. He faced Michael. His gaze had not once looked toward Isabel. "It's been a long time," he said.

Michael's expression was indecipherable. "Did you hire someone to have me killed?"

"No," Henry answered. "Nor did my father."

"What makes you so certain?" Michael asked.

"Because if he'd hired someone to kill you, you'd be dead."

"Just as Aletta Calendri is?" Michael's eyes had gone bright with suppressed anger.

Henry did not take offense. Instead, he said, "There was a time we were closer than brothers, and now we know each other so little."

"It's been a while since we last spoke," Michael said.

"Ten years . . . and our last conversation was an argument over Aletta."

"We're going to have another argument now," Michael assured him. "You believed I murdered her. You testified against me. Your father actively pursued seeing me hanged."

"Like everyone else, I thought the worst." Henry shook his head. "I don't know what I believe anymore."

"You have changed your mind?" Michael suggested, his voice dangerously silky.

Henry took a step closer to Michael. He spoke as if they were the only two in the room. "Even during the trial, I didn't believe you were the sort of man who could kill. Besides, it was you she loved. I was the one torn with jealousy."

"And I'm the one who has believed all these years that you killed her out of anger and left me to take the blame."

"No, Michael, I did nothing of the sort. The night of the murder, everyone saw me in my club getting drunk because my best friend, the man I loved as much as a brother, had stolen the woman I believed I loved more."

Michael cut the air with a sudden movement of his hand. "You lie!"

"I do nothing of the sort. It was investigated. You were so busy with your own defense you couldn't pay attention. They asked me questions. I proved *my* innocence."

The last was a direct reference to the fact Michael could still fall under suspicion.

Her husband looked away a moment, before turning back, and asking, "What have you been doing with Riggs if not planning a convenient place to ambush me?"

"Riggs is my wife's godson," the marquis said. "He's here this evening at my wife's invitation for her birthday."

Michael shook his head. "I saw you and Riggs at a tavern called the Crow," he told Henry. Isabel recalled that was the name of the place the driver who had tried to murder them had made his contact.

"The Crow is a popular place," Henry said, "because it is so close to the government buildings. You saw us together last night."

"I did."

"Richard came to me," Henry said, "because

he's had this change of heart. He's decided to become responsible. Partly through your influence and partially through mine. He decided if we could change and make our lives better, then so could he. He's accepted a commission to India."

"And·what brought about this wondrous change?" Michael asked skeptically.

"My sister," Henry said.

Isabel didn't realize who he was talking about until they all looked at her. She took a step closer to her husband.

"Richard fell in love," Henry said, "with your wife. He didn't realize how much she meant to him until you married her. He believes he could have had her if he'd made an honorable offer instead of an insulting one. He went a bit mad for a week or so. Brawled a bit and carried on. You remember how it was. I intervened. I understood how it felt to have a woman choose you, over myself."

"I have no regrets in marrying Isabel," Michael announced proudly. "But Aletta would have made your life hell, Henry. She was that kind of woman. The only person she loved was herself."

"So his mother and I have told him over the

years," the marquis said. "She was never worth your devotion," he told his son. "Ever."

"You haven't married?" Michael asked.

Henry frowned. "I could. I've not been ready."

The marquis grunted an opinion. "Perhaps if this woman hadn't been murdered, my son wouldn't have made her into such a saint. He has an obligation to his title, and still he hasn't married. He's the only one who even remembers who she was." His disdain for his son's sentiment was obvious.

But Michael's reaction was different. "Good God," he said quietly, "I was such a clod." He shook his head. "I have no excuse. I drank a great deal. I was selfish." He paused. "I would like to believe I would not do that now."

Henry raised his shoulders but did not speak, and Isabel understood. He'd loved and lost and dared not risk his feelings again. It didn't matter that the woman was not worthy of him. Unrequited love hurt.

And suddenly, in this half brother, she saw herself.

All her life, she had been searching for love. She'd wanted it from a mother who lived with her own bitter disappointments and from a father who might have sired her but was no parent.

In truth, the only person who had really given a care to her comings and goings had been her stepfather. He'd educated her and provided food and shelter. He'd made her strong enough to fend for herself.

And then Michael had come along with his dangerous quest and, without realizing it, she had let down her guard. She'd fallen in love. A love he didn't return . . . but she now understood that taking that risk was better than living the shadow of a life she'd lived before. The life Henry lived.

"Aletta Calendri sounds like she was interested in only her own desires," she said to her half brother. "Such a person can be destructive. Your father is right. You need to go on with your life. It's sad to realize that you've been mourning all these years for something that really never was."

He didn't like her saying such, but Isabel didn't care. For her, the link between them was severed. She looked at the marquis and his son and saw strangers.

She turned to Michael. "There is nothing more to be accomplished here. They had had nothing to do with the attempts on your life." She laid her hand on her husband's arm. "Let's go home."

Michael looked down at her hand and into

her eyes, and she wondered if he understood that her anger was gone. The circumstances that brought them together were no longer important. What mattered to her was her future. And right or wrong, she wanted it to be with this man.

Maybe someday he would return her love, but for the moment, it didn't matter. It was enough she loved.

Her husband took her hand. "We're sorry to have disturbed your evening." He led her to the door.

The marquis's voice stopped them. "You know, you are quite an interesting woman, Mrs. Severson. Completely different than I expected."

There had been a time when to have received even that faint praise would have meant everything to Isabel. Now, she thought he sounded rather silly. "Unfortunately, you are not what I had hoped for," she said, and walked out the door Michael held open for her, her head high.

Out in the hall by the dining room, many of the marquis's guests lingered, all agog for whatever tidbits of gossip they could gather. Richard stood back, away from everyone. Isabel mentally wished him well with his new life, but she did not stop.

The marchioness sat near the dining room door in her wheelchair. Isabel could feel her watching them leave. She sensed the woman's sadness, but that was not part of her life. Not anymore.

She tucked her hand in the crook of Michael's arm, and they went outside to the waiting hack, where he helped her up into the box as if it were the most natural thing in the world. They drove off.

They'd not gone long before Michael reined the hack horses to a halt. He faced Isabel. "I want you to know you made a choice back there in Elswick's library. You chose me." He said the words almost defensively.

"I know," she said, meeting his gaze with a steady one of her own.

"I won't let you go," he continued, as if she hadn't spoken. "And I may never clear my name, Isabel. I may have to leave England. I won't leave you behind. I'll take you with me, even if I must carry you kicking and screaming and vowing to hate me all your days."

Isabel heard what he didn't say ... and thought *what fragile creatures we all are, needing love and yet so afraid to open ourselves to its possibilities.*

She was not going to be afraid. Not any longer. She would take the risk.

"I could never hate you, Michael," she said. "I love you."

Sixteen

❧❀❧

"*Y*ou love me?" Michael repeated dumbly as if amazed.

She nodded. "I admit, it is rather foolish of me—"

"No," he broke in. "It is the least foolish thing you've ever done. You *love* me?" he had to repeat, wanting to hear the words from her lips one more time before he could believe.

"I love you."

If the heavens had opened with choirs of angels, Michael could not have been more overjoyed. He stood, right there in the box, the world suddenly aglow with possibilities.

"Even after all the mistakes I've made in my life and with you?" he had to ask. "No, wait.

Don't answer that. Don't ever say another word."

She listened, wide-eyed.

"I know," he admitted. "I'm acting like a madman and yet, suddenly, everything makes perfect sense. For the first time in my life, it all matters."

Michael reached down, took her by the arms, and brought her up for a kiss. He kissed her long and kissed her hard. Right there, in the middle of the street, standing in the hack's box, and he didn't care who saw him.

When he was done, she had to lean against him for support. *She loved him.* Almost reverently, he brought his hand up to her face, awed that this beautiful, vibrant woman loved *him*.

"Michael," she whispered, "let's go home."

Home. She'd used the word before, but now it meant something.

The anger that had been inside him for so long evaporated. He hadn't even realized it had been there until it was gone, and he felt new and whole.

All because of this one woman.

"Let's go home," he agreed and, after they'd both sat, picked up the reins and could have flown the hack back to their house.

Bolling opened the door. If he was surprised

to see his employer driving a hired vehicle, he didn't betray it by look or comment.

Michael placed his hands around Isabel's waist but didn't set her on the ground. Instead, he lifted her in his arms and carried her into the house.

"See to the vehicle, Bolling," he tossed out as he passed the butler.

"To whom does it belong, sir?"

"I believe it is mine now," Michael said, climbing the stairs.

Isabel had her arms around his neck. "Do you remember the last time you carried me up stairs?" she asked slyly.

"As if it were last week," he answered, and she smiled.

Isabel. His wife. His love.

He reached to open the bedroom door but it opened for him. The maid who had defied him earlier stood waiting for her.

"Becky, I won't be needing you tonight," Isabel said calmly.

"Yes, ma'am." The maid ducked her head and slipped around them.

"Is there anyone else waiting for us?" Michael asked.

Isabel laughed. "We don't have that many servants."

"We've seen them all tonight," he vowed, and kicked the door shut before setting her on her feet. Her maid had a fire burning in the grate, and the bed was turned down. Candles burned on the side tables.

Isabel rose on her tiptoes to kiss him, but he pulled back. "No, not yet. There is something I must say, and if I don't do it now, my courage will leave me," he told her.

"What is it?"

He took her shawl, which, even after the adventures of the night, still shimmered with the golden threads, and tossed it aside. He pulled off her gloves, taking his time, putting the right words together in his mind.

Holding her left hand, he said, "I want us to start our marriage from this night on. This is the day we shall remember as our wedding date."

"Why is that?" she asked, watching him carefully.

Michael didn't flinch from meeting her eye. "Remember when the Reverend Oxley told us that we were the celebrants of our own marriage?"

She nodded.

"Well, I am calling upon the sacrament here

and now, Isabel. You mean everything to me." No words he'd ever spoken had been more heartfelt.

"You are my family," she said simply. "I was hurt when I thought you used me and, yet, I love you. I have no pride around you."

Michael went to his knees in front of her. He pressed his lips against the gold wedding band, before saying, "Isabel, I love you."

Her breath caught in surprise. She came down to him. "What did you say?"

"Words I never thought I would say to anyone. Words I once thought meaningless. I love you." He repeated them again because the sound of them filled him with such a sense of wonder. "I believe I've loved you from the first moment I saw you."

She shook her head. "Oh, no. You may have lusted for me, as I did you, but love—?" She laced her fingers with his. "Love came when we weren't looking," she said quietly. "It humbled me to realize I couldn't be angry at you, not when I loved you."

"Through you, I've learned to forgive. I can let go of the past, Isabel, but I don't ever want to lose you."

He lifted her hand and looking into her eyes

said, "I, Michael Andrew Severson, take you, Isabel Halloran, for my lawfully wedded wife. To love and cherish, to honor all the days of my life."

Her eyes shiny with unshed tears, she replied, "And I take you, Michael, to be my husband. To love you and honor you and keep you close to my heart—"

"Please, never let me leave that place," he requested, his own eyes burning. "I have been in such darkness. You are the light, Isabel. Together, we are one, and no one can tear us apart."

"Not even ourselves," she whispered.

"No," he agreed. "We chose each other."

"We *choose* to love each other."

"May God bless our union."

Isabel smiled, and he didn't think anything could be more dear to him than his wife's smile. He leaned forward to seal their vows with a kiss.

Isabel met his kiss. Their lips touched, and it was as if a current flowed between them. Anything was possible.

They had always been compatible as lovers . . . but now their lovemaking took on deeper meaning. They took their time undressing each other. He knew where she tickled. She understood how to master him. There was laughter and kisses and everything there always had been, and yet it was not the same.

It was *more*.

They soon found themselves in the bed. Michael settling himself between her legs, feeling the draw of her heat. Her body curved to meet his. He was, physically, a powerful man, and right then his desire for her was most evident.

She smiled, knowing.

"I love you," he vowed, entering her. He filled her deep and knew that being this connected to her gave life meaning.

They began moving, the dance as old as time—but for them, this night, it was new and fresh.

She held him closer, her lips against his shoulder, and repeated his name over and over. Had it ever been like this between them? He couldn't recall. Together they moved toward completion—and yet, when it came it was nothing that they'd ever experienced before.

The earth rocked on its foundations. Time lost meaning. She cried out his name, and he swallowed the sound with his kiss.

His sweet, brave Isabel. She meant everything to him. Without her, he would be lost.

And she knew it. Once he'd not believed in

love. Now he whispered his love to her over and over.

What was happening between them wasn't just nature but creation.

Isabel hugged him close, humbling him with the generosity of her love. His senses were full of her. Never before had he felt so vital and alive.

Slowly, they drifted back to reality together, and it was still as sweet.

Michael slid off her but cuddled her close. He reached for the bedsheets, pulling them up over their bodies. Gently he kissed her temple, her eyes, her cheek, her chin. "My wife," he murmured sleepily.

She nestled close to his chest, her hand possessively on his hip. "My husband," she answered. He smiled, his eyes closed, and together they fell asleep.

Isabel woke to discover her husband awake and studying the ceiling. She pushed her hair back. The candles burned very low. "What is it?" she asked.

"I had the dream again. I didn't think I would have it now." He turned to her, shadows in his eyes. "Why does she come to me now?"

"Tell it to me." She listened as he repeated everything as it had been before. "Perhaps you had it again because of the attempt on your life," she suggested.

"No, I'm missing something. She's warning me that it isn't over." He looked to her. "I want it to be over."

"I know." She rested her hand on his chest.

He brought it up to his lips and kissed the tips of her fingers. "I love you. I don't want anything to hurt you."

"It won't," she said. "Dreams are also the sign of a vivid imagination." It was a pat response she'd often given her young charges when they couldn't sleep.

"Ask Alex. He will tell you a dream can foretell one's destiny."

Isabel raised herself up to look down in her husband's face. "Not this one," she said fiercely. "This one is your past." She brought his hand to her breast, right above her heart. "I am your future. Set your demons to rest, Michael. Let me guard you."

Michael held her long and hard before rolling her back on the mattress and making love to her again. However, after he had fallen asleep, she was the one who lay awake studying the ceiling with unseeing eyes.

Silently bartered with Aletta's ghost. *Let him be.* "He's mine," she whispered.

There was no answer.

But deep in her woman's soul, Isabel knew that sooner or later, there would be a reckoning.

Isabel refused to fear the future. As the weeks passed, she had discovered her place in the world. It was beside Michael . . . and it was enough.

In turn, he appeared to have entered a new stage of his life. He rarely spoke of the murder. It was as if he'd come to a conscious decision to focus on their future.

Of course, Isabel was no fool. She insisted Michael travel with a guard. In spite of two attempts on his life, he refused. So, when Alex returned, he and Isabel hired a man to keep a discreet eye on her husband and follow him until he returned home.

However, as the days turned into weeks, she began to hope that the past would stay buried.

Michael and Alex kept their London office. Isabel and Michael fully intended to make their home there. Of course, there were still whispers and rumors around Michael's name. One didn't attack the marquis of Elswick during his own dinner party and escape gossip. However, neither Isabel nor Michael gave a care to what people thought anymore. They were too busy planning their lives.

The house in Mayfair became a home. *Their* home. The decorator that Wallis thought Isabel needed was never called. Instead, Isabel and Michael enjoyed exploring the city and searching for just the right items that suited their tastes.

They purchased colorful India carpets and chairs made of precious woods. Silver was chosen for their table and pots for their kitchen. Michael's cook decided to go off sailing with Alex, so they tested cooks and settled on a gentleman from Italy who had quite a way with the French methods of sauces, and, of course, he needed a complement of kitchen staff.

Isabel moved down the hall into Michael's bedroom. Her maid Becky had suggested that it was more the fashion for husbands and wives to have separate suites of rooms. Isabel didn't care about being fashionable. She wanted always to sleep next to her husband.

Every night, when they went to bed, she fell asleep touching him in some way or the other. Most often they slept curled up with her back against his chest. This was her favorite, because he'd often wake her in the middle of the night to make love.

Otherwise, she would sleep on her stomach, her hand tucked between his body and the mattress. Michael would stroke her hair, and she'd drift off into the sweetest dreams.

Every day she told Michael she loved him. She couldn't say the words often enough. And he felt the same. He'd say them when they were alone or beside each other in church or in a crowded bank. He'd say them for her ears alone or when everyone could hear him.

One morning, she was sitting over breakfast when Alex arrived. He and Michael were to be at a meeting with wool merchants. Instead, he was there.

Michael had told Isabel that Alex followed Indian time, which meant he did things as he deemed them necessary, not according to the clock. Isabel suspected Alex just didn't like meetings.

And Michael didn't want to go sailing and roaming the world.

Their differences made for a good partnership, and their shipping venture prospered. They had two ships—the *Sea Serpent* and one Alex had purchased and christened the *Warrior*.

He was to leave that afternoon to go fetch it from Portsmouth. Isabel enjoyed teasing him about the name.

Having missed the meeting, Isabel asked Alex if he wished to join her for breakfast. He was happy to do so, and she realized she appreciated his friendship. He was a generous man who had extended his deep respect for her husband to herself.

This morning he pleased her by saying, "I've never known Michael to be so settled."

"We're both happy," she told him.

"And he never broods anymore?"

"Not that I know of. The wonder of all wonders is we're starting to find friends, albeit slowly. There is some stigma attached, but time will help."

"Good." Alex reached across her for cream to pour into his tea and caught a glimpse of the floor plan she was sketching. "What are you designing now?"

"A nursery," she said dreamily—then could have kicked herself.

Alex's eyes widened.

"Don't tell, Michael," Isabel begged.

"Michael? A father?" He set aside his spoon.

She nodded. She had no doubt she was increasing. She was starting to show all the signs that meant that she had conceived the night they had repeated their vows.

It made this baby all the more special.

"I've been waiting until I was certain," she said. It was easy to be frank with Alex. The Shawnee side of his nature seemed to make him more aware of the natural order of things than an Englishman would be. "There are some small signs, but . . . ?"

"When are you going to tell Michael? Wait, don't do it until after we get the provisions for this next journey ordered. He won't be worth anything once he hears this news and will expect me to do my own accounting." He shook his head and sat back. "Michael. A father." This time the words sounded more definite. "You've completely changed his life."

"He's changed mine." She ran her fingers lightly over the vellum sketch. "When do you leave, Alex? I don't know if I can hold off telling him much longer. Having confided in you makes the possibility all that much more real."

"In two days, provided the *Warrior* is ready. We're heading to Spain again, then Morocco." Alex grinned, a happy man. He liked sailing his ship, and he liked being in charge without Michael pestering him over details.

"I'll try to hold off two days," she promised. "But my husband is an observant man. He could notice."

"Not with the wool merchants irritating him," Alex said, then his expression turned thoughtful.

"What are you thinking?" she asked.

"That I will have to come up with a new name for my friend."

"For Michael?"

"He has a Shawnee name—Lone Wolf. It no longer suits him."

"And what name would you choose?" she wondered, stirring cream into her morning tea before taking a sip.

Alex considered the matter less than a second before daring to suggest, "Happy Rabbit?"

Isabel almost spewed her tea in the most unladylike way. She and Alex both started laughing, so they didn't hear Wallis's arrival until she walked into the breakfast room. She was dressed entirely in ice blue, the color a good complement for her blond beauty. "It sounds as if you are enjoying yourselves this morning?"

Bolling, who had just come out from the kitchen with Isabel's toasted bread, didn't hide his frown. The butler did not like Lady Jemison. "My lady, I didn't hear the door."

"A maid opened it," Wallis said breezily, pulling off her gloves, but then paused. "This isn't Michael."

"No, it is Mr. Haddon, Michael's business partner," Isabel said.

"The Indian," Wallis realized. She offered her hand.

"The sister-in-law," Alex countered. Isabel wondered if there was a touch of sarcasm in his tone. One never could tell with Alex. He bowed over Wallis's hand with a gallantry Isabel had not known him to possess. "It is a pleasure to meet you, Lady Jemison."

"And I you," she said, her voice deepening and her eyes sparkling with interest. He pulled out a chair for her next to his, while Isabel wondered what it was about blondes that made all men a bit balmy?

Isabel pushed her drawing away from Wallis, not wanting her sister-in-law to make any connection to the truth the way Alex had. "What brings you here so early this morning?"

"Is it early?" Wallis asked.

"For you."

Her sister-in-law laughed indulgently, her gaze sliding to Alex. If she worried that his attention had wandered, she needn't have. He was watching her every movement.

"I came to invite you and your husband to dinner Friday evening. We haven't seen each other for some time."

Isabel didn't want to go. But she could think of no excuse not to. "That would be nice." Why would Wallis trek all the way to her house before noon to offer a dinner invitation?

"What tribe are you, Mr. Haddon?" Wallis purred.

"He's half-Shawnee," Isabel interjected.

"Which half?" Wallis asked slyly.

"The best half," Alex replied without missing a beat.

Wallis gave her tinkling laugh, and Isabel wanted to gag. Her exasperated gaze met Bolling's, and she knew the butler shared her opinion. She decided to take action. "Unfortunately, Wallis, as much as I enjoy your visits, I have an appointment I must keep." It was far too direct a hint to be polite, but Isabel didn't care.

However, it was not a good ploy for separating Wallis and Alex. The two of them "discovered" they were going in the same direction, and Wallis offered Alex a ride. Isabel wanted to pull her friend aside before they left and warn him to be careful.

She didn't. There wasn't time to do so, and she had to accept that Alex was a grown man . . . with, apparently, a grown man's taste. But she was disappointed in him, although not in Wallis. After seeing the other side of Carter in the library, the one he didn't show the public, she understood why her sister-in-law would look to other men. The best news was that Alex was leaving that afternoon.

Meanwhile, Isabel had tasks around the household she had to finish. Today, Wednesday, was Cook's day off after breakfast. Most of the footmen also received the afternoon off as well.

Isabel enjoyed having the house quiet and to herself. She used the time for planning the week's activities and catching up on correspondence and household business. There was also another task before her, one that she was having great difficulty accomplishing but felt she must because Michael had asked it of her—write her stepfather.

Michael had suggested they visit him. Her feelings were ambivalent. Love had tempered her old view of him and given her a clearer perspective upon her own behavior back then. She now realized how much he had sacrificed for her mother and her. The air needed to be cleared between them, and yet what would she say? She was having difficulty even writing a letter asking if they could visit.

About midafternoon, she received a note by messenger from Michael asking her to send Bolling to him with some papers he'd left in the library. Since her husband still preferred not to have a secretary or valet, Bolling often acted in those capacities. It was unusual for Michael to forget any detail in business, and Isabel made a mental note to tease him about it later.

Up in her bedroom, Isabel sat at her desk and took out fresh paper and ink, determined to get the dreaded letter to her stepfather out of the way. The right words were slow in coming. She'd always called him Mr. Williams. Her half brothers called him Papa. When she was younger, she'd done so, too, but as the years had passed, and her resentments grown, she'd needed to keep distance between them.

For the first time, Isabel wondered if she had been responsible for the rift between them. It hadn't been intended. She'd been too young to understand her own feelings.

Becky brought her a tray from the kitchen of cold chicken, cheese, bread, and wine. Isabel was more than ready for a break.

"Has it started raining yet?" she asked her maid.

"No, but the skies threaten to open at any

333

time, ma'am," Becky answered, plumping the pillows on the bed. "I brought you some mulled wine. I thought it would taste good on a day like today."

"Thank you." Isabel sipped the wine and found its sweetness to her tastes. The baby forming inside her must like it.

"Ma'am, would it be possible for me to have some free time this evening?" Becky asked.

"Are you going to be walking with Langston again?" Isabel asked.

Becky blushed. She'd been keeping time with one of the footmen. "He may go with me," she admitted. "My cousin has returned from the army, and I'd like to see him this evening if I might."

"Of course," Isabel said. She knew how important free time was to a servant. "Who is here?"

"Mr. Bolling."

"That is fine," Isabel said. "My husband will be home shortly. You have a good time."

"Thank you, ma'am." Becky left the room in a rush.

With a sigh, Isabel went back to her letter and crossed out most of what she had written. She finished her wine and put the cup on the tray.

Outside, came the first rumblings of thunder.

Isabel hoped Becky had made her way to her cousin before the downpour.

Those plumped-up pillows called to her. Her words on the paper were looking more and more like meaningless scribbles, whereas a nap seemed a very good idea.

Isabel gave up writing her stepfather just as the first big drops of rain hit the window. She blew out the candle, so tired, she could barely make it over to the bed. She didn't even bother kicking off her shoes.

She thought she dozed. She wasn't certain.

The bedroom door opened. Her eyes half-shut, she saw Michael standing there . . .

No, it wasn't Michael.

The man had the same set of the head but the shoulders were different. They had been bent by time.

"Carter?" she whispered.

"Yes, it's me," he answered.

Isabel tried to raise her head, but couldn't. It wasn't as if she were in pain. Actually, she felt quite pleasant, and she understood Michael's dream.

"Why did you kill Aletta Calendri?"

He walked to the side of the bed and smiled down at her. "Ah, Isabel, you are far too smart for your own good. It shall make me sad to kill you."

Strangely, his words didn't alarm her. She supposed she had been drugged. Who would have thought it? And while her limbs felt useless, her mind was working.

"You told me you knew Michael killed her," she said.

"I lied."

Seventeen

❦

*M*ichael sensed something was wrong the moment he entered the house. Bolling wasn't at his post, and all was entirely too quiet. No candle burned; no fire gave off heat in the grate.

Or did the heavy rain outside his door fuel his fears? The skies had opened, and the downpour seemed to deaden all sound.

He'd learned to listen to his instincts. He didn't call a greeting but quietly slipped out of his damp greatcoat, placing it on the floor with the stealth of a hunter.

Alex had sent a note about Wallis's visit to Isabel that morning. It had been an unusual action for such a woman, and the sort of thing both of them had been waiting for.

Michael had never doubted Aletta's killer would someday find him. But he was shocked by his own suspicions.

He wanted to believe Wallis decided to rise early that morning and had good reason to pay a call. Wallis, one of Riggs's lovers.

Then there was the man they had caught in Portsmouth early that morning in the act of sabotaging the *Warrior* so it would sink with Alex and all on board. He had been hired at the Crow, just like the robbers who had waylaid his and Isabel's coach.

Always the Crow.

Where Riggs went.

Even though he was rumored to be far away, Michael didn't trust him. In truth, Michael hadn't seen anything harmless in anyone since he'd set foot on English soil. Nor did he trust Isabel's maid, whom Wallis had recommended. He'd never felt comfortable around her, so he'd assigned Langston to keep watch.

That afternoon, Becky had left the house with her packed bag and climbed into a hack. Either Isabel or Langston would have told him if they'd known Becky was leaving his employ. She'd climbed into a hack, and Michael was glad he'd taken the precaution. Ladies' maids did not hire hacks.

Something was afoot. While Langston continued to follow Becky, and Alex went to Portsmouth with the bailiff to gather evidence against Riggs, Michael had decided to come home. What harm could there be in seeing with his own eyes that the wife he loved so much was well and happy?

Now, as he climbed the front stairs of his house, careful where he placed his feet, keeping even his breath quiet, he prayed he was wrong.

At the top step, he looked down the hall. Their bedroom door was the only one open. That was not unusual, but it added to his anxiety.

Isabel was his life. If anything happened to her, he would never forgive himself—

He heard her voice. She was in the bedroom talking to someone, and Michael's knees almost buckled with relief.

God, he was a suspicious fool. But what was he to think after they had received word of the attempted sabotage?

He shook his head, relieving some of the tension in his shoulders and started for the bedroom, anxious to see his wife—

Carter's voice stopped him in the hall. "Why does any man kill someone?" his brother asked rhetorically. "Didn't we discuss this once? Cain and Abel?"

"Cain and Abel," Isabel murmured. She didn't sound like herself.

Michael flattened himself against the wall and began moving toward the bedroom.

"Tiresome, but true," Carter said. "I must admit, I didn't plan for Michael to become involved. He did that to himself by being where he shouldn't have been."

"What do you mean?" Isabel asked. Her voice sounded as if each word was almost too heavy to say.

"You didn't know how my brother was in those days. He wasn't like he is now. Back then he was completely arrogant. Cocky. Too handsome for his own good. Women fell over themselves to get to him. Of course, he didn't have money or a title or even a real reason to get up in the morning. He was a shallow wastrel with a pretty face."

Michael reached the bedroom. Peering around the corner of the doorjamb, he caught sight of Isabel stretched out on the bed, her head on a pillow, her hands neatly folded on her stomach. Carter sat on the edge of the bed beside her. His body faced the door although his attention was on Isabel.

They appeared completely at ease with each other and for a sizzling moment Michael's mind jumped to the worst conclusion until Isabel said in that lazy, distant voice, "Michael isn't like that."

She had been drugged—and Michael knew what his dream had meant. It was all there. The woman on the bed . . . and his brother.

Betrayal cut through him. He reeled with the realization. The one person he hadn't suspected was Carter, and now he realized he should have. With a faith born of childhood, he'd trusted his brother. Michael had not even given his father as much credit as he had Carter.

"No, he has changed," Carter was agreeing. "More's the pity. I think I preferred the man he was back then. Made me feel better about myself. Now, it's as if I'm the failure. People look at the two of us, and I come up lacking."

"Jealous," Isabel mumbled.

"Yes, I'm jealous." Carter shook his head. "It would have been better for me all the way around if they had hanged him."

On the other side of the door, Michael replaced bitter disillusionment with steel resolve. He clenched his fists, ready to strike hard when his wife's next question held him in check.

341

"Why did you kill her?" Isabel asked.

"It was an accident. I hadn't planned to. It just happened."

"You were at her apartment," Isabel said, a sign that, even with her senses dulled, her sharp, disciplined mind was still working.

"We both were," Carter said. "I was in her bedroom, waiting for her, when Michael arrived. Aletta would do that, make a man think she was going to give him some and slip away. She told me to leave, and there he was, so drunk he'd passed out on her couch. Can you imagine how I felt?"

"Angry," Isabel whispered.

"Yes, I was angry. No one ignores me. Not after they've taken my money."

"Not drunk now."

"Michael? No, he appears to have become a paragon of virtue," Carter said sarcastically. "But back in those days he was sloppy, he was such a sot. And the women loved him. I couldn't understand it."

"Richard didn't help . . . ?"

"Richard? Are you referring to Riggs?" Carter laughed. "He had nothing to do with this."

Isabel didn't answer.

Carter waved a hand in front of her face. "Asleep?" He sighed and picked up a pillow. "I'm sorry, Isabel. I must do this." He started to place the pillow over her face.

Michael charged into the room, cuffing his brother on the side of the head, then physically taking him by the collar of his coat and throwing him up against the wall. He held him there, his forearm against Carter's throat. He could kill him right then, but after ten years, he wanted answers. He wanted everything.

"Go ahead!" Michael demanded. "Finish the story. There was more to it that night. It was no accident." *He knew that.*

Carter was choking, his face turning blue as he struggled to breathe. Michael let up on the pressure.

"She did it to herself," Carter managed. "You heard?"

"Some." Their faces were inches from each other.

"Do you remember anything at all?" Carter asked.

"I saw you that night," Michael said. "The two of you were shouting. You shook her, and she fell." He'd seen his brother kill her and had blotted it out of his liquor-poisoned mind.

"It was an accident," Carter said. He was no longer unemotional. It was *his* life he feared for now. "Aletta told me to leave. Said you were there. She laughed, Michael. Said she had her choice of two brothers and chose you. Do you know how she made me feel? She was such a bloody little tease, and she wanted to toss me out. She shouldn't have talked to me that way."

Michael didn't say anything.

"Yes, I shook her," Carter confessed, "but I didn't kill her then. She fell and hit her head on the edge of the bed. It was an accident. I didn't mean to do it."

"But she was suffocated."

"Yes," Carter said. "I picked her up, Michael, and put her on the bed. I was sorry. But she came to her senses, saw the blood from the cut on her head, and started screaming—"

In the back of his mind, Michael could hear her calling to him for help. He'd been unable to comprehend what was happening.

"—I wanted her to be quiet," Carter said. "She wouldn't. She was going to wake you. So I put the pillow over her face, just to shush her a bit. I didn't mean for her to stop breathing. It was an accident, Michael. It was."

"Why didn't you tell the court that?"

"I was scared." Carter wet his lips. "I didn't plan for it to go the way it did. I took you with me when I left. My thought was to get us both away, but someone had seen you arrive."

"You could have said something."

"No, I couldn't." Carter closed his eyes, his regret seemingly genuine. "There are many things I wished I'd done that night. I shouldn't have gotten so angry. We both, you and I, had such terrible tempers in those days. You understand."

"Why did you let me take the blame?" That was the crux of it. All these years, Michael had wavered between thinking he might have done it and refusing to believe he had. His life had been a living Purgatory because of his brother. "You could have told everyone it was an accident. They might have believed you."

Carter shook his head. "Not Father. You know how he was, Michael. I couldn't face him."

"He disowned me." The pain was still there.

"Well, at least you weren't the heir. You can never understand the pressure of the title, how difficult everything is."

Michael stepped back from his brother. "I don't know you. I may never have known you."

Released from Michael's hold, Carter slumped against the wall. "We'll go to the magistrate now," Michael said, unable even to look at his brother. "We'll tell the story. There is a chance they will believe it was an accident."

His concern now was for his wife. "What did you give her?" he demanded, going toward the bed.

"Tincture of opium. She'll be fine."

Michael placed the back of his fingers against her cheek, just as an ominous click sounded behind him. He turned around.

Carter had regained his balance. He stood tall, a gun in his hand. It was a small pistol, the sort that could be concealed. The click had been the sound of it cocking.

Michael didn't feel fear. He'd faced death before. "Why?"

Carter actually laughed. "I'm broke. The duns hound me, and my lovely wife keeps spending. As your sole male relative, I inherit your wealth and, if all goes as planned, your savage partner will soon follow you out of this life."

"You could have asked me for money. I would have given it to you."

"And expect me to pay it back—"

"No," Michael said, shaking his head. He took a step toward Carter. His brother raised the pistol higher, a warning for him to stop.

"I know the man you have become, Michael. You will never stop searching for Aletta's killer. This"—he nodded to the pistol—"solves many problems, including answering the question in people's minds as to whether you *were* Aletta's killer."

"Why is that?"

"Because you are going to be accused of killing your wife in the same manner."

"And for what reason?" Michael challenged.

"Riggs. Did you know he had an affair with Isabel? I couldn't believe my luck in learning that. Wallis fancied Riggs, but apparently he lost interest in her because he'd become enamored by Lady Baynton's governess, who just so happened to be Isabel. Wallis was furious to have been unceremoniously dumped for a servant. Understand, I was only peripherally aware of all this. It was a stroke of luck actually. However, my awareness of Riggs led to the information that you were to accompany him to a hunt party out in Rutland. I arranged a hunting accident for you. I don't think most people would have cared if you lived or died back then. You weren't very well liked, Michael. Your questions and accusations made people nervous. Isabel has changed a lot of that for you."

He was right. His wife had opened doors that had previously been closed. "Was Riggs ever an accomplice?"

"Unwittingly. Of course, he can't testify against me. He is now far away in India."

"You tried to kill me a second time."

"I tried to have both you *and* Isabel removed," Carter answered. "You can't imagine how frustrated I've been. Murder is not an easy thing to plan."

"I imagine it is easier when it is spontaneous," Michael answered, forcing himself to control his anger.

"Yes," his brother admitted, "and less a burden on the conscience although I shall manage to live with myself. After that last attempt failed, I've had to bide my time. It's been difficult."

"And you are doing this all for money," Michael said, letting his scorn show. He looked his brother in his eye. "Kill me, but leave Isabel out of this." He thought about the guard Isabel had hired to keep watch over him. The man usually stationed himself across the street in the park when Michael was home. If he could get Carter to fire and miss, then perhaps it would alarm his bodyguard enough to come and help.

"I can't, Michael," Carter said. "She's breeding, and I don't want to share the fortune. She also isn't as gullible as you were. Your wife has a quick mind. It's led to her undoing."

Michael felt as if he'd been punched in the head. "Isabel is pregnant?"

Carter smiled. "I heard that directly from her maid. The husbands are always the last to know. I could never tell with Wallis. Two sons and I never had an inkling until she made an announcement. Of course, her maid always knew."

Isabel carried his child. The love they had for each other had manifested itself in a child. It was a sacred and powerful moment—one that gave Michael the strength he needed.

He moved fast and low, head down, charging his brother and hitting him full force before he could fire. Michael reached for the gun and there was a moment when they both had their hands on it. Of course, Carter had his hand close to the trigger. Michael kneed him and, with a grunt, Carter let go, throwing it aside so that Michael couldn't have it.

Both hands free, Carter grabbed Michael by the neck. They crashed into the dresser, knocking over candlesticks and a mirror. Carter fought for his life. He knocked Michael to the ground and picked up a side table to smash over him. Michael kicked Carter's legs out from under him. His brother crashed to the floor.

Michael was younger, stronger, and angrier. Using his body weight to gain the upper hand, he rose over his brother and slugged him with everything he had.

Carter went limp.

Michael waited for him to move. He didn't. He was still breathing, but he was out cold.

It was done. It was over. But Michael felt no triumph.

He rose to check on his wife, when he realized they weren't alone.

Wallis stood in the doorway, Carter's pistol in her hand.

"Hello, Michael."

"I don't suppose you've come to help me?"

She shook her head. She had one of her feathery hats on, and the ostrich plumes bobbed with her movement. "I've been here all along. Downstairs. Carter wanted me to hide in case you returned before he finished with Isabel. I heard the two of you fighting."

Michael took a step toward her, and her grip tightened on the pistol. "I'm a good shot," she said. "Perhaps not as good as you are rumored to be, but I will hit you. It's still primed."

He held up his hands. "I don't want you to do anything foolish."

"I won't," she said evenly. On the floor, her husband groaned, regaining consciousness.

Michael took a step toward her, trying to take advantage of her lapse of attention.

"Don't move," Wallis warned.

"I'd hoped you weren't a part of this," he said.

"I must be," she replied sadly.

"Are you doing it for the money, too?"

"I do it for my sons," she said. "They don't have much of a father. He's almost ruined us all, but there you have it. He's the man I married, and I must support him."

Carter reached up and grabbed the spread on top of the bed to help himself up. He shook his head as if clearing his brain.

"Wallis, are you certain you can get away with murder twice?" Michael asked. "You met Alex. We caught the man who attempted to sabotage our ship. Alex will avenge my death."

"I can handle him," she said confidently.

"Did you know he sent me a note after your meeting? He's already suspicious of you. We both have been of everyone." Everyone, that was, except Carter.

"I wish I wasn't a part of this, Michael," Wallis said stiffly.

Carter rose to his feet. Wallis glanced at her

husband, then back to Michael. "I've wished that for a long time, ever since Carter murdered that actress and dragged me into it. I would have been happier if he hadn't told me. If I'd thought you were the guilty one."

"So, you've known all along."

She nodded. "Unfortunately." She paused a moment, then confessed, "Do you know I used to love Carter at one time? I adored him—all the way up until he made me his accomplice in Aletta Calendri's murder. My poor sons."

"Then free yourself of it," Michael urged quietly.

"I can't," Wallis said. "There's too much at stake."

Michael gambled everything he had on his sister-in-law. "Wallis, kill me, but spare Isabel. She's innocent in all this. She's going to have my child. You can't let her die."

The news rocked her back. She looked to her husband in confusion. "Is this true?"

Carter was more concerned with the blood at the corner of his mouth than his wife's conscience. "Your Becky told me. It only gives us more reason to see her dead. Can't keep her alive."

"Except now, instead of two people, you are

involving me with the murder of a child," Wallis answered.

"The child's not born yet," Carter said flatly.

She looked at him in horror. "Did I never know you?" she wondered. "Are we strangers?"

Carter made an impatient sound. "Here, give me the damn gun. You go downstairs, and I'll come get you when I'm done."

"No," Wallis said. "I'm not doing this, Carter, and I'm not letting you do it." She turned as if to run from the room but her husband jumped for her, knocking her to the ground.

Michael rushed to help Wallis. He saw the gun in Carter's hand. Wallis struggled to turn over, shoving her husband just as the pistol went off.

Carter stiffened. He sat back on his heels and looked down. He'd turned the weapon in his own direction and shot himself in the chest at close range.

He stumbled up to his feet and looked down at his wife in amazement.

"I didn't—I couldn't," Wallis whispered.

He looked at Michael. "I shot myself." He sounded slightly amazed. The pistol dropped from his hands, and he fell to his knees.

Eighteen

Michael moved to his brother and lowered him to the floor. The wound was mortal. Carter started having difficulty breathing. Michael held him in his arms.

"Is he going to live?" Wallis asked, her tone edged with hysteria.

"Why don't you go downstairs?" Michael suggested quietly.

Instead, she leaned over her husband. Carter looked up at her. For a long moment, they stared at each other.

Wallis broke the silence first. "I did love you, Carter. At one time, I cared for you very deeply."

Struggling for breath, he asked, "Then why . . . didn't you . . . do . . . what I said?"

Tears welled in his wife's eyes. "For my sons." It was the same reason she'd given for having a hand in his plans. "And because I couldn't kill a baby. I couldn't have that on my soul."

"Go on," her husband said harshly. "Leave me be."

Wallis scrambled to her feet and went out in the hall. A second later, Michael heard her break down into sobs.

Carter frowned at Michael. "Don't . . . trust . . . women."

They were his last words. A beat later, he died.

Michael closed his brother's eyes and laid him on the floor. Outside, the rain continued at a steady pace. He rose to his feet and went to his wife.

Isabel slept peacefully, blissfully unaware of what had transpired around her. Michael took her into his arms and carried her out of the room and away from all the ugliness.

Isabel recovered from her opium-induced sleep without any ill effects.

An inquest was quickly organized to look into the circumstances surrounding Carter's death. Michael welcomed the opportunity to clear his name and was gratified when Wallis testified to the truth. Her testimony was substantiated by the maid Becky.

The judge at the inquest ruled that Carter had shot himself. The ruling didn't make the following days any less stressful. The gossips went wild.

Michael accompanied Wallis to the boys' schools to bring them home. It might have been simpler to have sent a coach, but Wallis knew they would be upset by their father's death.

Jeremy and Wallace had both been the light of their parents' lives. They appeared to be good boys who had respected their father and thought of their uncle as a murderer. Breaking the news to them was not easy, especially since rumor traveled faster than Michael and Wallis.

By the time they arrived at Eton, the oldest, Jeremy had already heard many of the stories concerning his father's death. He refused to see his mother, and that cut almost destroyed Wallis.

"I must talk to him," Michael told the headmaster.

"He is being very firm in his decision," the gentleman said.

"He's a boy. Tell him I will see him."

The headmaster did not dare defy Michael.

He met Jeremy in the headmaster's gloomy office. When the boy entered the room his carriage was so erect Michael sensed he might break if he bent even the slightest bit. Therefore, he was not surprised when Jeremy refused his offer to sit in the chair across from his.

"I'd rather stand, sir." He spoke to Michael as if he were a stranger . . . and, sadly, he was.

"You look very much like your father," Michael said. It was true.

"Thank you."

"You know who I am?"

"Yes, sir," Jeremy's voice had gone fainter.

"I'm sorry," Michael said, meaning the words.

For the first time, his nephew looked at him. His eyes were shiny. "I wish you had been the guilty one," he said, his voice tense with emotion.

"I know."

There was no other way to deal with this issue than honesty. "Here, sit," Michael said.

This time, Jeremy practically collapsed in the chair.

"You have a great weight on your shoulders," Michael began. He would not talk down to his nephew. "You are going to be named the earl of Jemison."

"I know, sir."

"There are responsibilities that accompany a title."

"Yes, sir."

"One of them is seeing to the family."

The boy nodded. Michael wasn't telling him anything he didn't know.

"I loved your father."

Now he had Jeremy's attention. "I looked up to him," Michael said. "I tried to follow in his footsteps."

"You ruined him." The boy's face was tight as if he suppressed all emotion.

"No, we all make our choices, and your father made his. He chose his own path, Jeremy, but it doesn't have to be yours."

"I know that." There was such pride in those words.

"Your brother needs you, as does your mother."

The child in him surfaced at last. "They say she killed him," he said, looking to Michael. "Is that true?"

Michael leaned forward. "No."

Jeremy swallowed. His anger and fear battled with his love of his mother.

"She did the right thing, Jeremy. Your father

attacked her. The shooting was an accident. He had the gun in his hand, not her. And I will be honest. He wanted her to kill me and my wife. If she had gone along with him, both of your parents would have been charged with murder. A man can't run forever from his actions. The truth would have been known sooner or later."

"I don't want to believe he murdered anyone." Jeremy swung around to Michael. "You were the bad one. We all hated you."

This is what Carter had done. The legacy he had left behind.

Michael was determined to see it end here.

"It's always a challenge when you believe one thing, then you discover you had been told a lie."

"My father wouldn't have lied to me."

"No, your father wouldn't. And I like to think the brother I once had would not have done so either. But life changes us, Jeremy. Like the heroes in those Greek myths your tutors force you to read, each of us is given a set of challenges. We are tested and expected to face those tests with courage. My brother failed in many ways to meet the challenges he was given, but not in what he felt for his sons. Both of your parents loved you very much."

There had been a time when he would not

have used that word "love." Now he knew how important it was.

"If he had truly cared for me," Jeremy said, "he would not have disgraced his name. And my mother would not have—" He broke, unable to finish the sentence.

"Your father left her no choice," Michael said. "I know it is hard to understand. I don't completely grasp all of his reasons. I do know a challenge is before you. Someone must take up the family mantle. Someone must lead us through this."

His nephew looked at him with doubtful eyes. "You are the earl. It's in your hands."

Michael waited, hoping he'd said the right words.

"I don't know if I can," Jeremy admitted. He was so bloody young.

"I will be there to help you, and so will your mother. She believes in you. She knows you will be a fine earl. A great one."

"I'm not good at my studies," Jeremy confessed.

"You can change that," Michael assured him.

His nephew considered the matter a moment, then said, "I can."

Michael smiled, and Jeremy gave a shy smile back.

"Your mother would like to see you. We need to speak to your brother and want you to come with us."

This time, Jeremy didn't hesitate. "I want to see her, too."

The reunion between mother and son was heartfelt. Michael knew it would take a great deal to steer his family through this crisis, but at least the healing had begun.

The funeral was held as soon as the boys reached London. It was a somber affair and poorly attended. Isabel thought that a shame.

Michael had said the final prayer over his brother's body. All hearing him speak were deeply touched. Then he and Carter's sons threw the first handfuls of dirt on the coffin.

A trust was set up for the boys, financed mostly by Michael. He told Isabel his brother's estate was worse than he had even imagined. However, with sound management, he hoped he could turn it around.

Wallis closed the London house and retired to the country. She had become a very somber woman. She stopped by to see Isabel before she left.

The two of them had never spoken about the events of that afternoon. Their talk always centered around Jeremy and Wallace and other safe topics, and so it was that day.

However, as she was leaving, Wallis said, "I sold my emerald earbobs. I wanted to pay for my husband's headstone myself."

"Wallis, Michael and I would have covered that." They had paid the other funeral expenses.

"I told Michael no," Wallis said. "It was my way of forgiving Carter. Michael understood."

Isabel put her arms around her sister-in-law's shoulders. "Please, Wallis, forgive yourself."

"I will." The older woman stepped back. "In time." She took Isabel's hand. "You haven't said anything, but I want you to know how blessed you are to have a child on the way. My sons mean everything to me."

"You know about the baby?"

Wallis nodded. "Michael does, too. I didn't know if you knew that or not. It came up during the scene with Carter." She gave Isabel a quick kiss on the check and left.

Thoughtfully, Isabel walked to her husband's study. Since that afternoon, he did most of his work at home. The door was half-open and she could see him bent over his ledgers. Alex wanted to buy another ship and it was up to Michael to handle the details.

Sunlight fell across his desk from the window

that overlooked the garden. He appeared thoroughly frustrated by the numbers.

"I didn't say anything because I wanted to be certain," Isabel said without preamble.

Michael looked up. His hair was mussed where he'd run his hand through it. He didn't pretend to mistake her meaning. "I know."

"But you wondered?"

His lips curved into a rueful smile. "Every man would wonder such a thing. But I trust you, Isabel. I knew you would say something when the time is right."

"I worried about that opium Carter gave me." She walked into the room and around his desk to where he sat.

He pushed his chair back, inviting her to sit on his lap. She covered his hand with hers and pressed it against her stomach. "I think the baby is still there. I spoke to Mr. Talmadge." He was a physician. "He thinks all will be fine, but we will have to wait until the baby begins moving."

Michael nodded, his expression sober. "It will be all right, Isabel."

"I pray it is so."

They were interrupted by Bolling. "I beg your pardon sir, but a gentleman from Higham in Lancaster has just delivered this package for Mrs. Severson."

Higham was her village, the one where she'd grown up. Isabel rose and took the cloth pouch the size of her palm and letter from the butler. Her name was addressed on the outside. "Is he still here?"

"No, ma'am. He said he was delivering for a friend and left."

Isabel nodded. She knew who the friend was. She recognized her stepfather's handwriting. "Thank you," she said to Bolling, dismissing him.

Michael waited until after the door was shut. "Do you know who it's from?"

"My stepfather." She walked back to the desk and stopped, staring at the package.

"Open the letter," Michael instructed.

Isabel broke the seal. It was a short note. Her stepfather was not one to waste words, but what he wrote touched her deeply. Her lower lip started to tremble, and she struggled to keep back tears. Without a word to Michael, she yanked open the strings of the pouch and poured the two pearl hair combs onto the desk.

"What are those?" Michael asked.

"They were my mother's. Oh, Michael, I have been so wrong."

"About what?"

"Him." She held up the letter. "He sent those

two combs to me. I thought he wanted to keep them for himself. I thought he didn't care for me. Now . . . ?"

"What did he write?"

She read to him, "My dear stepdaughter, I have heard of your marriage. May you find much happiness." It sounded so perfunctory. But then the tone of the letter had changed.

"I know in my grief for your dear mother I wasn't much of a father to you. I spoke hastily and have regretted my words many times these past years. I pray you can find it in your heart to forgive an old man who was foolishly in love. These combs were my wedding gift to your mother. I held on to them after she died, but now you can make better use of them. Think on her when you wear them and of your stepfather, who tried in his fashion to be a parent to you all these years. Your brothers wish you well and perhaps someday our paths will cross again."

He'd signed it "Papa."

Isabel swiped a tear away from her cheek with the heel of her hand. "I feel silly."

"Why?" her husband wondered.

"Because"—she took a moment to collect herself—"all these years I thought he didn't care at all, and I was the one who kept us from being closer. I knew he wasn't my real father."

"You were waiting for the marquis," Michael said, understanding.

"Yes, even while this man clothed me, sheltered me, and taught me what I needed to know in life. I see now that when I left, we were both so lost in grief over my mother's death that we allowed ourselves to misunderstand each other."

"I will take you to see him," Michael offered.

"Yes," she said thoughtfully. "Perhaps the time has come." She picked the combs up off the desk. Her husband's money could buy her anything she wanted, but nothing could be more precious than these.

"Let me go write him," she said, and left the room. Upstairs, at her desk, she pulled out pen, ink, and paper. The afternoon was sunny, not dreary as it had been that last time she'd attempted to write him. She set the combs on the corner of her writing desk.

This time, the words were not so difficult to find. All she had to do was start with *"Dear Papa, thank you . . ."*

January 1804

What miracles a year could work!
They had just come from church.

Michael stood in the hall, his daughter in his arms, and let Bolling help him remove his coat. Diane Isabel Severson was still red-faced from her crying fit.

His wife took the baby from him. "She hasn't liked anything this morning, from getting dressed in the lace and ruffles of her christening gown to having the waters of baptism poured over her head. Poor baby."

Diane pouted prettily for her mother.

From the moment Isabel had felt the baby stirring in her womb, she had taken on a radiance that only made her more lovely every day.

Their baby had been born healthy and strong, a circumstance for which Michael thanked God every day.

"I thought the bishop went far too long," Michael said. "I'm not so certain he wasn't more worried about my soul than Diane's."

Isabel laughed. She wore her mother's pearl combs in her hair. "He thought nothing of the sort. Come along, baby, let us go see your grandpapa."

Michael followed them down the hall to the dining room, where everyone had gathered.

When he'd purchased this house, he'd not even been able to imagine it brimming with love and good wishes as it did now.

Mr. and Mrs. Oxley had traveled from Rutland. The vicar had stood beside the bishop and added his blessings on the baby's head.

Alex poured wine for Wallis, who looked relaxed and at peace. Her sons stood close by. Alex had promised to take them—and Isabel's half brothers Terrance and Roger—sailing on the morrow. All four boys were of the same age, and Alex would have his hands full with such a group. Michael had no doubt his friend could handle such a motley crew. All four boys were more than a bit in awe of their uncle Alex, who seemed to relish the role.

Alex's path had yet to cross his infamous father's, but Michael knew it would happen. His friend had confided that the night of Diane's birth he'd had a dream of seeing his father again. It was destined.

Isabel's stepfather was there, too. They had visited him in the summer, and he and Isabel had become regular correspondents. All grudges had been buried. It was good to know Diane would have a grandparent.

Alex cleared his throat, gathering everyone's attention. "Since I am the godfather, I shall propose the toast," he said. He looked around to make certain everyone held a glass except Isabel and Michael.

"To Diane," Alex said. "The most beautiful baby in the world."

"Hear, hear," Mr. Oxley said.

"May her future be filled with happiness, prosperity, and love."

"To love," the others echoed.

"And to Isabel," Alex continued. "A woman of good sense and grace."

"Hear, hear," Michael said, and kissed his wife.

"And to you, Michael. My friend. May you always be as happy as you are at this moment."

Michael put his arms around his wife and

child. Isabel leaned back against him, and he knew in that moment he was the richest of men. Life had meaning.

He had come home.